I'm So Happy for You

Also by Lucinda Rosenfeld

I'm So Happy for You

a novel

Lucinda Rosenfeld

BACK BAY BOOKS
Little, Brown and Company
NEW YORK BOSTON LONDON

Back Bay Books / Little, Brown and Company
Hachette Book Group
237 Park Avenue, New York, NY 10017
Visit our website at www.HachetteBookGroup.com

First Edition: July 2009

Back Bay Books is an imprint of Little, Brown and Company. The Back Bay Books name and logo are trademarks of Hachette Book Group, Inc.

The characters and events in this book are fictitious. Any similarity to real persons, living or dead, is coincidental and not intended by the author.

Library of Congress Cataloging-in-Publication Data
  Rosenfeld, Lucinda.
  I'm so happy for you : a novel / Lucinda Rosenfeld.— 1st ed.
    p. cm.
  ISBN 978-0-316-04450-9
  1. Best friends—Fiction. 2. Female friendship—Fiction.
3. Jealousy—Fiction. I. Title.
  PS3568.O814I42 2009
  813'.54—dc22   2008045124

10 9 8 7 6 5 4 3 2 1

RRD-IN

Book design by Brooke Koven

Printed in the United States of America

for the munches, senior and junior: jc, bc, and cc

Nothing fortifies friendship more than one of two friends thinking himself superior to the other.

HONORÉ DE BALZAC, *Cousin Pons,* 1848

I'm So Happy for You

I.

SINCE WENDY MURMAN had begun trying to conceive, eight months earlier, having sex with her husband, Adam Schwartz, had turned into something resembling a military operation: spontaneity and passion were discouraged; timing and execution were everything. Late one Sunday night, however, Adam, ignoring the calendar — it was day twenty-four of Wendy's cycle — pressed up close against her in bed and ran his right index finger along the elastic waistband of her underwear. Wendy's first instinct was to tell him to let her sleep and save his genetic material for the following week, but she didn't want to offend him. She was also flattered to think he was still so attracted to her.

Wendy was weighing her options when the phone rang in the living room. Pushing Adam away from her, she swung her legs over the side of the bed and stood up.

"Can't you just let the machine pick up?" Adam grumbled into his pillow.

"I'll just be a minute," Wendy said hurriedly on her way out the door.

The living room was pitch-black, and Wendy rammed her shin into the side of the coffee table. With one hand, and in agony, she clutched her leg; with the other, she felt around for the receiver, which was still ringing. She finally located it on the floor, sandwiched between the previous week's issues of *The New Yorker* and *In Touch Weekly*. Earlier in the evening, she'd been reading a ten-thousand-word article about melting ice caps by Elizabeth Kolbert, only to be distracted by a cover headline asserting that Jennifer Aniston was back on the dating market. Poor thing had apparently been dumped again. Or at least according to *In Touch* she had been. "Hello?" she said.

"We-e-endy," came the tremulous response.

Just as Wendy had suspected when she heard the phone ring, it was Daphne Uberoff, her best friend since college. Although it was after midnight, Wendy wasn't surprised to hear her voice. With every passing year, Daphne seemed to grow needier. Wendy felt increasingly responsible for her mental and emotional well-being. She cared for Daphne; she also hated the idea of missing some fresh drama in Daphne's life. "Daf," she said in the most compassionate tone of voice she could muster, "what's going on?"

"I'm sorry I'm calling so late." Daphne followed her apology with a hiccuping sob reminiscent of bathwater being sucked down the drain of an old tub. "But I'm not okay."

"Is it Mitch?" asked Wendy. It was mostly a rhetorical question, since it was always Mitch, as in "Mitchell Kroker Reporting Live from the Capital." He was fifty, with the wrinkled and vaguely sulfurous complexion of a golden raisin. From what Wendy could gather, Daphne saw more of him on TV than in real life. This was possibly due to the fact

4

that, in addition to being married to someone else (a weather-woman named Cheryl with immovable hair), he lived in D.C., while Daphne lived in New York.

"He called me when he got into town tonight." Daphne was practically hyperventilating. "We were supposed to see each other, but I was already feeling really frustrated because he was only going to be here for like a few hours"—audible inhale—"so I said I felt like this hotel he checked in and out of, and he said he was sorry I felt that way, but he was giving me all the time he had to give"—audible inhale—"so I said that wasn't enough anymore and that I needed to know if this was leading anywhere and he said"—choking sob—"he said that if I needed the promise of a commitment in the future, we shouldn't see each other anymore because he could never live with himself if he left the kids at least not until they're out of the house which will be in like two hundred years at which point I'll be like TWO THOUSAND!" Daphne began to weep.

"Oh, Daf, I'm so sorry," said Wendy, resisting the urge to point out the errors in Daphne's arithmetic. "He's such a fuck-ing disappointment!" She tried to sound impassioned both in her sympathy and her outrage. It wasn't easy. Wendy had heard endless variations of the same woeful tale before. Daphne had also asked her to interpret countless emails and voice messages from Mitchell, none of which said anything of note. Wendy prided herself on being a good friend and knew that Daphne was going through a rough time, but she'd grown impatient with her old friend's steadfastness in the face of so much privation.

On rare occasions when Mitch was feeling romantic (i.e., immediately before sex), he'd tell Daphne that he fantasized

5

about the two of them running away to some beachfront bungalow on the Turks and Caicos Islands. Never once, however, had he offered to leave his wife. Never once—as far as Wendy knew—had he even used the "L word" to describe his feelings for Daphne. From what Wendy could tell, the only thing Mitchell Kroker had to offer was the prospect of sharing his suite at the Essex House hotel, on Central Park South, every now and then when he happened to be in town.

It was also true that Wendy had grown weary of the story line and longed for a new character, a new development— anything to advance the plot.

Her wish was granted shortly thereafter. But it wasn't the plot point for which she'd hoped. "I feel like dousing myself with gasoline and lighting a match," Daphne announced through her tears.

"Daphne—take that back right now!" cried Wendy, even as she thought: *right*. She'd heard it all before. And before that, too. Daphne threatened to kill herself so often that her threats barely registered with Wendy anymore—even as Daphne's methods kept getting more grandiose. Once, she'd promised the mellow fade-out of pills. Now she was pledging pyrotechnics.

"Why should I?" said Daphne, still weeping. "What good am I to anybody?"

"You're good to a lot of people," said Wendy, although she couldn't think of anyone in particular.

"I'm going to be alone my whole life," declared Daphne.

"That's not true," demurred Wendy. "Mitch is the one who's going to be miserable and stuck in his awful marriage. And you're going to be madly in love with someone else. And then, I swear, you're going to look back and wonder what you were ever doing with the guy."

"Wasting two years of my life," Daphne said with a sniffle and a quick laugh.

To Wendy's relief, the tears seemed to have dried up, at least for the moment. "Listen," she said, "I want you to call Carol tomorrow, as soon as you wake up." Carol—as all of Daphne's friends knew, since Daphne began so many of her sentences with "Carol thinks"—was Daphne's therapist. "And then, what about going to get a massage or something? I think you need to do something nice for yourself right now."

"The only thing I need right now is a new prescription for Klonopin," said Daphne.

"Take a Klonopin if you have to," said Wendy. "Just promise me you won't take more than one."

"I feel like swallowing the whole bottle — "

"Daphne!"

"What?"

"You're scaring me again."

"I'm not going to swallow the whole bottle. Okay?"

"Do you promise?"

"I promise!"

"Because you don't need drugs. You just need to get rid of Mitch."

"So I can sit here by myself feeling even worse?"

"Daphne, I swear, you're going to be alone for, like, five seconds," said Wendy, glancing at the clock on the cable box. It was twenty to one. Her eye fell to the DVD player. She still missed her old VCR. Just when she'd finally learned to program it—five years after purchasing—the technology had

7

changed again. Plus, there had been something weirdly satisfying about the buzzing noise it made when sucking video-tapes into its gullet. Also, the new remote had four separate "play" buttons; who had the energy to read another manual and find out why?

"Yeah, sure," said Daphne.

"You don't believe me, but I'm right," said Wendy.

For several more minutes, the conversation continued in a similar vein, with Wendy offering sanguine prognoses regarding Daphne's future, and Daphne rebuffing them, even as her protests grew audibly weaker, possibly on account of the tranquilizer she'd just swallowed.

By the time Wendy hung up, she felt assured that Daphne would do nothing more dangerous than fall fast asleep for the next thirteen hours. Which was fine for her, Wendy thought. Daphne hadn't had a real job since her midtwenties, when she'd been an editorial assistant at a city listings magazine. Not that it had been a "real" real job. It had been Daphne's responsibility to "write up" the sample sales each week. (*X's micro-weight cashmere separates will be 70 percent off retail. . . .*) These days, she filed "reader's reports" for a small film production company — three or four times a year.

As Wendy contemplated Daphne's schedule — or, really, lack thereof — she felt an old kernel of resentment rising to the surface of her consciousness. Wendy was a senior editor at *Barricade,* a left-wing news biweekly that had been founded on the campus of the University of California at Berkeley in 1968 and relocated to New York during the Reagan era. There was a movement afoot to transfer the whole operation onto the Web. But for the moment, at least, the magazine was printed on the equivalent of developing-world airport toilet paper. It claimed a subscription base of 90,000, every two weeks, though Wendy suspected that at least 40,000 of those were free subscriptions to public libraries and extinct hippie communes. She also assumed that the only people who read *Barricade* already agreed with the editorials it ran (and she edited). But at least she was contributing to the dialogue.

Unlike Daphne, Wendy also woke up for work.

But then, other people's good fortune didn't necessarily exist at her expense. At least this is what Wendy had been encouraged to believe by her own therapist — or, rather, *former* therapist — Marcia Meltzer, PhD, MSW, CSW. (Wendy had fired her after she raised her rates, then refused to continue submitting bills to Wendy's health maintenance organization, which reimbursed a modest but still significant 35 percent of Marcia's fee. There had also been tension between the two of them after friends invited Wendy and Adam away for a long weekend. Hoping not to be charged for the missed session, Wendy had left a fraudulently rheumy message on Marcia's answering machine, claiming to have the flu. Marcia had charged her anyway.) Besides, Daphne's good fortune didn't currently extend very far, Wendy reminded herself on her way back to the bedroom — despite the fact that Daphne's HMO continued to cover 80 percent of the cost of seeing Carol, which also seemed a little unfair.

"Sorry," said Wendy.

Adam was sitting up in bed now, his reading light on and a free humor newspaper in his lap. ("Man Eats Sandwich," read the front-page headline.) No doubt he'd picked it up at the local coffee shop where he spent a substantial portion of his own "workweek," Wendy thought. A couple of months earlier, he'd quit his job as the copy chief of a respected financial news Web site to write a screenplay. At the time, she'd been tempted to tell him that screenwriting was a skill like any other that took years of practice, whereas he was just a novice. But she didn't want to be the one to spoil his fantasies. He was her husband, after all. She wanted to believe in him. And she was conflict avoidant. And he'd been bored with his job. And she couldn't exactly blame him for being so. How many more S's could he be expected to add to the oft-misspelled "Dow Jones Industrials Average"? So she'd agreed to support him for a year, during which time, in theory at least, he'd write a first draft.

From what Wendy suspected, in two months, Adam had failed to complete a first sentence. The evidence: the triple-digit iTunes charges on their joint credit card bill, the fact that he changed the subject every time she asked to read something, the pervasive smell of marijuana on his jackets and sweaters, the random afternoon sightings of him and Polly, his beloved geriatric Doberman pinscher, meandering through Prospect Park. In that moment, however, Wendy's frustration with Adam's lack of a career was tempered by the recollection that she'd rejected his advances in order to take Daphne's call. No doubt he'd be feeling hurt. He was apparently curious, too. "So, what's the latest in Daphne-ville?" he asked as she climbed back under the comforter next to him. "Any thwarted carjackings? Accidental crack binges?"

"Oh, just the usual," said Wendy. "Mitch still isn't leaving the weatherwoman. Plus now Daphne's threatening to light herself on fire. Which is why I was on the phone so long."

"Now she's threatening to burn herself alive?!" Adam

looked up, his brow knit to convey horror and fascination in one. "You've gotta be kidding."

It had occurred to Wendy on more than one occasion that it was their mutual love of stories that connected her and Adam above all else: gossip, literature, comedy, tragedy, political plots, plots of old TV shows; it was all the same to them; it was all titillating. "I don't think she was being any more serious than usual," she said, feeling guilty but maybe not that guilty for using Daphne's misery as a marital healer. "But I guess you never know for sure."

Adam slowly shook his head and laughed. "Can you explain to me why it's always the most beautiful women who end up so completely fucked up?"

"Do you really think she's still that beautiful?" asked Wendy. Because it was one thing for her to admit that Daphne was gorgeous, and another for her husband to confirm it. "I mean, she obviously was ten years ago."

Adam shrugged. "Well, maybe she's not as beautiful as she used to be. But she's still about two hundred times more attractive than that nightly-news weenie she's screwing."

"Tell me about it," said Wendy, relieved by her husband's retreat but still feeling insecure. "Will you kiss me again?" she said, sidling back up to him with a scrunched face.

"I tried to kiss you before," he said, his eyes back on his newspaper. "But apparently you had more important business to attend to." It was as if Adam had suddenly remembered that he was miffed. At the pained expression on Wendy's face, however, a sly smile took hold of his own. He placed his paper on his bedside table. Then he said, "All right, you have one final chance to experience the great gift of my body." Then he reached for Wendy, and she melted into his mouth and into his embrace. Even after seven years together, she still relished the plumlike taste of Adam's lips, as well as the ropy feel of his surprisingly muscular arms—surprising because he was so slight.

"I love you," she mumbled into his chest.

"I love you, too," he said. "Even though you're obsessed with another woman."

"You're so funny," she said, nestling even closer.

But as Adam took her hand and placed it on his crotch, once again Wendy had to fight the urge to recoil. Only there was no way out this time, no needy friend to save her from her own arousal. So she relented. And in the end, she was glad that she had, glad to think she'd made Adam glad; glad in the way that, at a certain age and a certain number of years into marriage, unplanned sexual activity rewards its participants with a real sense of accomplishment.

Or maybe just the conviction that their marriage is likely to last another year.

The next morning, as Wendy made her way up Broadway to her office, she was aware of her stride being longer than usual. For the first time in weeks, she wasn't about to be late for work. It wasn't the thought of editing angry diatribes on the Guantánamo Bay prison camp or the lack of federally guaranteed health insurance that spurred her forward, however; it was the prospect of sending two emails, both of which she'd carefully composed in her head on the subway ride from Brooklyn.

Arriving at her cubicle—only senior staff had offices—

Wendy switched on her ancient PC, which took six minutes to load (*Barricade* was perpetually short on funds). After establishing a weak Internet connection, she opened her email program, whereupon the usual hodgepodge of absurdist pornography ("XXX Girl Scouts $3.99"), unsolicited pitches ("Like Gandhi before him, Hugo Chavez . . ."), and left-leaning political missives ("Sign This Urgent Petition to Stop Bush's Illegal . . .") trickled in. Generally speaking, Wendy believed that adding her name to a document, even if it was never read by anyone with any power, was the least she could do to better the world. But at that moment, the least she could do seemed like too much. She was more concerned with solidifying her position as Daphne Uberoff's best friend, even though she knew it was juvenile and possibly even pathetic of her to care about such designations. She opened a new message and began to type:

Hi sweets. I just wanted to see if you were feeling any better??
Call any time and/or if you need ANYTHING. At the office all
day. I know you're going to get through this. Thinking of u, W.

Wendy addressed her second message to her and Daphne's mutual friend — or, really, Daphne's friend and Wendy's longtime nemesis — Paige Ryan, a six-feet-tall senior analyst for a Manhattan-based hedge fund, where she researched overvalued stocks that the fund then sold short with the aim of making a killing when the price subsequently fell. (At the moment, she was concentrating on the retail sector.) But Paige made a great show of giving a large percentage of her salary to worthy causes, thereby making herself beyond reproach.

She was also always mailing Wendy and Adam invitations to benefit parties they couldn't afford to attend, then calling attention to their absence.

Paige had been a college classmate of Wendy's, as well. Back then, she'd been best known for launching SAD, a nationwide advocacy group for college students suffering from depression and anxiety. Despite her lifelong commitment to battling mental illness, however—and while there was every reason to believe that Paige herself was perpetually despondent—she'd never admitted to feeling anything less than peachy. What's more, those who made the mistake of suggesting otherwise risked being subjected to a fusillade of vituperation—those, for instance, who expressed sympathy over Paige's recent divorce, as Wendy had. ("What do you mean you're sorry?" Paige had snapped at her. "Sorry for what? Antoine and I came to a mutual decision we were both happy with. Case closed. Maybe you're sorry about your own marriage. But I'm not about mine.")

Wendy essentially loathed the woman. But she was Daphne's "other best friend." In some bizarre way, Wendy felt sorry for her. It was also common knowledge that Paige was an excellent point person to have during a crisis, if only because grappling with other people's distress and dysfunction was as close as she came to having a hobby. Not that Daphne's phone call from the night before necessarily constituted a crisis. Even so, Wendy felt compelled to keep Paige abreast of the situation:

P. Not to be alarmist—I think/hope she was just being dramatic—but Daphne called late last night and threatened to kill herself again. (Mitch, of course.) She promised me she'd call

14

Carol in the morning, but it probably wouldn't hurt if her
friends checked up on her, too—hence, my email to you. Anyway, hope things are well on your end. (I'm sure they are.) Yrs,
W.

Both emails sent, Wendy turned her attention to her editorial assignment for the day: an opinion piece arguing that the
Medicare prescription drug benefit had been a cynical give-
away to "Big Pharm," with the secret purpose of bankrupting
the federal government, thus leading to a permanent downsizing of the social safety net. *Barricade* had published a nearly
identical piece just the month before. But it was rhetoric, not
repetition, that concerned the magazine's top brass. Wendy's
initial editorial move was to cross out the first sentence, which
referred to the Republicans as "avaricious profiteers." (The
phrase seemed redundant, not to mention a little heavy-
handed.) "Let's start here," she wrote in the margin next to
sentence two. She'd only just begun to get her head around
sentence three—"While the military-industrial-pharmaceu-
tical complex siphons billions off the slumped backs of the
elderly and the incapacitated . . ."—when Paige's name came
blinking into her in-box.

To Wendy's secret shame, the sight of it filled her chest
cavity with what felt like a fresh burst of oxygen. Though she
mostly believed she'd reached out to Paige on Daphne's behalf, Wendy was also aware of being a horrible gossip. Moreover, gossip didn't fully exist for her in all of its nuance-laden
splendor until she'd shared and parsed it with someone else,
preferably someone who knew all the parties implicated.
Abandoning her editorial assignment, Wendy opened Paige's
message and began to read:

Wendy,

Please understand that I am AT WORK RIGHT NOW—and therefore NOT AT LIBERTY TO DISCUSS THESE SORTS OF PRIVATE MATTERS IN DETAIL. That said, the news is indeed distressing, and I will of course call Daphne at the first opportunity that presents itself. In the meantime, I think it would be prudent for one of us to contact Richard and Claire (Daphne's parents) and let them know what has transpired. In the bigger picture, I think it may also be time to confront Mitchell himself—not my first choice, obviously. But, then, Carol seems to be of limited help, and, quite frankly, I've run out of other ideas.

As for Daphne just being "melodramatic"—until the veracity of that statement is proven, Wendy, I don't think this is the time for us to be closing our eyes and hoping for the best.

As for me, I'm quite well, thank you—just sorry to have missed you at my multiple sclerosis benefit last night! We raised 325K, a record for the organization. I guess you've been busy. Perhaps there's reproductive news of which I'm unaware?

      Paige

"Wendy," someone was saying behind her head in a gravelly voice. "Do you have Leslie's copy yet?" (Leslie, whose full name was Leslie Fletcher—and who, for the record, was a man—was the writer of the Medicare piece.) Quickly downsizing Paige's email, Wendy swiveled around in her desk chair, only to find herself staring into the pockmarked face of *Barricade*'s executive editor, Lincoln Goldstein.

I'M SO HAPPY FOR YOU

Ordinarily, Wendy would have felt compassion for someone who had such a glaring cosmetic defect as Lincoln's. But "Missing Linc"—as Adam had nicknamed him—had a way of squinting as he spoke, one side of his mouth raised in a half smile, as if he were "in" on the fact that she spent a good portion of her workday emailing friends, playing solitaire, shopping online for furniture and clothes, perusing soul-deadening celebrity gossip Web sites, and generally pursuing cheap thrills that had nothing to do with fighting the forces of fascism in Washington and elsewhere.

But then, considering the paltry salary she was paid, Wendy didn't see how she wasn't entitled to a certain amount of personal time. Not to mention the occasional white lie. "I just got the piece this morning," she told Lincoln. (In fact, it had come in on Friday.) "I should have something for you to look at by this afternoon." With that, she straightened her spine against the back of her chair, the better to block her computer screen, which was currently blank.

She watched Lincoln's eyes case her cubicle and linger on the Duane Reade pharmacy shopping bag that sat on her desktop, as if it surely contained goatskin condoms for her lunchtime pleasure, when, in fact, it contained an ovulation predictor kit, an antiperspirant, and a three-pack of Hanes Her Way cotton briefs, because wearing nice underwear had come to seem as superfluous as having sex during the "wrong" time of the month. (It was rare for Wendy to buy new underwear at all; she tended to wear hers until their crotch panels were discolored and their waistbands had begun to sprout threads in the manner of carrots and potatoes left too long in the bin. It wasn't clear if Adam noticed, or minded.)

"Please forward it to me as soon as you finish," said Lincoln.

"Will do," said Wendy with a perky smile intended to combat his mocking and mistrustful one.

He probably stood there for only forty seconds. To Wendy, it felt like an eternity. Finally, he disappeared. Then Wendy reopened Paige's email, her anger metastasizing with each sentence she reread.

She found the opening one, with its gratuitous caps and simultaneously self-aggrandizing and punitive tone, possibly the most egregious. (While Paige was essentially adding zeros to the stock portfolios of rich guys in Connecticut, she apparently imagined herself to be running the World Bank.) Though Wendy's blood boiled with near-equal vigor as she reviewed the fifth: *I've run out of other ideas?* As if it were Paige's problem to solve! (And as if Daphne had called *her* the night before.) It was so typical of Paige to claim Daphne's unhappiness for herself, Wendy thought. She was further enraged by the parenthesis containing the words *Daphne's parents*. (As if, after sixteen years of friendship, Wendy didn't know the first names of Daphne's family members.) Clearly, Paige was trying to prove that she was better friends with Daphne than Wendy was. Never mind the chastising tone of "I don't think this is the time . . ."

As for the implication that Wendy had been too busy having sex with her husband to attend Paige's MS benefit, the charge was so risible that Wendy had trouble feeling offended.

The real question, Wendy thought as she closed Paige's email, was why she couldn't keep her mouth shut. She knew this was what Adam would say if she told him what had hap-

I'M SO HAPPY FOR YOU

pened. She could already hear him going off: *Paige Ryan is a shrew and a control freak. Why can't you accept that? Just because Daphne is friends with her doesn't mean you have to be. Also, why are you going around talking to other people about Daphne's private business? She called you—not the* New York Post.

Adam would be right, of course. At the same time, he clearly believed himself entitled to hear every last Daphne Update. (Apparently, he didn't belong to the group herein identified as "other people.") It also seemed to Wendy that Adam discounted the pleasure to be found in having an arch-enemy. It gave you something specific to feel indignant about when the larger injustices (murder, famine, disease, the fact that some people got pregnant without trying) were beyond your control. It made the landscape more colorful, too, like the weeds that filled in abandoned city lots. For these reasons—and also due to a lifelong need to have the last word—Wendy spent the next twenty-five minutes composing a reply that struck just the right neutral, even pleasant tone that subtly reclaimed the mantle of authority for herself while shaming Paige. She finally settled on:

P—
Please do let me know if you reach D and learn anything more. In the meantime, I have to admit I don't see the point of contacting Richard and Claire right now (i.e., I don't think it would accomplish anything more than antagonizing D). I'm afraid I feel the same way about contacting Mitch. Plus, in his case, if D found out that you or I had gone behind her back, it might have the unintended effect of bringing the two of them closer—at least in D's mind.

At this point, my sense is that D mainly just needs her friends around her—and also, yes, Carol. True she's been unable so far to get D away from M. But she's still a medical professional, which neither of us is.

Meanwhile, very sorry to miss your benefit last night. I only wish Adam and I had the funds to go to stuff like that! But until *Barricade* goes "public"—and Vulcan Capital starts buying shares in it ☺—I'm afraid it's unlikely.

As for baby making, I'll keep you posted if and when it ever happens.

W

It was only after clicking "send" that Wendy realized her error in including the word *ever* in her final sentence. There was only one way to deal with Paige, Wendy had learned over the years, and it was to censor all traces of vulnerability in one's self. (And here she'd practically lit the way to the front door of her heart.)

Several minutes later, a new message arrived from Paige, along with a group email from the husband of Wendy's friend Pamela. Even without the subject heading, "New Addition," Wendy could more or less guess the news the latter message contained. The last time she'd seen Pamela—by coincidence, several Saturdays before, in Prospect Park—she'd been thirty-eight weeks pregnant (and jogging). Even so, Wendy decided to open Pamela's husband's email first:

Please join us in welcoming into the world Lucas Henry Rose, born on October 2, at 8:32 PM—in a taxi stuck in traffic on the FDR, en route to New York Presbyterian Hospital—weighing 10 pounds, 11 ounces. Baby and Mommy are well, and Daddy is thrilled. (Todd.)

Wendy was thrilled, too. She also felt envious of Pamela's reproductive success, if not of the manner in which she'd achieved it (or the monstrosity of the child she'd been forced to deliver). But she'd already found a way to justify the news in her head, so it wasn't as threatening as it might have been. For one thing, Wendy reminded herself, Pamela had been married six months longer. For another, she was eight months older. She was also Pamela Jane Rose. Which is to say, perfection personified: not just beautiful and successful—she was a senior producer at a critically acclaimed television news program—but a phenomenal cook, a former Rhodes Scholar, and the ex–backstroke champion of Southern California. She was also really nice and therefore unhateable. Finally, she was one of the few women Wendy knew who didn't spend 50 percent of her waking hours complaining about her life. Not that she currently had much to complain about. But even when she had—even when she'd been single and diagnosed with a rare form of lymphoma—she'd claimed to savor each living moment. Just as now that she was healthy again and married to a bestselling novelist who was also drop-dead gorgeous, independently wealthy, always home, and committed to fifty-fifty parenting, she claimed to be the luckiest woman in the world. Most of the time, Wendy found Pamela's upbeat attitude refreshing and even inspiring. At other times, she found it deeply threatening, insofar as it threw into doubt the legitimacy of her own chronic discontent. She wrote back:

Dear Pamela and Todd, I'm so happy for you guys!!!!! That's wonderful news. Can't wait to meet the little—or, I really should say, quite LARGE—fellow. Did he really come out in the cab? Insane. Only you. Congratulations and much love, Wendy

With a sense of foreboding, Wendy then opened Paige's reply to her reply:

Wendy,
I am afraid you have more faith in Carol than I do. Despite her master's degree in social work, calling the woman a "medical professional"—it seems to me—is a bit of a stretch. But, then, I know how you people in the media business like to throw around words!
        Meanwhile—f.y.i.—I just read a very interesting article about infertility among women in our age group. It turns out that most of the issues (tube blockage, lack of cervical fluid, etc.) have their origin in STDs. Which is not to say you have one. Still, it might be worth checking. Also, if it's been six months, you really should seek help. Unfortunately, at our advanced age, the chances of conceiving plummet with every passing month. Luckily, none of this affects me, not only because I've never had an extended promiscuous period(!), but because I'm more committed to battling overpopulation than I am to any narcissistic need to see my cheekbones replicated in another human being. But, then, that's just me.
        Paige

Newly confirmed in her suspicion that Paige Ryan was a close family relation of Satan's, Wendy hit "delete." She was about to return to Leslie Fletcher's overwrought Medicare editorial when she discovered that Pamela had already written back:

> wen, thanks for the sweet note. can't wait for you to meet the babe! meanwhile, can't believe how hysterical everyone gets about childbirth. yes, i would have preferred a hospital (vs. taxi) delivery. but, really, it was so *not* a big deal. like a few bad menstrual cramps. (whatever.) i'm a little sore this morning. i mostly just feel bad for the cabbie! (kind of made a mess of his backseat—whoops.) i only wish he'd accepted my check for new upholstery. . . .
>
> anyway, should be heading home from the hospital in a few hours. any chance you and adam want to come by for dinner tonight? i have this great recipe for lasagna i want to try. xxoopammy

Pamela's superwoman act had the occasional, paradoxical effect of making Wendy feel the need to deride herself as scum personified. She wrote back:

> P, You are a champ for making it through labor unscathed! Having zero tolerance for pain, am hoping for a high-risk pregnancy, so I can schedule a C section. Though equally possible I'll never get pregnant and end up adopting a spina bifida baby from China. In any event, would so love to come meet Baby Luke tonight. But, tragically, being an alcoholic depressive, I already have drink plans. (Not sure what Adam's doing. Not that he ever tells me anymore.) Maybe I/we could come by this weekend?? And, wait, I should be cooking YOU lasagna. Unfortunately, being a total failure of a woman, I don't know how. (Amazing Adam hasn't left me already.) XXW

Again, Wendy clicked "send," only to be sidetracked by yet another arriving email. This one was from her friend Sara, a strawberry-blond intellectual property lawyer and Houston-reared heiress whose highly effeminate men's magazine "style editor" fiancé of four years, Dolph, was widely believed to be gay—hence his refusal to set a wedding date:

> Wendy, I heard from Paige that Daphne is threatening suicide again?? Is it true??? Sounds like you two have the situation under control, but please please please let me know if there's anything I can do. Love, Sara

The gossip chain had apparently just begun: Sara's email was closely followed by one from *her* best friend, Gretchen Daubner, a mite-sized workaholic UNICEF executive who rarely saw her two-month-old twins, Lola and Liam, conceived on Gretchen's third round of in vitro fertilization. (Wendy had yet to see them, either, though not for lack of trying.) Gretchen's email arrived with a "high priority" flag, though in truth almost all of her emails did:

> wen, i heard from sara that daphne tried to kill herself? is she okay?????? please let me know what the situ is a.s.a.p. (leaving for congo in an hour.) so worried, g

Wendy promptly replied to both women, assuring them that the situation was "under control." Then, if only to be sure that her assessment was correct, she called Daphne. But Daphne's cell and home phones both rang straight to voice mail. Not wanting to appear overbearing, Wendy left no messages. Instead, she called Adam to tell him about Pamela and

24

Todd's baby — "That's nice for them," he said — and also to report that she hadn't heard anything from Daphne, *and wasn't that kind of strange?*

"She's probably been kidnapped by aliens," he offered.

"I hope you get kidnapped by aliens," she told him.

"Maybe I already have," said Adam.

"Good — more room to stretch out in bed," said Wendy, who both cherished her husband's sense of humor and also wished that, if only once in a while, he'd give a straight answer, however stupid the question was.

The majority of Wendy's friends had stopped eating muffins years earlier, after *New York* magazine ran a damning exposé revealing that they were nothing more than glorified cake and possibly even more caloric. Preferring denial, Wendy devoured a corn muffin and lentil soup with the conviction that she was eating a healthy lunch. Then she headed over to Zara to check out the sale racks.

She returned to the office an hour and twenty minutes later with a top she realized retroactively was made of cheap fabric, was a shade of green best described as "broccoli," and was already missing a button. On the other hand, it had been marked 70 percent off. And the only thing Wendy hated more than missing a sale was getting ripped off. (To her lingering resentment, *Barricade's* copy chief, Hal Mooney, had surprised her on her thirty-fourth birthday the year before with a pizza party in the conference room, then asked her for a twenty to help cover costs.)

After stuffing her shopping bag in the bottom drawer of her desk — there was always the chance that Lincoln would come calling again—Wendy checked her in-box. To her surprise, there was still no word from Daphne. Surely by now the Klonopin had worn off, Wendy thought. And though Daphne had no job, she owned a BlackBerry and was therefore never far from email (and rarely missed an opportunity to write back, especially when the subject was herself). Maybe she was simply feeling too numb to express the humility and renewed vigor that were expected in scenarios such as these, Wendy reasoned. Or maybe she'd gone in for a special "double session" with Carol. Armed with these two possibilities, Wendy reopened Leslie Fletcher's Medicare editorial and attempted to apply herself to her job.

But her mind kept straying from the villainy of health maintenance organizations to the mystery of Daphne's whereabouts. At four o'clock, an email arrived from Wendy's insanely thin perpetual grad student friend Maura. It came as a welcome distraction from both topics:

> W, Will you forgive me if I cancel drinks tonight? Just totally wiped out from the weekend. (Have been working like a dog. Or is it a mule?) Anyway, am *finally* seeing the end of the diss. Am thinking now that I might be able to finish by next summer, or, if not next summer, definitely next fall/winter/spring. (We'll see.) But can we reschedule for next week? Promise to get to some kind of stopping point by then. Sorry again, M

Wendy was disappointed if not surprised. Whenever she made plans with Maura, she assumed there was a fifty-fifty chance of Maura's canceling. This was because although Maura had the least taxing schedule of any woman Wendy knew (with the possible exception of Daphne), she apparently

26

found her days to be stressful and action packed in a way that only an unstructured life of relative idleness could seem. Maura had been about to finish her dissertation — on the role of jugglers in the Scottish Enlightenment — for at least ten years. However it was that Maura actually spent her days — dotting and undotting i's? — it didn't apparently involve eating. Wendy had never seen her consume anything more than a handful of nuts off the bar. The few times she'd invited Maura out to dinner, Maura always claimed to have dined at home. So Wendy had learned to ask her out only for drinks, though she sometimes refused those, too. How was it possible that the most unstable person Wendy knew (again, with the exception of Daphne) was also the only one ever to have been released by her therapist in less than a decade, Maura's therapist reputedly having told Maura that they had "nothing more to discuss" and that their "work [was] complete"? Wendy's hypothesis was that Maura's therapist had simply lost patience and/or decided that Maura was too far gone to be helped.

Wendy wrote back:

Dear "Professor McLane,"
Bummed you can't make it tonight! But very exciting that you can finally see the finish line. (Keep up the good work.) And don't worry about tonight. I'm pretty beat, anyway. Up late last night dealing with Daphne. (Don't ask.) Let's talk next week?
Luv, W

Caffeine, Wendy thought. She strode the necessary twenty steps to *Barricade*'s decrepit kitchenette, where she ran into Lois Smith, the magazine's octogenarian receptionist, dressed in a purple muumuu and brown suede Birkenstocks in which her unaccountably bare and shockingly bulbous toes shone a frightening shade of deep purple. Lois had been a major player in the Adlai Stevenson campaign in 1956. She was also senile and often forgot whom she was putting calls through to. She sometimes forgot their names, as well. "Hello, Wilma," she greeted Wendy.

"Hi, Lois," said Wendy, lacking the energy to correct her (and also fearful that Lois might be offended if reminded of the fact that she'd essentially lost her mind). "How are you?"

"Troubled, my dear," said Lois, pressing down on her cane as she made her way to the sink with an ancient-looking Tupperware vat that bore the traces of a surfeit of mayonnaise. "America shouldn't be fighting France's colonial wars."

"Very true," said Wendy, nodding.

Returning to her cubicle with a lukewarm cup of Lipton—the coffee machine had been broken for two months and the office manager laid off—Wendy was amazed and alarmed to discover that it was already three thirty. Was it possible that she was still on page two of Leslie Fletcher's Medicare editorial? Guilt-ridden, she turned off her Internet connection.

At four thirty, feeling cut off from the world, she turned it back on. She had no new email. Yet again, she called Daphne. Both lines still rang straight to voice mail. She checked the headlines. Then she checked a Web site devoted to celebrity baby making, where she learned that Gwyneth Paltrow was pregnant with a second child. Though Wendy's life bore as much resemblance to Gwyneth's as a chimpanzee's did, her mood quickly soured. In search of a distraction from her distraction, she called up the secondhand furniture listings on Craigslist, where she conducted a search for a new (old) dining room table, preferably with built-in leaves. Wendy and Adam's apartment didn't have a separate dining room, but she figured they could always push a larger table against the wall of the living room when it wasn't in use. Moreover, although Wendy was a horrible cook and rarely entertained, her self-image rested in no small measure on seeing herself as the kind of person who threw raucous dinner parties complete with meaty stews in giant Le Creuset pots and bawdy banter about what ever happened to Monica Lewinsky and her blue dress. . . .

Somehow, it had become six o'clock. Wendy checked her email a final time. A freelance war zone journalist currently residing in Iraq had written to propose an article on the epidemic of "plastic bags caught in trees" along the streets of Baghdad. Wendy figured the guy was drunk. That or he was suffering from some kind of post-traumatic stress disorder. Either way, she decided to deal with his email tomorrow.

She figured she'd finish editing Leslie Fletcher's Medicare editorial the next morning as well. She was tired and hungry. And Lincoln had already left the office for his weekly watercolor class at the New School. After shutting down her computer and gathering together her belongings, Wendy called Daphne a final time.

A recorded message announced, "Mailbox full."

Wendy's mind began to race. What if this one time Daphne had actually made good on her threats? (What if she'd really lit herself on fire or, more realistically, swallowed the whole bottle of Klonopin?) Only, the bottle must have been almost empty, since she'd alluded to needing a new prescription. But even if she'd had only a week's supply left, there could be trouble. As Wendy considered the nonchalance with which she'd parried Daphne's earlier claims, she envisioned her old friend lying in a pool of vomit on the black-and-white-checkered floor of her bathroom.

Just as quickly, she pushed the picture away, telling herself it was ghoulish and absurd to imagine such things. Everyone agreed that Daphne was, above all, a top-notch actress. At the same time, Wendy knew she'd never forgive herself if something had happened to Daphne and she hadn't gone to check on her. Wendy couldn't bear the idea of Paige getting there first, either.

Daphne was the last of Wendy's friends to live in Manhattan. The rest had joined the exodus to Brooklyn — Sara to Dean Street in Boerum Hill; Gretchen to Kane in Cobble Hill; Pamela to the North Slope; Paige to tony Columbia Heights, overlooking the Promenade, in Brooklyn Heights; and Maura to the more-coming-than-up area around the still-polluted Gowanus Canal.

Since her late twenties, Daphne had lived in the pied-à-terre that her parents had purchased twenty years earlier on East 36th Street, near Second Avenue. The bedroom was small, the living room was a little dark, the ceilings were lower than you'd think they'd be in a prewar building. Plus, the block was permanently congested with traffic vying for entry into the Queens Midtown Tunnel. But it was more or less her own. And it had always secretly irked Wendy that while she and Adam struggled to pay the ever-increasing rent on their attic floor-through in an undistinguished brick row house on the southern edge of Park Slope, Daphne had to contend each month with only a modest maintenance fee.

Wendy had been there to visit so many times before that the doorman waved her through without making any attempt to announce her arrival. "Is she up there?" she asked, mostly to be polite, while skirting the rubber plant, Barcelona table, and chrome-and-black-leather Brno tube chairs that comprised the lobby decor.

"Haven't seen her since yesterday," he replied, unintentionally fueling her fantasies.

Wendy stepped into the elevator and pressed the button for the ninth floor. As the numbers lit up one after the other, she found her mind returning to the image she'd conjured before she left the office — of Daphne sprawled on the floor in a pill-induced stupor. The elevator shuddered to a stop, then opened onto the dimly lit mauve hallway that Wendy knew so well. She walked ten steps to the right, pressed Daphne's buzzer, and waited.

There was no immediate answer. Fifteen seconds went by, then thirty. Maybe Daphne was asleep. Or maybe she'd slipped out for an emergency pack of cigarettes while the doorman was in the restroom. But what were the chances of that? Daphne had officially quit smoking two years ago. Which was to say that, like Wendy and everyone else she knew, Daphne now limited her cigarette intake to infrequent "borrowings" from other people's packs. As Wendy buzzed again, she felt her heartbeat accelerating.

After another ten seconds went by without an answer, a surge of panic climbed the length of her chest, clamping down on her lungs and threatening to close her throat. It was a physiological reaction she still associated with certain traumatic childhood incidents—getting locked in her great-aunt's bathroom in Wilmington, Delaware, with the wallpaper featuring Victorian corset advertisements, getting separated from her mother at a carnival in the Adirondacks near Lake George. She could still remember how the tinny tunes emanating from the arcade game booths seemed to mock her abject terror, how the circling lights of the Ferris wheel mimicked her spinning head. "Daphne, it's me—Wendy," she called out, her face leaning into the crack between the door and the wall. Still, there was no response. "Daphne!" she called again, louder this time. "Please!"

Suddenly there was movement. Rustling. Footsteps. The clinking of a chain. The door cracked open, revealing a bare leg and a flushed cheek, followed by Daphne's short silk bathrobe with the Japanese leaf pattern. "Daphne!" Wendy cried again, this time with relief. She felt her breath returning to her, the world coming back into focus. (It was one thing to love stories and scandals—another to wish to be among their leading characters.)

"Wendy." Daphne spoke in a squeak. "What are you doing here?" Her cornflower blue eyes were popping and blinking. Her upper lashes were dotted with what appeared to be clumps of yesterday's mascara. A single silken head hair had become affixed to her cheek, its tip flirting with the corner of her mouth. Wendy also couldn't help but notice that even in disarray, Daphne looked beautiful—like some kind of French film star, with her pillowy lips, her gazelle's neck, her almost marmoreal skin. (She had only one visible flaw: a barely perceptible scar that started at the left corner of her mouth and zigzagged down the side of her chin like a tributary to a great lake, the remnant of a childhood accident involving a diving board. Maybe Wendy was the only one who'd ever noticed.)

"I was—I was worried about you," Wendy stammered. "I mean, is everything okay?" She couldn't tell if Daphne was happy to see her or not. And the not knowing unnerved her. She felt as if she'd missed some essential plot point, had accidentally skipped ahead to chapter seven without first understanding chapter six.

"You're sweet to check on me," Daphne answered with a shy smile. But her eyes fell to the floor as she spoke. And she still hadn't opened the door to its full capacity. That was when Wendy caught sight of him: a half-dressed man with a tangled mat of salt-and-pepper chest hair, taking a seat on Daphne's sofa. He had a television remote in one hand and a glass of something cold in the other. "I'm just having a little talk with Mitch," Daphne mumbled at the carpet, her shoulders hunched around her breasts, as the petals of a tulip close in around the stamen during bad weather.

Anger instantly displaced anxiety in Wendy's mind. She was furious at Daphne for making her worry for no reason. She was furious at herself, too, for being such a fool: she should have known that Daphne would be back with the guy the next night. Wendy supposed she ought to be relieved as well to find that Daphne was okay, insofar as having Mitch back in her bed was Daphne's version of okay. Only, how could Wendy feel relieved when she felt so stupid? So duped? So unwelcome? So convinced that the man was ruining Daphne's life? "Sorry—I didn't mean to disturb you guys." Wendy unleashed a bitter laugh as she began to back away from the door, her right palm raised.

"No—I'm sorry," said Daphne. "I shouldn't have called you last night when I was upset. It was selfish—"

"Everything okay out there?" It was Mitchell Kroker Reporting Live from the Sofa.

"Everything's fine," Daphne called back to him, frantically whipping her head around to face her lover. Then she whipped it back to face Wendy. "I know what you're thinking," she said with a cringing expression. "But it's not like that."

But now Wendy felt like the humiliated one. It was bad enough to be exposed for a worrywart and a fool, but to be placed in the role of moral authority was even worse. It made Wendy feel as if she were overinvested in Daphne's life, and as if she didn't have one of her own. It also reminded Wendy of the way things had been in college, back when her main identity had been Daphne Uberoff's Best Friend. At least, that had been her secret fear. "I don't care *what* it's like!" Wendy cried. "It's your life. Just do me a favor, and next time you're feeling suicidal at one AM, don't wake me up to tell me you're going to kill yourself and then not answer your phone for the next eighteen hours. Anyway. Whatever." She laughed again. "Good luck working things out with Mitch." She turned her back and started down the hall.

"Wendy!" Daphne called after her. "Please. I'm really sorry. . . ."

But Wendy kept walking, didn't answer, didn't know when she would. She and Daphne had had fights before. Or, rather, Wendy had got mad at Daphne. That was the usual pattern. It was built into their relationship that Daphne was the vaporous, unstable, self-absorbed, inconsiderate one, while Wendy was the consistent, solid, better friend. But within forty-eight hours, she always forgave and forgot. Some part of her was probably still flattered by the fact of her and Daphne's friendship—felt it made her more exciting where she'd always feared to be dull, effortless where she'd always imagined herself to be plodding. Another part probably felt guilty that she was happily coupled and Daphne not. (It made the universe seem upside down.) Then there was Daphne's difficult family situation back home in Michigan. Wendy felt bad for her about that, too.

Besides, who doesn't secretly love just a little bit more than usual the "best friend" who's busy fucking up her life for no apparent reason, especially when that "best friend" used to have it better than you?

But in that moment, Wendy found her supplies of sympathy, sycophancy, and schadenfreude all used up. Next time the phone rang after midnight with tales of heartsickness and neglect, she'd let it ring, she told herself. (Next time, she'd be too busy having sex with her husband.) And why hadn't she been the night before? That was the part that humiliated Wendy the most—that she'd been so desperate to take Daphne's call. To Wendy's relief, the elevator was still on the ninth floor. She got in without looking back.

2.

ENDY HAD NO memory of actually meeting Daphne—maybe because from the moment they met, it was as if they'd always known each other; they were already, instantly best friends, holding hands on their way to class, Wendy in her "uniform" of ripped Levi's and a black leather jacket, Daphne in red lipstick and clacking heels, her shiny black hair parted on the side and hanging over one eye, her pterodactyl fingers festooned with cocktail rings. She saw herself as some combination of the fictional character Holly Golightly and the forties film star Veronica Lake. She was frequently in tears. She laughed a lot, too. Daily life presented itself to Daphne, in turn, as a Puccini opera and some hilarious inside joke. There were always boys, later men, one after another, sometimes at the same time. "Josh will kill me if I sleep with Eduard," she complained to Wendy one brisk March afternoon of their sophomore year, her eyes narrowed to convey the difficulty and complexity of the situation in which she found herself. "But I'm also really attracted to him. And I don't know what to do. Will you come with me to his place tonight?"

"He's your friend!" protested Wendy, wary of looking like a tagalong.

"But his roommate, Boaz, will be there, too."

"Not that pasty-faced guy."

"He's cute!"

"Please — he looks like he has TB." The weekend before, Wendy had accompanied Daphne to the Friday night hip-hop party at the African American student union, where Eduard and his posse had stood together in the corner, laughing and dancing in place and wearing what appeared to be the same chain-link-patterned button-downs and Girbaud jeans.

"Well, his family owns diamond mines in Guyana, plus a bathing suit company in Brazil," said Daphne.

"I'm so impressed," said Wendy, who secretly, sort of, was.

"Pretty pleeeaaasssseeee?" Daphne angled her head entreatingly.

"Fine." Wendy ultimately consented with a heavy sigh, as if the sacrifice were large, even though it was no sacrifice at all. For in anointing Wendy her chief confidante and protector in times of trouble, Daphne had infused their relationship with a combination of intimacy and obligation that, to Wendy, felt like family. Or, at least, what Wendy, who had grown up with a single mother and no brothers or sisters, imagined family to feel like. (From what Wendy gathered, her father, Donald, if not a one-night stand, had been no more than a two-or-three-night one; Wendy had met him only twice — both times during her childhood. From what she remembered, he looked distressingly like the bearded "lover" illustration in her mother's semihidden copy of *The Joy of Sex*. The last Wendy had heard, he worked in forest preservation and lived in Washington State.)

But it wasn't just that Daphne made Wendy feel needed. It was that Wendy had never felt so clever, so convinced that the world was tamable, so excited to be young and alive, as she did in Daphne's company. And if most of the excitement belonged to Daphne, it was also true that Daphne had the ability to turn even the most mundane encounter (a chance meeting with a TA in the grocery store, an awkward kiss from a frat boy) into a triumph of wit and ingenuity. In that way, she made Wendy feel like part of the Big Story. And if Daphne had a tendency to make everything about herself, she was also warm and loving, even if her expressions of affection sometimes seemed insincere.

"You're my favorite person in the entire world," she told Wendy before air-kissing her in the vicinity of both cheeks. "Do you want to borrow something to wear?"

Wendy picked a stretchy geometric-patterned minidress and a navy blue men's blazer out of Daphne's vastly superior wardrobe. But no sooner had she got in the car — Daphne drove her father's old Saab — then she began to regret her outfit. She wished she'd worn her ripped Levi's. She felt too exposed — not just physically. (Wendy's other greatest fear about her friendship with Daphne was that people would think she was trying to be Daphne; Wendy knew enough to know she never would be.)

In college, all the rich foreign guys hung out in one clique. The majority hailed from Western Europe. Thanks to a couple of charismatic Iranian-American premed students whose families had emigrated to the US after the overthrow of the shah, however, they were collectively known around campus as the "Persian Versions." Nearly all the PVs lived off-campus, most of them in a four-story luxury apartment complex that overlooked a roaring river that ran along the outskirts of campus. Eduard de Hurtado, who was from Madrid by way of Monte Carlo, and his roommate, Boaz Rothschild Heidelberg, who was from Caracas via Switzerland, lived on the top floor. "Hellllooooo?" Daphne called out as she opened their door, Wendy one step behind. (That Eduard and Boaz left it unlocked made them seem even richer than they probably were.)

The two girls found the two boys seated on a deep-pile white rug. Eduard was smoking a cigarette, his blond hair pulled back in a ponytail, his knees bent and splayed, his back pressed against a low-slung beige sofa, while Boaz, his legs crossed in a modified lotus position, transferred the contents of a zip-lock bag into the bowl of a grotty-looking pipe. Pink Floyd's *Wish You Were Here* was playing on the stereo. A thick glass coffee table piled with newspapers, ashtrays, and a box of imported marzipan had been pushed off to the side. Behind them, a set of sleek glass doors with gleaming gold hardware led to a wrought iron balcony. At the sight of Wendy and Daphne, Eduard rose to his bare feet and exclaimed, "Las muñecas!" His spider legs were encased in tattered blue jeans, his sculpted chest in a tight raspberry-colored Lacoste polo shirt. Although Eduard was a chain-smoker who never exercised, he had the build of a championship swimmer.

Boaz, who was smaller and slighter, was wearing a pair of Adidas track pants and a wrinkled white button-down that appeared not to have been laundered in several months. His beard was stubbly. His eyes were bloodshot. He was deathly pale. At best, he was interesting looking. He didn't get up.

"Huh," he said, before returning to his drug-related activities.

"You remember my roommate, Wendy — right?" said Daphne.

"Encantado," said Eduard, slowly pressing his lips to the back of Wendy's hand.

"Hey," said Wendy, who was still trying to figure out what *muñecas* were. She thought back to Spanish class. Apples? No, that was *manzanas.* . . .

Now Eduard turned his full attention to Daphne, whom he kissed on both cheeks, then again on the first cheek, muttering, "Guapacita" between each peck. Then he said, "Please — you will sit," and motioned for Wendy and Daphne to join him and Boaz on their shag rug.

"Aren't you guys going to offer us a drink?" asked Daphne, tugging at her own miniskirt.

"Impatience!" declared Eduard. Then he raised one eyebrow. "A quality I like in a woman."

Wendy rolled her eyes at Daphne, who laughed and said, "Eduard — you are so full of shit!"

In time, Eduard produced a bottle of Campari and another one of club soda. He pushed the glass table back onto the rug and placed the bottles on top of it. Soon, Wendy found herself in possession of a highball glass filled with an orangey pink liquid that tasted like cherry-flavored cough syrup. "Yum," she said, then felt stupid for having used such an infantile expression.

It was another five minutes before Boaz opened his mouth. "Ganja?" he said, lifting his pipe and eyebrows at Wendy.

Finally, she'd been given an opening to display her keen wit. "No, thanks," she answered. "I only use herbs when I cook."

Boaz knit his brow in confusion. Or was it contempt? In either case, Wendy's joke had fallen flat. She felt like disappearing into the flokati rug. "Wendy's just kidding around," said Daphne, clearly trying to help out. "She doesn't actually cook."

Daphne declined Boaz's offer, too. (For all her other indulgences, she wasn't a pot smoker.) So the boys began to pass the pipe amongst themselves, their thumbs pointing up and out as they positioned a pink plastic Bic lighter over the bowl. Soon Boaz was doubled over with laughter and muttering, "Detective Asshole requests your presence."

"You are kindly requested to wait in the waiting room, Señor Asshole," Eduard replied, eliciting a new round of convulsions.

"Hey, it's bad manners to tell private jokes in front of visitors," said Daphne.

A minute earlier, Pink Floyd had gone quiet. Eduard took the opportunity to grab her hand and say, "You select the next song. Yes?" Encountering no protest, he led Daphne over to the stereo—leaving Wendy alone with Boaz.

Maybe she wanted to impress him. Maybe she was just trying to fill the time. Maybe she was hoping the pot would relax her. "Is there any left of that?" she asked, motioning at the pipe with her chin. "Maybe I'll have one hit."

"Please," said Boaz, crawling over to where she sat. He placed the pipe in her fingers, then held his lighter over the bowl as Wendy slowly breathed in. . . .

The pot—or maybe it was hashish—burned her throat. It also made her feel less negative toward Boaz. Genesis's *Three Sides Live* had replaced Pink Floyd. "Follow you, follow me," sang Phil Collins. Behind her, Wendy could hear Daphne giggling, "Shuuut uuuppp!"

"Come — we go to the balcony," said Boaz, holding out his hand.

Wendy took it, unable to think of a reason not to.

A rope hammock had been strung up between two of the balcony's sides. In the darkness it reminded Wendy of a giant spiderweb. Boaz climbed in and she followed, inching her buttocks across the net, then lifting her legs over the side as carefully as she could so she wouldn't expose her underwear. In the process, their ankles brushed against each other, imbuing Wendy with sudden longing for a romantic attachment of her own. For a few minutes, the two of them lay motionless and silent, listening to the frenzy of the river below. Finally, Boaz spoke: "We are insignificant specks on the earth's surface. You realize that, finally."

"On the other hand, trees and rocks don't have brains," offered Wendy, with the hope of saying something interesting and provocative that would set her apart in Boaz's mind. "So maybe we are special."

"How do you know trees don't have brains?" Boaz shot back.

"I don't know for sure!" Wendy laughed, taken aback by his accusatory tone.

Boaz pulled a pack of Rothman cigarettes out of the pocket of his rumpled shirt and slowly lit one. Then he turned his gaze on her — in the darkness his eyes looked like pink marbles — and smiled smugly. "Why is it that you feel you must try to be agreeable?" he asked.

Enraged by the suggestion, Wendy strained to think of a comeback that would shame and embarrass him. But the pot made her brain feel like sludge. All she could get out was: "That's a very rude thing to say to someone you don't know."

"I saw you inside." Boaz gestured with his cigarette toward the glass doors. "You feel overshadowed by your friend. You should have more confidence. You're attractive, too—in a more unconventional way."

Blood rushed to Wendy's cheeks and temples. With one line, Boaz Rothschild Heidelberg had destroyed her entire fantasy of herself and Daphne as a meeting of equals, each with her own attributes, neither more powerful than the other. "Fuck you!" she cried, furiously extricating herself from the hammock. "You don't know anything about me."

But he does, Wendy was thinking as she yanked open the sliding doors and reentered the living room.

She found Daphne seated on the low-slung sofa beside Eduard, who was running his hands through her mane and flicking his tongue at the underside of her neck while she moaned, "You know I can't" in a supple voice that was clearly lacking in conviction. Neither one of them seemed to register Wendy's entry. And Wendy suddenly didn't have the nerve to disturb them, to remind Daphne that she'd promised they'd only stay an hour, to jolt Daphne out of her enchanted world.

That was what it was like to be one of the beautiful people, Wendy thought as she skulked down the hall toward the front door, the Gipsy Kings' "Bamboleo," which had replaced Genesis on the stereo, growing fainter with every step. Your own life was so vivid that you barely noticed anyone else existed. It never even occurred to you to look, never mind to care what other people thought of you. That was the secret: the secret of obliviousness. You could act as hysterically as you wanted, but since it was always ultimately about your own reflection, no one ever really got under your skin.

The next morning, Daphne accused Wendy of abandoning her, and Wendy didn't argue otherwise, if only because she couldn't bear to admit what had happened with Boaz.

Looking back, it seemed to Wendy that as needy as Daphne frequently acted, she'd always had a way, however unwittingly, of making Wendy feel even needier.

But that's ancient history, Wendy reminded herself on her way out of the 9th Street station in Brooklyn. It wasn't Daphne's fault that some rich Venezuelan in college had made Wendy insecure about her looks and personality. It didn't matter, either. Wendy felt ashamed and embarrassed that she even *remembered* minor incidents from her late adolescence. Daphne probably had no recollection of who Boaz Heidelberg was, never mind Eduard de Hurtado. (Wendy was the type of person who remembered the name of every kid in her fourth-grade class.)

And when she thought about how much had changed in the fifteen years since that night! In her twenties, Wendy had worked hard to create her own identity and life apart from Daphne. Then, one day, she'd woken to find their positions seemingly reversed: Wendy's name published on a masthead for all the world to see, her bed and home full, while Daphne was anonymous, alone. Or at least most of the time she was. A homeless man, his beard caked with dirt, sat slumped in the stairwell that led to the street, muttering to himself. *Daphne isn't in that bad shape,* Wendy thought as she passed him. Yet there were few traces of Daphne's former glory—her free apartment, her fading beauty, a married guy who stopped by once a month when he happened to be in town.

Wendy, on the other hand, had a husband and a career. She had peace of mind, too. And if she'd never been a great beauty like Daphne—had always wished she were taller, had never liked her nose, had the typical complaints about her thighs—she'd reached a truce of sorts with her flaws. She was also proud of her long, thick brown hair. *I should feel sorry for Daphne,* Wendy thought. And she did. She also thought of the wonderful times they'd had together: their backpacking trip through Belgium after college, their "summer shares" in Fire Island (their last summer, Wendy had had to pry a deer tick off Daphne's leg—and had somehow enjoyed it), the countless alcohol-fueled confessions they'd traded at bars and restaurants and on each other's sofas over the years.

Even so, Wendy needed a break from Daphne's problems. She didn't even want to say her name out loud for a few days. Which was why, later that evening, back home in Brooklyn, Wendy told Adam she'd met up with Maura for a drink after work. (She knew he'd only ask her what she was doing at Daphne's place, then imply it had been Wendy's fault for showing up.)

"How's my Lady of Perpetual Graduate Student–dom?" he said.

"Oh, you know, toiling away," said Wendy, amazed at the facility with which she'd always been able to lie to her husband. "She's on some kind of cleansing grapefruit diet, so she didn't even drink." (Had that last detail really been necessary?)

And the next day at work, when an email arrived from Daphne, Wendy waited to open it until she'd finally finished editing Leslie Fletcher's Medicare screed. And when she did so, she performed a quick scan rather than conduct a careful exegesis, which would have been her normal inclination. It said: *So sorry for worrying . . . good friend . . . I know I'm pathetic . . . Obviously, I need help . . . I don't expect you to listen . . . Asking for your patience . . . Sorry again . . . Your friend, Daf.*

Fearing that not answering might be interpreted as a form of escalation—and also secretly eager to assert her superiority and indifference—Wendy wrote back, "D, It's fine. Let's talk later, W."

That's some sort of progress, she thought.

But by the following Sunday, Wendy's resolve to put distance between herself and Daphne had begun to falter. She woke that morning to find that she had her period again, even though she and Adam had had sex on two of her three most fertile days the previous month. That something she'd always taken for granted should turn out to be so elusive—that her life could be reduced to charting her menstrual flow on graph paper and examining her cervical fluid for signs of elasticity—made Wendy feel angry, ashamed, and disoriented. What's more, she had no one to complain to about how frustrated she felt at still not being pregnant. Bitching to Adam was out of the question. He would only remind her, as he always did, that they had each other (and Polly), which was the important thing.

And that he got tired of listening to her complain all the time.

And Wendy didn't feel right complaining to her other

friends who weren't married. (*At least you have a husband,* they were sure to think, if not to say.) She wasn't comfortable calling her friends who were already mothers, either. They were probably busy with their children, anyway—at least Pamela was. (Even though it was Sunday, Gretchen was probably attending a strategy session to end poverty in Africa.) Moreover, the pity in their voices—even if it was mostly projected; even if, in Gretchen's case, it was fairly clear she'd rather be anywhere than at home playing patty-cake with her twin babies—only made Wendy feel worse.

And for all of her problems, all of her hysteria, Daphne was the rare person who could hear other people's news and not immediately think about herself. Or at least Daphne gave that impression. (And was there really any difference?) Plus, on account of the many hours that Wendy had spent listening to Daphne talk about Mitch, she felt able to natter on about her own neuroses in a way she didn't with anyone else—especially now that she'd fired her therapist.

Wendy already missed the patter of their private language, with its rising and falling cadences, its ample use of hyperbole, especially on Daphne's part, too. "You're kidding!" she'd say. And "I'm dying!" And "That's just BEYOND!" Daphne's spoken English sometimes seemed to be composed entirely of exclamations. Which is maybe why Wendy never felt that Daphne was minimizing her pain.

And even though Wendy was the one who was supposed to be mad, she'd begun to worry that Daphne might be mad at her, too. (Why else had she not called?)

And what if Paige had stepped in to fill the void created by Wendy's retreat?

It was also true that Sundays had always depressed her.

There was too much pressure to relax. And the apartment seemed too quiet, even with Adam in the living room. Or maybe it wasn't quiet enough. She could hear him all the way across the apartment, crunching loudly on tortilla chips while he watched the Sci Fi Channel on TV.

And was it Wendy's imagination or, since the advent of text-based communication, did the phone never ring anymore? Then it did. . . .

The caller ID said "J. Sonnenberg." Wendy didn't know anyone by that name. But she was bored and curious. (She was always curious.) And the receiver was right next to her on the bed, where she lay leafing through a home furnishings catalogue, simultaneously loathing and longing for the fantasy of generically upscale domesticity intimated by a photograph of an immaculate suburban "mudroom" with individualized footwear cubbies labeled "Aidan," "Zach," and "Olivia." "Hello?" she said.

"Ohmygod, I'm *so* glad I reached you."

"Daphne?" said Wendy. It sounded like Daphne's voice, albeit dumped in a vat of honey.

"You're still furious at me, aren't you?" said Daphne.

"Forget about it — really," Wendy told her.

"Really?" said Daphne.

"Really," said Wendy.

"I'm so *beyond* relieved you're saying that. So, how are you?"

"Since you asked, terrible," said Wendy. "I got my period again this morning. I feel like I'm never going to get pregnant. Plus, I feel like I can't talk about it with Adam anymore.

He just gets mad at me for not being happy with what we have." Admitting her frustration to Daphne made Wendy feel as if a huge load had been lifted off her back.

"SWEEEEEETIE!" cried Daphne. "First of all, you're totally going to get pregnant. It just takes a while at our age. And then you're going to completely forget about this whole period of your life. In the meantime, OF COURSE you must be dying of frustration. Anybody would be—except maybe a Zen Buddhist. I mean, we're goal oriented. That's just who we are. Forget about Adam. Just talk to me. Men never understand this stuff anyway."

But Daphne understood. Or seemed to understand.

"Maybe you're right," said Wendy, feeling better by the second. "I mean, I hope you're right."

"Believe me, I'm completely and utterly right."

"Anyway. How are *you?*"

Daphne let out a mellifluous sigh before she announced in a singsongy voice an octave higher than normal, "Well, I'm in love. And no, not with Mitch. I met someone. I'm actually at his apartment right now."

In love—since Monday? "You're kidding!" said Wendy, as startled as she was suspicious. "That's amazing."

"No, *he's* amazing," said Daphne, lowering her voice to connote the seriousness of the situation. "I mean, he's possibly the greatest person ever—like maybe in the history of mankind."

Was Daphne dating Jesus? Gandhi? Hugo Chávez? "My god," said Wendy. "Who is he?"

Daphne's voice returned to the soprano range. "Well, his name is Jonathan. He's a lawyer. He's thirty-seven. Never married. Jewish—you know me!" She laughed. "Most importantly? He's literally the sweetest man I've ever met. I mean, he's beyond sweet."

"And you met him where?"

"Mortifyingly enough, at the gym. I mean, we'd seen each other there before, but we'd never spoken or anything. At least, I don't remember speaking to him. Though he *swears* he told me I left my water bottle on the Lifecycle or something a few months ago and I thanked him. But whatever. Tuesday morning, we were on adjacent treadmills, and we started talking. And we've basically spent every waking hour together since then."

"That's insane!" said Wendy, still struggling to believe. Daphne had the worst taste in men of anyone Wendy knew. Rich, married, arrogant, obnoxious, and over forty-five was her usual formula. She'd also seen Daphne rush into "serious" relationships before, only to find that they were flings at best, and cruel jokes at worst. Wendy didn't know if she had the energy to see her through another disappointment, another punch line that wasn't all that funny. "So you think it's for real?" Wendy knew as soon as she'd said it that it had been an unsupportive thing to say.

Daphne's voice sharpened. "What do you mean, do I think it's for real? I know it's for real!"

"Well, it's very exciting," said Wendy, anxious to make amends.

"Thanks, Wen," said Daphne, sounding wary if marginally less defensive.

"Of course —"

"So anyway, listen to this. Yesterday, Jonathan gave me this silver tennis bracelet from Tiffany's, engraved with both of our initials and the date we met. How insane is that?"

"Insane."

"I mean, it was literally the corniest present anyone's ever given me. But at the same time — honestly? — I was practically crying when he gave it to me."

"My god, he must be incredibly in love with you already," declared Wendy, suddenly feeling defensive on her own account. It had been years since Adam had given her any jewelry. Now that she thought about it, he'd never given her any jewelry, other than her wedding band, which — now that she thought about *that* — they'd ordered together (Adam had gotten a matching one) and paid for jointly. Actually, Wendy had paid, and Adam, who had no savings at the time, had promised to pay her back for at least half the cost — a promise that had become moot after they got married and merged bank accounts. Not that he'd accumulated any savings since then.

"Well, I don't know how in love with me he is," said Daphne. "But, at the risk of jinxing things, I honestly think this might be it. I mean, I don't think I've ever felt this way about anyone."

"Well, it's great news," said Wendy. And it was. Wasn't it? If Daphne was to be believed, she'd finally broken free of Mitch's grip. What's more, from how Daphne had described him, Jonathan Sonnenberg was precisely the kind of man who Wendy and her friends had been exhorting Daphne to date. He was available, he was age appropriate, and with any luck, he was not dependent on antipsychotic medication that he occasionally forgot to take.

Yet there was an unreality to Daphne's voice and words that Wendy felt somehow irked by. Only seven days earlier, after all, Daphne had been threatening suicide. From the way she was acting now, it was as if Mitchell Kroker had never existed—and that, by association, Wendy hadn't spent hundreds of hours of her life listening to Daphne prattle on about the guy.

Or was Wendy being ungenerous, petty, even? No doubt Daphne was in the myopic first throes of, if not love, then at least infatuation, when the world receded from view leaving nothing in its place but the two of you. Wendy recalled having briefly inhabited this particular desert island with Adam, although she could no longer remember what the sand had felt like beneath her feet.

"Well, I can't wait for you to meet him," Daphne was saying.

"Well, I can't wait to meet him!" said Wendy.

"Maybe the four of us could meet for dinner next week? We could even come out to Brooklyn—"

"That would be great," lied Wendy, who reserved a special dread of group restaurant expeditions, if only because someone always ordered three appetizers and four times as much alcohol as everyone else and then, when the check came, suggested they split the bill evenly.

"Terrific," said Daphne. "Why don't you talk to Adam and I'll talk to Snugs and then we'll talk again in a day or two."

"Snugs?" said Wendy, knowing full well to whom Daphne was referring. It just seemed unfair that Daphne should have an "adorable" inside-joke nickname for the guy after six days.

"Oh, sorry!" Daphne giggled. "That's my little pet name for Jonathan. He's so into cuddling that I started calling him Snuggle Bunny. Then it got shortened to Snuggle, then Snugs."

"It's very cute," said Wendy, reminding herself that she had an affectionate nickname for Adam, too: Mr. Potato Head. Though hers was critical as well as affectionate, insofar as its origin lay in what she deemed to be the beginning of jowls on her husband's face.

Adam had a new nickname for Wendy, as well: Pope Wendy, because, according to him, just like the pope, she was "only interested in sex for procreation." With every new menstrual cycle that failed to produce an embryo, Wendy found the joke a little less funny.

After Wendy hung up the phone, she went into the living room, where Adam sat on their pilling Ikea sofa, Polly panting at his feet, and said, "Hey." She was excited to tell him Daphne's news. She thought he'd be excited, too. Some insecure part of her thought he'd be less likely to leave her if she kept the stories coming. She was mad at him also—for never buying her a bracelet. She was mad at herself, as well, for caring about something as superficial as jewelry.

"Huh," Adam grunted without looking up.

Wendy sat down next to him and folded her arms across her chest, a signal of irritation she knew he'd fail to notice. There were crumbs everywhere, which annoyed her further. Why couldn't he keep the chips in his mouth? She figured she'd let *that* complaint go, too. What was the use? Adam was a slob; that was just who he was.

He was watching *The Twilight Zone*. It was that famous episode where a guy on an airplane looks out the window and sees a boogey man balanced on the wing. All the flight attendants think he's crazy because every time they look, the boogey man disappears. Then the station switched to a low-budget commercial for a nearby Hyundai dealership. Bunting filled the screen. Rebates were promised. "So, Daphne met someone," Wendy began. "Some lawyer guy who's madly in love with her and already got her an engraved bracelet from Tiffany's."

"Let me guess," said Adam. "This one isn't quite as married as the last one, though, technically, he's still married."

"You're so hilarious," Wendy replied as she frequently did — only with more aggression. As if he wasn't actually that hilarious.

But if Adam detected anger in her voice, he ignored it. "Any chance you want to make us eggs?" he said, his nose suddenly burrowed in her neck.

"Make your own damn eggs!" she said, pushing him away.

"Purty please. I'll have sex with you every day next month — "

The tears came on suddenly, collected in the corners of her eyes, where they shimmied like disco dancers. "I got my period this morning," she choked out.

"That was pretty obvious," said Adam.

"How did you know?!" asked Wendy, an octave higher than normal. Just like Daphne. (She was still shocked by how well her husband could tell what she was thinking, even when he didn't appear to know she was alive.)

"Because you've been moping around the house ever since you woke up," he answered. "And now you're upset that Daphne found another married guy to buy her some heinous ankle bracelet from Tiffany's."

"It was a regular bracelet, not an ankle bracelet!"

"Same thing."

"You're such a Mr. Potato Head," declared Wendy. But now she was laughing, too—laughing and dabbing at her eyes with the backs of her hands and nestling into the crook of Adam's arm, and thinking that things weren't so bad after all. Daphne Uberoff wasn't such a bad friend. Adam Schwartz wasn't such a bad husband, either. (She loved their private, nonsensical language, too.) And if there wasn't much romance left to their romance—and he didn't currently earn a living wage—he had a special talent for making upsetting things seem amusing. And that was something—really, more than something.

And when she woke before dawn, as she frequently did, her mind agitating preemptively with the dread of being unable to fall back asleep—moreover, of feeling that she'd never make up the hours, never catch up—she'd press her chest and belly into the back of his T-shirt, letting his body warm hers and his heartbeat reset her own.

"And you're my special Pope Wen," said Adam with a quick squeeze. "But can we talk about it in a few minutes?" (The show was back on.)

The news of Daphne's burgeoning romance spread rapidly through the social circle that she and Wendy shared, with reactions ranging from cautious optimism to outright euphoria. The general feeling was that Jonathan, whoever he turned out to be, couldn't be any worse than Mitch. Wendy took no small measure of pride in knowing that she'd be the first to meet him. The four of them (Wendy, Daphne, Adam, and

Jonathan) had made plans to meet for dinner the following Thursday, at a bistro in Fort Greene.

The restaurant had been Wendy's idea. She and Maura had eaten there several times over the summer — or at least Wendy had eaten and Maura had watched her do so. The food was casual French. The decor was funky. The lighting was dim but not too dim. Most significantly to Wendy, the prices were reasonable. It was also loud enough in there to fill any gaps that arose in the conversation. (Wendy expected there might be a few.) She was further hoping that Adam would get a kick out of the waitstaff, which was composed of extremely attractive Quebecois lesbians. Adam preferred diners to restaurants, and eating at home on the sofa while watching TV to both. He'd also expressed "zero interest" in meeting Jonathan. And Wendy was always feeling guilty about dragging him places, even though it seemed to her that they never went anywhere. "I really owe you one for this," she told him as they took their seats on what appeared to be a church pew, beneath a vintage poster for Courvoisier depicting a cancan girl in a fur stole and nothing else.

"You can pay me back in sexual favors," said Adam.

"There's something in your hair," said Wendy, ignoring the provocation.

"What?" He ran a hand through his curly mop. Several seconds later, it emerged with the crumbling remnants of a maple leaf.

"Did you and Poll go to the park today?" she asked.

"The park?" He wrinkled his brow. "No. Why?"

"I was just wondering how the leaf got there," Wendy said, shrugging.

Adam shrugged, too, as he ground the remains of the leaf into his hand. "Must have fallen from the sky," he said. He took a sip from his water glass. He looked around. Then he said, "Damn, the waitresses are really hot here. Are you sure they're lesbians?"

"You're turning into a dirty old man," said Wendy.

"Turning?" he said.

Wendy flashed back to their first date, if you could call it that. The two of them had met at his favorite coffee shop, a hole in the wall on Thompson Street in Manhattan, where they'd sat on a bench out front, smoking cigarettes that Adam had rolled for them in tissue-thin Drum papers and talking about their jobs (Wendy was an editorial assistant at *The Village Voice;* Adam was a production assistant at i.Guide.com) and their childhoods (from what Wendy could gather, Adam's had been happier than hers). After their first kiss—later in the hour, on that same bench—he'd turned to her and said, "It's cool hanging out with you." Maybe it wasn't the most romantic line ever uttered.

Somehow, Wendy had been touched. Somehow, she still was.

Maybe it was the distinctive way Daphne walked or, really, slinked, her hips forward, her back straight, her shoulders slightly rounded—the lower half of her body seemed to move without the assistance of the top—but as soon as she entered any room, Wendy had always been able to spot her. That evening was no exception. "Here they are," she said, as the brown velvet curtain that separated the dining room from the door billowed behind two slim figures.

Upon closer inspection, Daphne was wearing a low-cut beige tunic sweater and a pair of off-white jeans that hugged her thighs. Her hair was dark, her skin was pale to the point of translucent, her eyes were the same color as Windex. After all these years, her beauty still startled.

Jonathan Sonnenberg turned out to be an equally handsome specimen of Homo sapiens. He had bright brown eyes, a sculpted chin, the same glossy black hair as Daphne, and the smooth, tan complexion of someone who'd been well taken care of in life. He was wearing an expensive-looking navy blue suit jacket over a crisp white oxford shirt with French cuffs. His hair was parted on the side and formed a swoosh over his forehead. As he approached the table, his mouth was raised in a smile that suggested amusement at some larger irony to which the rest of them were unlikely ever to be privy.

"I'm so, so sorry we're late," Daphne began breathlessly. "We literally couldn't find a cab anywhere!"

"Don't worry about it," said Wendy. She stood up to hug Daphne hello. Then she turned to Jonathan. "Hi, I'm Wendy," she said. "It's so nice to meet you."

"Jonathan Sonnenberg," he replied while making slippery contact with her right hand. "And a pleasure it is."

"And this is my husband, Adam Schwartz." Wendy motioned to her right.

"Hello, and I like the T-shirt," said Jonathan in a mocking tone.

"Thank you," said Adam with an exaggerated smile that clearly belied offense.

Wendy felt embarrassed and vindicated in equal parts. Before dinner, she and Adam had argued over his choice of garb.

Wendy had suggested he wear a collared shirt; Adam had insisted on donning his favorite faded blue T-shirt that read "Women Love Me, Fish Fear Me," a memento from the summer he'd spent in Alaska after college, working on a salmon boat. The previous year, Wendy had hid the shirt in the linen closet between two towels — with any luck, a first stop on the road to Goodwill. But Adam had ransacked the apartment until he'd found it.

"Well, I am so happy we're all here!" Daphne announced with her usual effusiveness. "And Wen — you look so great. I swear you get younger looking every year."

"Oh, please," said Wendy, waving away the compliment even as she basked in its aura.

"I understand you're turning twenty-eight this month," said Jonathan.

Wendy couldn't tell if he was flattering her or making fun of her. "Twenty-seven — please," she answered gamely, willing to give him the benefit of her doubt.

In time, a small woman with long bangs appeared with menus. "To drink?" she asked brusquely before they'd even had a chance to open them.

"I'll have a glass of the sauvignon," said Wendy, after confirming that it was the cheapest selection on the white-wines-by-the-glass list.

"That sounds perfect! One of those for me, too," said Daphne — to Wendy's relief. (Wendy had expected Daphne to order the eleven-dollar glass of Sancerre, oblivious as she'd always been to the cost of living.)

"And I'll have a Heineken," said Adam.

It was Jonathan's turn. His lips pressed together as if he were about to whistle, he reviewed the menu while Bangs lowered her lids over her eyes — or at least what was visible of them — as if she were about to fall asleep from boredom. Finally, he looked up and asked, "Do you have any American beer?"

"This is a French restaurant," the waitress answered tartly. "We have no American beer."

"But you have German beer," Jonathan pointed out.

"I tell you — we have no American beer!" Bangs said again, this time in a shrill tone.

"No need to get hysterical, woman," said Jonathan, slapping his menu down on the table. "I'll just have water."

"Perrier?"

"No, the kind that comes out of the *goddamn* faucet and I don't have to pay for!"

"Jesus Cristo," Adam muttered in a bad Spanish accent.

Again, Wendy felt her allegiances divided. Clearly, Jonathan was acting like a jerk. But the skinflint part of her was delighted to hear that he was failing to add to the dinner bill. At the same time, she felt an overwhelming urge to please Daphne — if necessary by pleasing her new boyfriend. "Don't you guys have Sam Adams?" she asked.

"Sam Who-is-this?" Bangs squinted at her.

"Sam Adams," Wendy said again. "The beer. I know I've had it here. Isn't it on tap at the bar?"

"I will have to check." The woman sniffed before stomping away.

After she'd gone, Wendy expected Jonathan to thank her for calling the waitress's bluff. But he said nothing. His eyes drifted away from the table. "So, Daphne tells me you're a lawyer," said Wendy, trying to draw them back.

"That is correct," he said.

"Wills and estates?" she blurted out, for no particular reason.

"I'm a federal prosecutor for the Southern District of New York."

"Oh!" said Wendy, straining to think of something civil to say, possessed as she was of a deep-seated bias toward public defenders, those champions of murderers, rapists, turnstile jumpers, and the wrongly accused alike. Finally, she came up with: "Well, that must be exciting work. Do you get to bust Mafia dons and stuff?"

"Occasionally," he answered.

"A few years ago I got obsessed with that tabloid story about that old guy who walked around the West Village in his bathrobe, pretending to be insane so he wouldn't have to stand trial. Remember him — the 'Odd Father'?"

"The majority of my work involves the war on terror," announced Jonathan.

Though Adam was essentially uninterested in politics, he'd found an opening. "War on terror," he said, shaking his head as he exhaled through his nose. "I fucking hate that phrase, man."

Jonathan didn't hesitate: "Are you denying that the West is engaged in a defining struggle against an international network of fundamentalist Islamicists who exhibit no respect for human life and who would like nothing more than to wipe us off the map?" he shot back.

There was an awkward silence. "Ohmygod — Wendy — did I tell you I got carded last week?" said Daphne. She scoped Wendy's face for a reaction.

"You're kidding," Wendy answered with somewhat less

enthusiasm. (She hadn't been carded in ten years. Which made her think that Daphne had been lying when she told Wendy she kept getting younger looking.)

"I'm not denying anything but you being a pain in the ass," said Adam. Wendy cringed. As obnoxious as she found Jonathan, her fight with Daphne was still too fresh to risk alienating her all over again, if only via Adam. Nor had she forgotten the reason for their dinner: they were there, after all, to laud Daphne in her long overdue subrogation of Mitchell Kroker for a man who was apparently, if unfortunately, available. But Adam wasn't finished. "Though I might also point out that the war in Iraq has nothing to do with your death-worshipping fundamentalist Islamicists," he continued, "since, for starts, Saddam Hussein was a secular leader who, if not a good guy, never threatened a single American interest."

"Hussein threatened Israel," said Jonathan.

"So?" said Adam.

"So I told the guy, 'You have no idea how happy you're making a thirty-four-year-old woman right now,'" said Daphne, as if her conversation with Wendy were the only one at the table. "So then—get this—I pull out my license, and it's EXPIRED, and the guy won't let me in! I mean it was just BEYOND."

"Israel's strategic interests are America's interests," said Jonathan.

"Wooooooooooeeee." Adam began to laugh in a staccato-like clip. "According to who?"

"According to me."

"What are you—the fucking secretary of state or something?"

"God, isn't it pathetic that neither of us drive?" said Daphne.

"Totally pathetic," said Wendy.

"Let me guess — you went to Bennington and majored in pottery," said Jonathan.

"Wesleyan, actually," said Adam. "And, for the record, I majored in European history."

"And when the next holocaust comes, remind me which of your favorite *liberal* European democracies you'll be jetting off to. Sweden? France?" Jonathan laughed knowingly.

"I'm sure as hell not heading to the country you're living in," said Adam.

"Jerusalem will miss you," said Jonathan. "Or, actually, maybe it won't."

"Sweetie — come on," said Daphne, stroking his arm and seemingly mortified, as well. Or was Wendy just projecting?

"Don't worry, I'll be in the West Bank, bulldozing some refugee camps. Oh — sorry — that will be you," said Adam.

"The Palestinians have as much right to the West Bank as the Aborigines — another *nomadic* people, though possibly not as homicidal a one," said Jonathan.

Daphne kept at it. "So I went to the DMV yesterday to get it renewed," she said, turning back to Wendy. "And I swear, I stood there waiting for, like, SIX HOURS. I mean, it was like everyone in the city was having their license renewed on the same day!"

"That sounds hellish," said Wendy. But she was no longer listening to Daphne. The Arab-Israeli conflict was one of the few subjects that made her feel as if she really *was* a politically engaged creature, as opposed to one who cared mainly about celebrity baby gossip. "Honestly?" she said, turning to Jonathan in a burst of anger and excitement. "I get so tired of people bringing up the Holocaust to justify Israel's occupation of the West Bank. Yes, the Palestinians have done some really odious things. But why should they have to pay for the crimes of the Nazis?" Feeling simultaneously triumphant and terrified, Wendy turned to Adam, who squeezed her thigh approvingly. Then she glanced back at Jonathan, whose face revealed further amusement. Finally, she looked at Daphne, whose eyes appeared in danger of popping out of her head. Guilt and embarrassment quickly replacing giddiness, Wendy swatted at the air and announced, "Anyway, enough politics for the night."

"Wendy is an editor at *Barricade* magazine," Daphne said to Jonathan.

"Not that old commie rag," Jonathan said, chuckling.

Again, Wendy felt fire in her chest. But Daphne's brow was now so deeply knit that a cleft had formed between her eyes. Wendy took a deep breath and said, "So, are you guys already planning for the holidays?"

"Well, Jonathan's family has a house up near Stratton," Daphne said quietly. "And I think we're going to go up there and do a little skiing. Or"—she laughed quickly—"in my case, sitting around the fire drinking hot chocolate and reading *Shopaholic* novels. Anyway, I think we're going to be there the whole time."

"Fun!" said Wendy as enthusiastically as she could manage. "And your family doesn't mind you missing Christmas?" As far as Wendy could remember, the Uberoff family Christmas, which took place in Daphne's hometown of Ann Arbor,

Michigan, was a fairly big deal. Never mind the fact that Daphne's mother, Claire, was in a wheelchair with late-stage multiple sclerosis.

"Well, we're going to do Hanukkah this year instead," Daphne said, turning to Jonathan with a demure smile, which he reciprocated with a proprietary arm around her squirrelly back.

A surge of rage toward Jonathan Sonnenberg pulsed through Wendy. Politics was one thing. Religion was another. Surely, Daphne wasn't going to give up her heritage for a man she'd met less than two weeks before. (While there was reason to believe that her maternal grandmother had been part Jewish, Daphne was essentially Presbyterian.) Or was it none of Wendy's damn business what religion Daphne did or didn't practice? And why did Wendy even care? Wasn't the important part that Jonathan seemed to make Daphne happy?

Bangs reappeared with their drinks, including a Sam Adams for Jonathan, which she plunked down before him, spilling some in the process. He didn't say thank you, and she didn't say sorry. She flipped opened her notepad and said, "To eat?"

Adam ordered the hamburger, Jonathan the steak frites, Wendy the coq au vin, and Daphne, as she always did, two appetizers. (Daphne always claimed to have had a "huge snack" just before she left the house.)

While they waited for their meals to arrive, Wendy struggled to keep the conversation going. Politics and religion were now off-limits. Jonathan didn't know any of the same people that Daphne and Wendy did. Wendy had already asked him about his job. And he seemed utterly disinterested in finding out anything more about Wendy or Adam than he already knew.

"So, have you guys been watching *Iron Chef*?" asked Wendy during one uncomfortable lull.

"What channel is that on again?" asked Daphne.

"The Food Channel," said Wendy.

"Oh. I'm not sure if I get that." She turned to Jonathan. "Do I get the Food Channel?"

"Beats me." He shrugged. It was his last contribution to the general conversation. He spent the rest of the evening nuzzling Daphne's neck, whispering in her ear, and, after their dinners finally arrived, nearly an hour later, eating off her plate.

Halfway through the meal, Adam turned to Jonathan and said, "Enjoying your French-I-mean-Freedom fries?"

"Is someone talking to me?" Jonathan asked. He turned around in his seat as if the voice had come from a neighboring table. Finding no one there, he went back to his dinner. To Wendy's relief, Adam left it at that.

Finally, dinner was over. The four of them passed through the velvet curtain and onto the sidewalk. A taxi pulled up as if on cue. "Good night, Brooklyn," Jonathan announced without eye contact, before he disappeared into the backseat.

Daphne lingered on the sidewalk. "Well, it was so great to see you guys. Adam," she said, throwing her arms around him, "I swear I haven't seen you in, like, a year!"

"That's not true," said Adam. "I see you every time you

come out to the Slope, which happens — wait — have you
ever been to our apartment? We've only lived there for four
years."

"Shuuut uuuup — of course I've been there!" Daphne said
with a broad grin.

"Suuuuure."

"You're so mean to me."

"It's only 'cause I love you."

"Yeah, sure — "

"I do."

"Prove it."

Wendy smiled. She'd always found it gratifying to see other
women flirting with her husband: it made him seem worthy of
flirting with and was therefore a compliment to her. She also
suspected that Adam enjoyed the attention more than he let on,
especially when it came from Daphne. It was she who had introduced Wendy to Adam. The three of them had been at a
party in the East Village thrown by an aspiring singer-song-
writer-womanizer named Donal Wendy-Couldn't-Remem-
ber-His-Last-Name, who wore women's headbands in his
lanky brown-blond hair. He and Adam had gone to college together. Daphne had slept with Donal once, or maybe it was
twice. (It was unlikely she remembered his last name, either.)
That was Wendy and Donal's only connection. But the few
times a year they'd see each other, he'd hug and kiss her hello as
if they were old and close friends. (For a while, for Wendy, the
city was filled with people like that — people who squeezed
her tight, and said, "Yo — Wen! — Where you been? —
Baby — I've missed you!" as if they'd actually thought about
her once since they'd last met. And then, one day, it was no
longer like that. One day, those same people started walking

right by her like the virtual strangers they actually were. And it was jarring but it was also kind of a relief.)

Neither Adam nor Daphne had ever satisfyingly described their meeting for Wendy. As she understood it, Daphne had plucked Adam off the sofa in Donal's living room with little more than, "Will you come meet my friends?" Then she'd dragged him through the crowd to Donal's bedroom, where Wendy stood talking to another now-lost acquaintance. "Wen—you have to meet my new best friend, Adam!" Daphne had said, her hand in his. "Isn't he adorable?" She'd laid her head on Adam's shoulder.

Always obliging, Wendy had said, "Hey."

"How are you?" he'd answered.

"Fine, except I can't breathe," she'd told him. It was one of those apartment parties that was so crowded you literally had to shove people out of the way—that or climb over furniture—to get to the other side of the room. (Somehow, only Daphne had managed to move freely.)

"I have clove cigarettes if you want one," Adam had offered. "They always drive away a few assholes."

Wendy had smiled, amused, and said, "I'm okay, but thanks." From the beginning, there had been an immediate connection between her and Adam—a shared misanthropy laced with humor and longing. Was that it? In any case, Daphne had done Wendy the biggest favor that a friend could do; hadn't she? And yet, over the years, Wendy had come to resent the fact that Daphne had found her a husband. It gave her too much power; it made Wendy feel indebted. . . .

"Daphne Uberoff." It was Jonathan, calling from the back of the cab.

"Well, I better run." Daphne threw her arms around

Wendy. "Thank you so much for organizing this. It was *beyond* great to see you guys."

"It *was* great," said Wendy.

"I'll call you tomorrow. Mwuh." Daphne blew a kiss in Wendy and Adam's general direction. Then she, too, disappeared into the cab.

As Daphne and Jonathan's taxi sped off, Adam turned to Wendy, and said, "It's official. He's the worst person on earth."

"What about that serial killer guy, Jeffrey Dahmer?" Wendy said, laughing, as they crossed Lafayette.

"He's dead," said Adam.

"He is?" said Wendy.

"He got bludgeoned in the men's room, like, his first day in jail."

"Bummer . . ."

They decided to walk home. Or, really, Wendy made the decision for them. The dinner had cost more than she'd anticipated, and a car service home was likely to add another ten or fifteen bucks to the evening's bill. Plus, it was a beautiful, crisp autumn night, the kind of night that, as a child, Wendy had associated with the knowledge that the holidays were all fast approaching, each—in theory, at least—with its own storehouse of treats. (In practice, holidays at Wendy's mother's apartment on the Upper West Side had mostly been dreary potluck affairs populated by a random assortment of neighbors, cat-sitters, and visiting professors at Lehman College in the Bronx, where Judy Murman taught in the women's studies program.)

"Anyway, serial killers don't count," Adam went on.

"Bin Laden?" suggested Wendy.

"I guess you have to give Sonnenberg credit for not incinerating thousands of innocent people in an office tower. Still, could you believe that line about the Palestinians? What an A-hole."

"At least he's not married, like Mitchell."

"He will be soon."

Wendy gasped. "Oh, god, you don't think—"

"I think indeed," said Adam as they headed east on South Portland. "The guy isn't exactly a bohemian type. And he's probably getting close to forty."

"I think he's thirty-seven."

"Well, then, he's probably anxious to populate his own land—you know, raise some nice Zionist children to populate Israel before those nomadic Arabs multiply the place into extinction."

"Stop, you're hurting me!" Wendy covered her ears. But her discomfort had found a new source: Adam himself. She couldn't help but wonder why her husband, essentially the same age as Jonathan, wasn't more anxious about repopulating his own land. At the beginning of the year, he'd finally agreed to go along with her plan to get pregnant—as far as Wendy could tell, only because she'd drilled into him the idea that time was running out. (Maybe it already had.)

Wendy spent the rest of the walk home pretending not to be upset. "What do you mean?" she'd say when Adam asked her why she'd fallen silent.

Forty minutes later, they turned onto Thirteenth Street in Park Slope. Exhausted, Wendy broke her rule about makeup removal and collapsed into bed. Shortly afterward, Adam joined her under the covers. She was just drifting off to sleep at twelve twenty, when the phone rang.

Her first thought was Mitchell Kroker. He still wasn't committing. He was never going to commit. Was Daphne ever going to move on? Returning to full consciousness, Wendy recalled that Mitch was now history and that Daphne was happily paired with Jonathan. So why was she calling so late? Had they already broken up? It seemed unlikely. Just an hour or two earlier, they'd been eating off each other's forks.

This time, the ringing seemed to be coming from Adam's dresser. Wendy stumbled out of bed and thrust her hand in the direction of the receiver. Adam was snoring lightly. He could sleep through anything. . . .

It was Adam's mother, Phyllis.

"Phyllis, hi," said Wendy. "Is everything okay?"

You weren't supposed to like your mother-in-law, but Wendy actually got along better with hers than she did with her own mother. This was maybe because talking to Judy Murman frequently made Wendy feel as if she were standing trial, whereas she felt loved and accepted by Phyllis no matter what she said. Though, admittedly, there were limits to what the two discussed—typically, deeply trivial yet somehow comforting subjects having to do with shopping and cleaning. (Adam's employment situation, for instance, went unmentioned.) "Ron's been in a terrible car accident," Phyllis announced, her voice breaking halfway through the sentence.

Wendy felt as if her head had detached from her body. Terrible car accidents were supposed to happen to other people, people on the eleven o'clock news. (And Phyllis was supposed to be calling about white sales at Bloomie's and how to wash cashmere in the washing machine—i.e., gentle cycle, cold wash, encased in a mesh bag.) "Oh, god! Phyllis. I'm so sorry," Wendy managed. "Let me get Adam." Her heart was beating so hard that it hurt her chest. "It's your mother," she kept saying to Adam. "Wake up."

Just as he kept muttering, "Sleeping," into his pillow.

"Adam. Please! There's been an accident!"

The next thing Wendy knew, Adam was standing in the window of their bedroom, facing out, one hand gripping his forehead, the other gripping the receiver. His hair was standing up. His boxers were down around his hips. His legs were splayed and squared like those of the high school wrestler he'd once been. "I don't understand," Wendy heard him say into the phone, his voice high and thin. And "What do you mean?" And "Where is he?" And "What are the doctors saying?"

Finally, he hung up. Saying nothing, he strode into the living room, threw himself on the sofa, and covered his eyes with his fists. "Dad was in a car accident on the Mass Turnpike," he began. "An SUV sideswiped him and he rolled over the divide. He was on his way back from a client dinner in Hartford. He's in intensive care, in a coma. They don't know if he's going to wake up." He let out a sob as he delivered the uncertain verdict.

"I'm so sorry," Wendy whispered into the darkness, her completely bald father-in-law's favorite joke rushing back to her: *A colleague of mine asked me if I was going to start wearing a rug. And I told him, "What's the point? Hair today, gone tomorrow."* Once, that punch line had made her recoil in horror; now it seemed eerily prescient. She felt terrified for Ron, terrified for Phyllis, terrified for Adam, terrified for herself, too. She wasn't ready for the older generation to die—or for that buffer layer between herself and Death to be removed. She wasn't ready to concede that she was "all grown up." Because if she was, why did she still so often feel like a little kid playing house?

3.

F WENDY AND Adam slept at all that night, it was only for a few hours. The next morning, Adam left on a train for Newton, Massachusetts, where his parents lived, and Wendy got ready for work. She'd volunteered to skip out and accompany him, but he'd declined her offer, promising to send for her only if his dad's condition changed. Secretly, she'd been relieved. She was bleary-eyed from lack of sleep. She didn't know what she could do up there, anyway. Some childish part of her couldn't deal with bad news, wanted to hide from it and pretend it had never happened. It was also rare that she had the apartment to herself. Plus, Adam had left his computer out, and she was dying to sneak a look at the "Screenplay" document on his desktop.

Wendy waited for the faint clack of the front door closing behind him. Then she sat down at his desk. Her heart was in her throat as she switched on his laptop, then double-clicked on the file. Seconds later, two sentences popped into view. The first read, "Concept: a nuclear disaster that reduces the sperm count of New York City's male population to zero." The sec-

75

ond said, "Hero: a sarcastic but essentially decent thirty-something househusband / former Web site copy chief trying to knock up his wife." The rest of the page was blank.

For a brief moment, Wendy allowed herself to feel amused, even hopeful, insofar as Adam's thinly veiled description of himself seemed to suggest that he was more intent on impregnating her than he'd previously admitted to being. After reflecting upon the situation, however, she felt deceived. So much for Wendy's "supporting the family" while Adam "pursued his art." Never mind the fact that the plot of his apparently unwritten movie sounded, to Wendy's mind, truly asinine. But that she should even be thinking about her husband's career prospects at a time like this! As Wendy closed the file, she felt deeply ashamed of herself.

Arriving late to the office, she sat down in her cubicle and pulled out *Barricade's* phone list. She had to call a writer about a piece on the Abu Ghraib prison scandal that was already two days overdue. She had the phone in hand when she thought of Daphne. Etiquette dictated that Wendy get in touch with her at some point during the day to say how much she'd enjoyed meeting Jonathan. It occurred to her suddenly that the news of Adam's father's accident might relieve the two of them of the need to discuss the previous evening, which had clearly been a disaster, in any detail. It was also rare that Wendy had a dramatic story of her own to relay. She put down the phone, opened a new message, and began to type:

> D, It was so nice to meet Jonathan! He's very handsome and smart—and also so clearly madly in love with you. It was really very sweet to watch. Also, thanks for schlepping out to

Brooklyn to see us. Hope the restaurant was all right. The wait-staff was really rude, I know, but the food was good, right? . . .

Meanwhile, some awful news on this end. Adam's father was in a car accident last night and is in intensive care up at Mass General—apparently in a coma. Adam left this morning on the train. I may or may not go up tomorrow morning, depending on the progress report. Anyway, just wanted to let you know what was going on here. xo W

Wendy was leaving a message on the Abu Ghraib writer's machine, threatening to waterboard him if he didn't get his copy in by the end of the day (a dumb joke, but then, eight hours were a lot of hours to fill), when her other line rang.

"Hello?" she said.

"WEN! I JUST READ YOUR EMAIL. I AM SO UNBE-LIEVABLY UPSET FOR ADAM!" It was Daphne, and she was practically screaming into the phone. "That is just horrible, horrible news. How is Adam doing?"

"To be honest, he seemed pretty bad when he left for Boston this morning," said Wendy, noting that Daphne sounded more upset than she needed to be, even if it was the role of "supportive friend" she imagined herself playing.

"Ohmygod, poor thing. I just feel so awful for him," Daphne continued. "And for his mother, too, of course."

"Yeah, it's really awful."

"If there's anything at all I can do on this end while Adam's away, PLEASE let me know."

"That's very sweet of you," said Wendy. "But I really don't think there's anything anyone can do in New York."

77

"I guess I could go up there—" Daphne began in a hesitant voice.

"I really don't think that's necessary." Wendy cut her off, taken aback by what she felt to be the presumptuousness of Daphne's suggestion. It wasn't as if Daphne and Adam were *that* close! But then, Daphne was probably only trying to be a good friend, Wendy reminded herself. And Daphne was an emotional person. She was a performer, too, but sometimes even her acts were born of authentic feelings. "But if you want to leave a message or something, I'm sure he'd appreciate it," Wendy went on, then wondered why she had.

"Do you think? I mean, that's the *least* I can do!" declared Daphne. "But wait—can you give me Adam's cell again? I know I have it somewhere. I'm just not sure where."

He doesn't have to pick up, Wendy thought as she read out the digits to Daphne. And besides, who knew: maybe he'd actually be touched. Then again, maybe he'd be mad at Wendy for spreading around his family trauma as if it were just another piece of idle gossip. "Meanwhile, it was great to meet Jonathan," said Wendy.

"Oh, I'm glad!" Daphne emitted a tentative laugh. "I have to admit I was a little worried when he and Adam got into the whole Israel thing—and then you, too!" She laughed again. "I hope you don't all hate each other now."

"Oh, please," said Wendy. "Adam loves talking politics. And, I mean, that's basically what I do for a living. You know, argue for the Left." She laughed herself.

"Really?"

"Really."

"Okay, well, I won't worry, then. Anyway, there're more important things going on right now. So, when did you guys get the news about Adam's dad? . . ." Wendy's plan had worked: for the rest of their phone call, Ron Schwartz remained the focus of their conversation.

Why was it, then, that Wendy hung up the phone feeling so unsettled?

Adam called at three o'clock, sounding glum but resigned. He'd already been to the hospital to see his father and to talk to his father's doctors, who reported that at some point, Ron might wake up. On the other hand, he might not. Conceivably, the situation could continue as it currently stood for months. Understandably, Phyllis was a mess. "Why don't I come up in the morning," offered Wendy, suddenly anxious to become involved (and still feeling guilty about having spied on Adam's computer).

But Adam said it was probably better if she waited until next week and that his mother wasn't "ready for visitors." Adam also said that since his brother, Bill, couldn't leave his family in Worcester for any extended period, he'd agreed to stay in Newton indefinitely. Wendy told him she understood on both counts. But secretly she felt on the one hand, hurt (was she really still a "visitor" in the Schwartz family?) and on the other, blue (it was one thing to have the apartment to herself for the weekend, another to be abandoned for weeks or even months).

And if Adam was always away, how would she ever get pregnant? How would he find a new job when his twelve months were over? (Almost three of them were already gone.) And would he use his father's accident as an excuse to get out of looking for one? Wendy had begun to suspect that her husband enjoyed his life of leisure a little more than he let on. At the same time, she was aware that to complain about his absence right then would make her look unspeakably selfish. (Before hanging up, she made Adam promise only to keep her posted.)

Her weekend free, Wendy made plans to visit Pamela and Todd and their newborn the following afternoon. After she hung up with Pamela, she called Daphne back to see if she'd come along. (Wendy tended to find baby visits less trying when they included other women who'd also failed to procreate.) To her relief, Daphne said she'd love to do so and that she'd call Wendy the next morning to confirm.

But the next morning, Daphne canceled, claiming to have a cold and not wanting to infect the baby. Wendy suspected she was simply feeling lazy. Not that she could blame her. Park Slope was a hike from Murray Hill. What's more, Daphne had always seemed wholly uninterested in children. So Wendy, bearing fresh strawberries and a slightly damaged infant bath set she now regretted having purchased despite its being 80 percent off (what if Pamela noticed that one of the comb's teeth was missing?), set out alone for Pamela and Todd's handsome brownstone duplex just off the park.

Lucas Rose turned out to be an absurdly cute baby with fat pink cheeks and a full head of platinum hair. He spent the entire visit sobbing inconsolably. To Wendy's incomprehension, Pamela and Todd didn't seem to notice, or mind. Flouting Wendy's explicit instructions not to cook, Pamela had "whipped up" a duck-and-white-bean cassoulet and a strawberry layer cake for lunch. Miraculously, she'd already lost all of her baby weight except for two pounds. She spent most of the meal peppering Wendy with solicitous questions about Ron's accident. (Daphne, a decent gossip in her own right—though she always denied it—had already relayed the terrible news to all their mutual friends.) Wendy spent most of lunch yelling, "Sorry, what did you say?" and secretly wishing someone would chuck Baby Luke out the window.

She left their apartment on the verge of tears, if only because they all seemed so happy—at least, Pamela and Todd did. She also had a splitting headache.

Wendy filled the rest of the weekend eating breakfast cereal straight out of the box and reading *Anna Karenina* (admittedly skipping the boring Levin/joys of agriculture sections in favor of Anna and Vronsky and their steamy if increasingly paranoid affair). In her newfound solitude, she felt alternately listless and liberated.

There was no news from Newton.

Daphne called Sunday night to find out how Ron was doing since she and Adam had last spoken (apparently he'd picked up when she called), and also to report that Jonathan had told her that he loved her and that she'd told him the same.

"Wow, it really *is* serious," said Wendy.

"Um, yeah!" said Daphne, as if Wendy's assessment were obvious.

Daphne also suggested that she and Wendy get together for a "catch-up dinner" the following week. "You must be so lonely without Adam," she said. "Jonathan and I had to spend the night apart two nights ago, and I swear my apartment felt like a ghost town!"

"I'm doing okay—it's a little quiet at home," said Wendy, who appreciated Daphne's concern but didn't find their situations comparable. "So when were you thinking in terms of dinner?"

"Well." Daphne let loose a long sigh, as if her jam-packed schedule required a lengthy mental scrolling. "This week is kind of crazy. Then Snugs and I are going up to his parents' place in Rhinebeck next weekend. But what about the Monday after that?"

"That's fine with me," said Wendy, for whom the proposed date sounded impossibly far-off. "Where do you want to go?"

"What do you say we do something totally 'old-school,' like go to the Odeon and eat hamburgers at the bar," Daphne suggested in a conspiratorial voice.

"That sounds perfect," said Wendy, who missed her "single girl" years and didn't miss them, in equal parts.

In the intervening days, Wendy received another invitation—this one from Adam, inviting her up to Newton the following weekend. Apparently, Phyllis was now ready to "see people." Happy to have been asked, Wendy told him she'd get the train up on Friday afternoon.

"Oh, and would you mind bringing my laptop with you when you come?" Adam asked before he hung up. "I want to try and get some writing done in the off-hours. Also, I could use a few extra pairs of socks. And underwear. If you don't mind—"

"No problem," said Wendy.

She felt like a terrible liar that morning as she zipped his computer into its case, as if it hadn't been opened since he left. Or was Adam, with his unwritten screenplay, the bigger liar of the two?

He was waiting for her on the platform. "Hey, Pope," he said, but not with the usual glint in his eye.

"Hey, Potato," said Wendy, hugging him hello. For a second, she thought he'd contracted a severe case of dandruff. Then she realized it was flurrying.

They walked back to the parking lot. Adam was driving his mother's previously owned Lexus. (Adam's family was well-off but maybe not that well-off; Wendy was never sure.)

They arrived back at the Schwartz's contemporary Tudor in time for take-out Chinese, a family tradition on Friday nights. Smelling of garlic sauce and talcum powder, Phyllis enveloped Wendy in such a tight hug that Wendy felt as if she were inside her mother-in-law's giant bra.

"I hope I can be helpful," said Wendy before extricating herself from Phyllis's coral-colored nails, which were digging into her back flesh.

But as Wendy soon discovered, there was little for her to do, other than to keep her mother-in-law entertained — a feat she attempted with repeated shopping expeditions to the Chestnut Hill mall. On their first visit, Phyllis bought herself wool slacks and Wendy a cute top (both of them off a sale rack at Bloomingdale's, but who was Wendy to be choosy?). After that, they just window-shopped.

Wendy also paid a visit to her father-in-law at Mass General. There was little reason to believe that Ron Schwartz even knew she was there. But the sight of him lying motionless, machinated, and with his mouth ajar — as if he'd been in the middle of a sentence when calamity had struck, as if nothing but a noun or a verb or even just an adjective stood between life and death — left Wendy deeply unnerved. The institutions she'd built her life around — her marriage, her job, her circle of friends, an unexplained passion for *Antiques Roadshow*—seemed suddenly as flimsy and immaterial as newspaper blowing in the wind. Or as her own father, Donald. Not that she considered herself to have suffered on account of his absence. Marcia used to speak of Wendy's "fear of abandonment" as if it were a proven fact. But who was to say you missed what you'd never known?

Then again, maybe we were all hopelessly predictable in our pathologies.

Wendy had come to Newton to support her husband and his family, but it had also crossed her mind before she left that she was likely to be ovulating that weekend. Having sex in your in-laws' house was, of course, a grotesquerie that was best avoided. At the best of times, there was the chance of an accidental walk-in. But even if there wasn't, the thought of one's father- or mother-in-law being treated to a rhythmic ballet through the ceiling as he or she tried to butter his or her toast was enough to dampen anyone's sex drive. That said, Wendy was determined to risk such a possibility in the name of a greater good: reproduction.

There turned out not to be any need. The ovulation predictor test sticks on which she urinated on both weekend mornings failed to turn deep mauve, suggesting that she was still several days away from her fertile peak.

Sure enough, the optimum russet shade appeared the morning after she returned to Brooklyn—alone, in a cold rain that later turned to sleet. Laying her hands across her chest, elbows akimbo, Wendy began to breathe in and out in a rhythmic fashion. She'd learned the technique at a Sudarshan Kriya "breathing workshop" at the Art of Living Foundation, which she'd attended two winters before at the urging of Marcia, whose other mantra about Wendy was that she needed to live more in the moment and stop racing toward the next thing. (True to her former therapist's accusations of impatience, she'd only made it through the first of the workshop's six sessions.)

Several minutes later, feeling exactly the same only winded, Wendy got dressed and went to work. *There's always next month,* she told herself on the subway ride. Besides, she had more to offer society than the next generation of human existence. The work she did at *Barricade* was important, serious, substantive. That very week, for instance, they were closing a special issue on the current administration's "crimes against humanity."

Of course, every issue of *Barricade* was, to some extent, about the current administration's crimes against humanity. But this one was going to be special. The editors had invited ten distinguished left-leaning intellectuals, entertainers, and pundits to contribute guest columns. The roster included Mohammed M. Mohammed, a Bethesda-born horticulture grad student at Ohio State University who'd been held in solitary confinement by US authorities for the crime of having the same name as a Yemeni money launderer with ties to Al Qaeda; Dotty Dolittle, a transgender humorist and author of the graphic novel *Eat My Bush;* and, thanks to Wendy—and, by association, Daphne—Daphne's father, Richard Martin Uberoff, a distinguished professor of Near Eastern studies at the University of Michigan and (in Wendy's private opinion) a charming if shameless egomaniac.

At various moments in the past, Wendy had taken to wondering if the enduring connection between her and Daphne could be explained by the fact that they both hailed from academic families. Yet where Judy Murman seemed to have a special talent for alienating the people around her, Professor Uberoff was a bona fide star. Since September 11, 2001, he'd made frequent appearances on radio and television, where he delivered debatably potted histories of Islam that stressed its essentially peace-loving nature. Even Lincoln had seemed impressed when, during a story meeting, Wendy had pulled out Daphne's father's name as a personal contact.

What Lincoln didn't realize was that although Wendy had ostensibly known Richard Uberoff for fifteen years, he still seemed confused about who she was. "Lovely to talk to you, Wanda," he'd bid her farewell on the phone after agreeing to pen a column.

Wendy found herself recalling how, several years into their friendship, Daphne had sent her a postcard from Costa Rica (where she'd been vacationing with her family) in which she'd misspelled Wendy's last name, turning the U into an E, and the A into a U.

Daphne called later that morning to see if she and Wendy could postpone their dinner plans for that evening. She and Jonathan had had a "late night" the night before, she explained, and she was feeling like she "just need[ed] to get in bed and vegetate."

"Also, the weather's sooooooo crappy," moaned Daphne, "I don't know if I can deal."

"It's fine — don't worry about it," said Wendy, as disappointed as she was dubious that a federal prosecutor would go out late on a Sunday night before work. But no matter. Daphne was right: the weather was pretty bad.

"Meanwhile, are you going to Sara's girls night on Thursday?" said Daphne. " 'Cause if so, I'll see you there."

Wendy found herself wondering if Daphne was trying to get out of rescheduling their dinner plans. Or was Wendy just being insecure? "Oh, right—yeah—I'll definitely see you there," she said.

With another free evening ahead of her, Wendy paid an overdue visit to the rent-controlled apartment on West 106th Street and Broadway in which she'd grown up and in which her mother still lived—alone.

Judy Murman had never remarried—or, rather, married at all. For a while, in the eighties, there had been Jack, the recovering-alcoholic candle maker from Brattleboro, Vermont. For unclear reasons, he'd eventually melted away along with his beeswax. Later, in the early nineties, Wendy's mother had "come out" as a lesbian. Though Wendy had yet to see her with a female companion or lover.

Judy came to the door that evening clutching Mary Shelley's *Frankenstein*. "Hello, Wendell," she said with a quick embrace. (Judy Murman was the only one who ever called Wendy by her given name.)

"Hi, Mom," said Wendy, following her mother into the living room, where she took a seat in the wicker "egg swing" that dangled from an exposed beam in the ceiling and began to turn from side to side.

Judy sat down opposite her on a faded blue sofa covered with cat hair. She adjusted her giant red glasses frames. "That's a handsome blouse you're wearing," she said, peering inquisitively at Wendy. Judy was wearing some kind of tunic sweater and an "ethnic" necklace with beads the size and shape of dog turds.

"Thanks. I was worried I looked like a giant broccoli floret," said Wendy.

"I wouldn't say so," said Judy.

"Meanwhile, Adam's father was in a horrible car accident and he's in a coma. So Adam's staying up in Boston with him."

"How terrible," exclaimed Judy. "Please send the family my best wishes."

"I will."

"I hope you're being supportive of Adam. This must be a difficult period for him."

"Of course I'm being supportive!" said Wendy, defensive already. At the same time, she felt the urge to shock her mother with her paucity of goodwill. "Not that Adam's being very supportive of me these days," she went on. "I'm paying all the bills while he pretends to write a screenplay about space aliens with low sperm counts. From what I can tell, he spends half the time I'm at work smoking pot in the park. Or at least he was before his father's accident." (Why did she act so brittle and unforgiving in front of her mother?)

Judy grimaced disapprovingly. "Wendell—you made a commitment to support Adam's creative work while you continued at the magazine. I think it would set a very unfortunate precedent if you went back on your promise to him."

"Who said anything about going back on my promise?" cried Wendy, growing more irritable by the second. "I'm not getting divorced! I'm just saying it's annoying."

Judy didn't answer.

"Also, speaking of low sperm count, I can't get pregnant," Wendy continued.

"It will happen when it happens," Judy said evenly.

"What's that supposed to mean?" said Wendy, who never stopped being hurt that her mother didn't display the usual desperation for grandchildren that other people's parents did. (*I only have two, you know* was among Phyllis's common refrains at every Schwartz family holiday — to which Adam and Wendy, if they were feeling indulgent, answered, *Two what? Grandchildren to spoil rotten* was the usual answer, typically delivered with an exaggerated wink and a vaguely sinister grin.)

"It means you waited a long time to have children," said Judy. "Now you're just going to have to be patient. And you're not going to get any closer to your goal by pressuring Adam, if that's what you've been doing."

"How do you know what I've been doing?" said Wendy, flinching at her mother's intuition.

"I have no idea what you've been doing!"

"Well, then, I'd appreciate it if you stopped guessing."

Judy grimaced again. It was clear she felt unfairly maligned. "Wendell — I'm just trying to be helpful."

"Thanks. Anyway," said Wendy, suddenly eager to change topics. "So, what's new at school?"

Judy cleared her throat. "Well, I'm teaching a graduate seminar called The Matriarchal Impulse in Early-Nineteenth-Century English Literature. And I have a few absolutely top-notch students this semester, especially a young man named Douglas Bondy, who's been working as my research assistant. He's really an extraordinary person. His mother was a crack addict. He essentially raised himself. All I can conclude is that his love of learning somehow goes deeper than —"

"There's a guy in your women's studies class?" Wendy interrupted. Her mother had a habit of talking up everyone but her own daughter.

"I've had many men in my classes!" declared Judy.

"Oh."

"And how are things at the magazine?"

"Fine. I just edited a special pullout section on Abu Ghraib."

Judy lifted her glasses into her silver mop, flared her nostrils imperiously, and looked away. As if she didn't want to be held accountable for what she was about to say: "I blame that crazed hawk Condoleezza Rice. I suspect she pressured all of them — Bush, Cheney, Rumsfeld, et al. — into this ridiculous war."

"I guess it's possible," said Wendy, who had noted before that her mother was the rare feminist who, in every conflict, took the man's side — at the expense of whatever woman could feasibly be blamed.

When Wendy got home, she called Adam to tell him about her visit to her mother's apartment. "She started attacking me the moment I walked in the door!" Wendy began. "I told her about your dad, and she immediately suggested I wasn't being supportive enough." She waited for Adam to argue otherwise.

But all he said was, "Yeah, she's a tough one, your mom."

"And then, immediately after, she was on me about putting too much pressure on you to have a baby. She also told me I waited too long to have children."

"Hm," said Adam.

"What?" said Wendy, further disappointed by her husband's neutral response.

"I guess I'm wondering why you open up to her at all about personal things, since she always seems to respond in a way that pisses you off."

Even Wendy had to admit that Adam had a good point. Which was maybe why she cried, "What? I'm not supposed to tell her your father is in a coma?!"

"You can tell her about my dad. But why tell her you're trying to get pregnant?"

"Okay, I'm an idiot for trying to share my life with my own mother!"

"You're not an idiot," said Adam. "I just don't like seeing you upset."

"I miss you," said Wendy, suddenly overcome by tenderness for her husband. Or was she simply feeling needy in a more generalized sense? "When are you coming home?" she asked.

"Wendy, you know I can't come home right now," he answered. (Adam only called her Wendy when she'd said something wrong.)

"I know," said Wendy, trying not to be hurt by the fact that he hadn't told her he missed her, too. "You're there for a good reason. I've just been lonely. I'm sorry — I can't lie about how I feel."

"Don't you think I've been lonely, too?" said Adam. "At least you have your friends around."

"I guess."

"What? Aren't you seeing Daphne and stuff?"

"She's been busy with Jerky Jonathan."

"Well, it's always like that at the beginning of a relationship. You and I didn't get out of bed for, like, a week after we met. Don't you remember? My mother was leaving all those frantic messages at my apartment." Adam chuckled at the memory.

"I remember," Wendy said softly, even though, nearly eight years later, the story mainly existed for her in words, interspersed with fuzzy images of him naked and kissing the back of her neck. Even so, she liked the idea of her husband reminiscing about their early days together; it made their love affair seem real, ongoing. "We were crazy back then."

"Listen," said Adam. "I miss you, too." Wendy's heart fluttered, even if, as usual, his expression of affection for her had been more reciprocal than spontaneous. "But my parents need me right now."

How could she argue with that? "I understand," she told him before she wished him a good night and hung up.

By Thursday evening, Wendy was so eager for the company of like-minded peers — and an excuse to consume excess quantities of alcohol — that she arrived fifteen minutes early at the Mexican restaurant on Smith Street where Sara had directed her six closest female friends to assemble. Not even the sight of Paige Ryan, second to arrive and dressed that evening in a black pants suit and four-inch-high stilettos, put her off. Following their email run-in the previous month, Wendy had decided never again to communicate in English with the woman. But with the second sip of her margarita, she'd softened her stance. So that her old nemesis struck her as a harmless if pitiable eccentric. "Hello, Ms. Ryan," Wendy began, as

Paige assumed the seat opposite her at a wooden table beneath a decrepit-looking piñata. "And how goes it in the world of ruthless capitalism?"

"If you're referring to the private sector and its notorious largesse, then the answer is, swimmingly," answered Paige.

"Glad to hear it."

"And the arena of naive left-wing journalism? Is it treating you well?"

"Very well, thank you," said Wendy.

Sara appeared next, followed by Maura, then Gretchen and Pamela. There were hugs and kisses all around. Wendy spent so much more time emailing her friends than she did seeing them in person that the sight of them in all their fleshy (and not-so-fleshy—a.k.a. Maura) splendor left her somehow startled.

Not surprisingly, Daphne was the last to show. (Wendy had long ago adjusted to Daphne's Lateness Problem by mentally adding a half hour to all of her stated arrival times.) She was wearing a pair of old brown corduroys, a mustard-colored V-neck sweater dotted with moth holes, and a navy blue pea coat whose epaulets had become detached from its shoulders. On anyone else, the outfit would have looked ratty. "I love my friends!" she was squealing as she approached the table, her arms outstretched, her head tilted just so. She hugged Pamela first and went clockwise around the table from there. When she got to Wendy, she announced, "Wen—I'm so sorry I haven't answered your email yet from this afternoon!"

Wendy felt embarrassed, lest anyone at the table think she'd lost the ability to receive an instant response from her reputed best friend. "Don't worry about it," she said quickly. In fact, as Wendy reflected on the email she'd sent—a request that Daphne pass on the name and number of her masseuse, so Wendy could give it to her friend at the dry cleaners, Grace, who was still sore from having been hit by a bus—she realized how random it must have seemed. In truth, she wasn't entirely sure why she'd written it.

"Is your dry cleaner okay?" asked Daphne.

"She's going to be fine," Wendy told her.

"Well, that's good." Daphne sat down at the one available seat—to Wendy's right—only to turn her attentions to her own right, where Wendy's do-gooder friend Gretchen sat. "So, am I wrong?" Daphne began, one eyebrow raised. "Or has a certain someone not been in Bali, honeymooning with their husband, four years after the fact?"

"Guilty as charged," conceded Gretchen.

"The only crime is the color of your face," said Sara. She turned to the others. "Gretch didn't get the memo on tanning."

"Thanks, Sar," said Gretchen, whose cheeks and forehead were indeed the color of a shiny penny. "Just like you didn't get the memo on not being a bitch."

"Hey, you two," said Wendy, secretly tickled to see Sara and Gretchen fighting. "No more bickering like an old married couple. You sound like Adam and me."

"Who's bickering?" said Sara.

"Not me," said Gretchen, shrugging.

"Do you and Adam really fight?" asked Pamela, looking mystified by the concept.

"It only turns physically violent, like, one out of three times," Wendy assured her.

Pamela, whose many virtues failed to include a sense of humor, looked even more stunned.

"Sara's just pissed she's part of an old *un*married couple," offered Gretchen.

"Thanks, Gretch," said Sara.

"Don't thank me," said Gretchen. "Thank Dolph. I'm sorry, but you should really give him an ultimatum already. I mean, how many years has it been now?"

"Someone get these two to arbitration," muttered Maura.

"Wait—time out!" cried Daphne, her palm raised. She turned to Pamela. "Pammy, I'm dying to know—how's Baby Luke?"

"A little colicky," Pamela said breezily. "But nothing we can't handle."

"He's also incredibly cute," added Wendy, who wanted it known that she'd already been over to visit.

"Thanks, Wen." Pamela smiled warmly. "I think he's pretty cute, too."

Daphne leaned in. "So, are you getting any sleep at all?"

"Not much," admitted Pamela. "But I always say—there's plenty of time to sleep when you're dead!"

"But what if you live to sleep?" asked Maura.

"Don't have kids." Gretchen laughed knowingly.

"Or hire a baby nurse, like Gretchen," said Sara. "And refuse to let her out of the house until the kids are eighteen."

Gretchen ground her teeth but said nothing.

"Or kill yourself now and get it over with," said Maura.

"Hey, no suicide jokes tonight," said Wendy with a surreptitious glance at Daphne to see if she'd caught the allusion. (There was no evidence that she had; she was busy making a sad face at a broken nail.)

"Well, I'm *dying* to meet him," said Daphne. "I'm *so* sorry about the weekend before last. I'm a horrible friend. I was just—"

"It's fine! Really." Pamela cut her off with a wave of her hand.

"Maybe I could come by next week?"

"Whatever works for you. Meanwhile, inquiring minds want to know—how is *your* new man?"

All heads now turned to Daphne, who pursed her lips and said, "He's great. Beyond great."

"So, when do we get to meet him?" asked Sara.

"Well, he's been in the middle of this *big case,*" said Daphne, seeming to savor the last two words. "But it's supposed to be over tomorrow, THANK GOD. So then I can start showing him off again. Actually, he's taking Monday off, and we're going to Sag Harbor for the weekend. But after that we're not going anywhere 'til Thanksgiving." She turned to Wendy. "Wendy and Adam already met him."

All heads now turned to Wendy, whose pride at being the "only one" competed with her discomfort at being called upon to confirm Daphne's choice of mate. "Well, to start, he's very good-looking," she began. It was the one positive thing she could say with conviction. And why was it that she hated to lie to Daphne, Wendy wondered, but not to her husband?

"He and Wendy have slightly different political outlooks," Daphne informed the group. "But otherwise you liked him, right?" She glanced back at Wendy.

"Of course! He was great. Super smart. And funny," said Wendy, wondering if her facial expression gave her away.

"Paige—don't kill me, but I promised him the three of us could have drinks sometime next week, or whenever you have time," said Daphne, reaching her hand across the table and laying it on Paige's arm. "His family is talking about investing in some friend of the family's hedge fund—some guy named Madoff. Jonathan's really worried they're making a big mistake."

"Delighted to be of service in any way I can," chimed Paige.

"And Sara, I can't wait for you to meet him, too," Daphne went on. "He's *such* a lawyer. He's always arguing about everything! The two of you are going to love each other. . . ."

It seemed to Wendy that for the rest of the evening, Daphne's conversation was directed at everyone but her. What's more, Daphne's body was turned at such an angle that Wendy spent dinner staring at her back.

Daphne returned from Sag Harbor the following Tuesday, but she remained unavailable to Wendy. Like Maura, Daphne had always been a champion canceler, and the problem seemed to have grown worse since Jonathan had entered the picture. On Thursday, Daphne flaked out of yet another dinner plan with Wendy, again citing a physical malady. (This time it was food poisoning.) Wendy began to wonder if her best friend was purposely avoiding her. In retrospect, she regretted ever having opened her mouth on the subject of the Palestinians the night the four of them had met. Of course, it was equally possible, Wendy told herself, that Daphne was simply preoccupied with her new relationship and ignoring all her friends equally.

The latter theory seemed less likely after Wendy learned that Daphne and Gretchen had dined together later that same week. But was that detail necessarily so telling? Maybe Daphne had been feeling better. And Wendy didn't invite Daphne along every time she had dinner with a mutual friend. In any case, there was no way for Wendy to know if Daphne was mad at her or not. Daphne had never been the type to tell you if you did something wrong. She'd just start ignoring you, which always made you feel a hundred times worse.

Meanwhile, Adam announced he was coming back to Brooklyn the following weekend. And Wendy rejoiced at the news, even though his visit stood to fall during her period.

She filled the idle hours before his return working on her cooking skills. Armed with James Beard's *Theory and Practice of Good Cooking* (1977), which had been left in the apartment by the previous tenants, she made, on successive nights, Braised Pork Hocks, Italian Style; Stuffed Breast of Veal; and Jeanne Owen's Chili con Carne. (Whoever Jeanne Owen was, her chili tasted like Polly's dog food. Which either was or wasn't Jeanne Owen's fault.)

In a semicharitable spirit — at some indeterminate point in life, she'd discovered that it made her feel good to be nice to other people — Wendy also brought a bag of groceries to the ancient, never married, retired merchant marine, Barney, who lived alone with his metal furniture, peeling contact paper, Wonder bread, and canned corn in a rent-controlled studio downstairs. (Hoping to "mix things up," she brought him wheat bread and canned peas.) And then, because no good deed goes unpunished, Barney made her sit down on one of his metal chairs and listen to stories about lovesick sailors threatening to jump overboard over "Orientals" they'd met in the South Pacific while escorting cargo ships of sugar.

The night before Adam's arrival, Wendy partook of her

favorite shame-inducing activity after smoking and masturbating: scouring reproductive health Web sites and message boards in search of useful tips / old wives' tales regarding the most expedient way to get pregnant.

To her disappointment, however, she found no new nuggets of wisdom, having already served Adam coffee before sex, ingested cough syrup to thin her cervical mucus, orgasmed first to favorably alter the pH balance of her vagina, and assumed the bicycle position for twenty minutes after the act. She ended up on a Web site about male infertility, half-convinced that Adam had an obstructed vas deferens thanks to a hernia operation he'd had ten years ago. This would explain why he'd gotten his college girlfriend pregnant but had so far failed to knock up Wendy. She had no proof, of course. But what if Adam knew more than he was letting on? Wendy couldn't help but think of the contents of his "Screenplay" file. Was it a mere coincidence that her husband was writing a movie about nonfunctioning sperm? Of course, there was always the possibility that something was wrong with Wendy's own reproductive system. As a general rule, however, she preferred to imagine that the blame lay elsewhere.

After exhausting the potential of her search words, Wendy found herself Googling Mitchell Kroker. If she didn't miss his presence in Daphne's life, she couldn't help but wonder how he was faring. Did he care that Daphne had left him? Was he drinking heavily? Had he already found a new mistress/girlfriend? Wendy had never thought he'd leave his wife for Daphne. Yet she found it equally impossible to imagine how, after an affair as passionate as she understood his and Daphne's to have been, he could return to his marriage as if nothing had happened.

Other than the time that Wendy had accidentally barged in on the two of them in Daphne's apartment the month before, she'd met Mitch only once. Near the beginning of his and Daphne's affair, the three of them had met for drinks in the lobby bar of the Four Seasons Hotel in midtown Manhattan. He'd been friendly enough, asking faux-interested questions about *Barricade*. ("So, is Charlie Kohn still beating around the place—or did he die yet?") But it had been clear to Wendy from the outset that he'd only been there as a favor to Daphne, and that he couldn't wait to leave, either out of boredom or because he was terrified he'd run into someone he knew. He'd spent most of the hour drumming his fingertips against the top of their bar table and checking his Rolex. Wendy felt as uncomfortable as she was fascinated by the way he kept looking over at Daphne.

As if he wanted to climb inside her skin.

Wendy knew it was creepy and uncouth to imagine your friends having sex with their husbands or lovers. Many times over the past two years, however, she'd allowed herself to picture Mitch and Daphne together. Sometimes, she envisioned him huffing and puffing atop Daphne's prostrate form, beads of sweat dangling from the undulating lines that ran across his forehead, lines so deep they resembled a seismograph printout after a low-level earthquake. But more often, Wendy pictured Daphne on top, naked and slithering across a transfixed Mitch as a snake traverses a mossy rock. It was the latter image that Wendy found the most erotic, not because she longed for Daphne to slither across her own body, but because she liked to imagine *being* Daphne. That is, what it must feel like to be possessed of a body like hers (a body that appeared at once breakable and omnipotent), and also to be on the re-

ceiving end of the kind of obsessive desire that Mitch clearly
had for her.

After clicking on the first search result, Wendy found herself staring at an "official" portrait and biography of Mitch,
courtesy of the television network at which he worked. His
face made pink and smooth, his smile rising higher on one
side than the other, his arms folded over each other like Yul
Brynner's in *The King and I,* Daphne's former lover appeared
to be ten years younger than he actually was, far nicer, and
made of wax. His biography seemed equally unreal. The last
line read, "Mitchell Kroker lives in Georgetown with his wife,
Cheryl (weatherperson at CBS affiliate WUSA), and his two
children." Wendy's search turned up nothing more revealing
than that — moreover, no evidence that he and Daphne had
ever known each other. And was it possible that Cheryl had
never found out, never would? And were other people simply
better than Wendy at letting things go?

Before shutting down her computer for the night, Wendy
also Googled Jonathan Sonnenberg. From what she learned,
after clocking several years at Schiffer, Wallengberg, Griscom
& Steinholz, he'd moved to the organized-crime and terror-
ism unit of the US Attorney's Office. True to Wendy's inqui-
ries at dinner that night, he'd also been involved in several
high-profile fraud and money-laundering cases involving the
Gambino crime family. For Wendy, however, such factual information paled in interest next to the snapshot she uncovered
of Jonathan on spring break in some tropical wonderland,
a decade or two before. His chest bare, his shorts Hawai-
ian, his arms dangling over the shoulders of his fraternity
brothers — the Greek letters on their T-shirts identified them
as such — he seemed even then to be brimming with self-

confidence. Wendy wondered if, late at night, alone and awake in a dark room, Jonathan ever had moments of self-doubt.

She also wondered what he and Daphne did together in dark rooms. When Wendy envisioned the two of them, she saw Jonathan running his hands through Daphne's tangled mane and moaning clichéd things like "You're so fucking beautiful"—while he received expert fellatio. Yet where Wendy had always somehow relished the image of Daphne and Mitch together, she found the one of Daphne and Jonathan vile.

Adam arrived home in a swirl of luggage and coats and soiled paper bags containing fast food he hadn't gotten around to finishing on the train. In his absence, Wendy had purchased an Indian bedspread and two velvet pillows to better disguise the Ikea sofa they couldn't currently afford to replace. Every night before she went to bed, she'd taken to straightening the spread over the cushions and angling the pillows against the sofa's arms. No sooner had Adam walked in the door, however, than the pillows found their way to the floor and the bedspread pulled away from the sofa, exposing its old, pilled upholstery. Wendy knew she was indulging her "fussy old lady" side, but his carelessness annoyed her. To add to her irritation, Adam seemed as excited—if not more so—to see his dog as he did his wife. Or was she looking for problems because she couldn't justify the truth, which was that she was mad at him for being away? As Adam stroked Polly's head, Wendy announced, "To be honest, as much as I love her, it's been kind of a burden having to walk her every night."

"You can't do me the small favor of looking after her at a

I'M SO HAPPY FOR YOU

time like this?" said Adam, his eyes narrowed to connote disbelief at her selfishness.

"Sorry," said Wendy. "It's just that I haven't been getting home from the office until close to seven"—it was a slight exaggeration, but still—"and it's pitch-black outside because of daylight savings being over. And it just doesn't feel that safe walking around this neighborhood alone at night." She'd come up with the second argument midsentence, and it struck her as rather ingenious.

"Not safe with a Doberman pinscher?" said Adam.

"Not a geriatric Doberman pinscher—no."

"So now you have to insult Polly, too?"

"I'm not insulting Polly—I'm just stating the truth. She's getting old!"

"Do you ever think about anyone but yourself?"

In her relationship with Daphne, Wendy was the giving one, and Daphne the taker. With Adam, it had always been the other way around. "Are you trying to start a fight?" she asked.

"I thought we were already having one," he answered.

The two made up, but only superficially. They took walks, made dinner, and snuggled in bed, but their fight lingered like cigarette smoke on a Shetland sweater.

On Sunday afternoon, before he left, Adam announced he was taking Polly back up to Newton with him. "We know when we're not wanted," he added.

Wendy didn't know how to answer. Adam had gotten it all backward, but it was too late to turn him around. The irony was that, watching the two of them drive off in a rental car, with Polly craning her neck over the passenger window, Wendy wondered if she might even miss Adam's lumbering, fart-happy old dog. She already missed Adam. At the same time, there was a way in which she was relieved to see him leave again.

Wendy spent the next week working on *Barricade*'s special anniversary issue on police brutality. ("A Brief History of Pigs" was the title of the opening editorial.)

Daphne called on the Sunday after the issue went to press. "Are you sitting down?" she asked.

"I'm actually lying down," Wendy told her. In fact, she'd gotten in bed early with *OK* magazine. Jennifer Aniston had apparently stopped eating. Some reality TV star Wendy had never heard of had a really bad cellulite problem. Wendy justified her need to consume mindless trash on the grounds that she didn't actually purchase it. For example, she'd lifted the copy in her lap from the nail salon at which she'd treated herself to a pedicure the day before. Of course, stealing had moral implications as well. But then, Wendy always made sure to lift the previous week's issue.

"Jonathan and I are engaged," said Daphne.

"Ohmygod, Daphne, that's wonderful news!" cried Wendy, whose first reaction was shock — if not at the news itself, then at how quickly it had all happened. Other emotions followed. She was excited to have such incredible gossip at her fingertips. She was sad to think she was losing her oldest friend to a man with whom she was unlikely ever to be close. She was relieved, even thrilled, to think that Daphne's problems, insofar as they were based on her failure to find sustainable love, had finally been solved — even as she felt irritated that Daphne should think that Wendy cared enough about her life to be at risk for fainting. Also, how could you know you wanted to marry someone after forty-one days in each other's company? Never mind the fact that it had taken Wendy approximately four minutes to decide that Jonathan Sonnenberg was a complete prick.

Wendy also couldn't help but wish that the transformation in Daphne's personal life had taken longer and been more emotionally wrenching. No one deserved to be that happy that fast. It was as if Daphne had snapped her fingers and fashioned a fairy tale out of a soap opera or, worse, a nightmare. (Now Daphne left messages at one PM, as opposed to one AM, saying things like, "Hi, sweets. We're heading out to the Hamptons. Just wanted to say hi before we leave. Call any time. Love you. Mwuh" without any trace of relief or regret.) For most people, actions had consequences. For Daphne, life was apparently just a series of independent vignettes. Which meant she'd gotten to live, too—had had torrid affairs and traveled to distant countries and taken illicit drugs in the Mojave Desert with members of the MI5—while Wendy made pasta, watched *Law & Order* reruns, and never went anywhere. At least that was how she imagined the disparity in their personal histories.

Daphne went on to explain that the proposal had taken place over dinner at Tavern on the Green, in Central Park, the night before. It was such a clichéd setting for a romantic moment—so corny, too—that, hearing this detail, Wendy's first instinct was to roll her eyes.

Her second was to wonder what she'd missed.

She'd always understood Adam's aversion to sentiment to be a sign of his intelligence—his coolness, too. But what if it turned out that when the violins played and the candles flickered in a dimly lit dining room, the heart really did swell? Wendy had lived in New York for thirty-five years and had still never set foot in the legendary restaurant. What's more, Adam hadn't so much proposed to her as, one evening at home in their old apartment, two days before Wendy's thirty-first birthday and four years after they'd met, he'd reluctantly agreed to go to city hall the next day. It had been the culmination of a long conversation, instigated by Wendy. As far as she could tell, Adam would have been happy to stay cohabiting forever. She'd finally worn him down with the argument that they were "waiting for the sake of waiting." Looking back, she supposed that, in effect, she'd asked him to marry her. But were there really any marriages that weren't precipitated by women? Maybe self-servingly, Wendy had convinced herself that the idea that men proposed to women was among the great myths of Western civilization. Now she wasn't so sure.

Now, as Daphne went on about the vintage of the champagne and the color of the ring box, Wendy found herself fighting the urge to blurt out Mitch's name, if only to remind Daphne that history went back farther than six weeks.

She didn't dare. Instead, like the old and dear friend she imagined herself to be, she cooed, "You're kidding," and "That's insane," and upon hearing that Jonathan had gotten down on one knee—just like in the movies— "Noooooooooooooo—you're lying" in the appropriate long-drawn-out decrescendo.

But when she hung up, the taste of acid filled her throat. How odd it was that friends could be the source of so much pleasure and solace, Wendy thought, with their constant assurances that you were all in it together, lamenting lost opportunities, laughing at inside jokes. At the same time, they could devastate you doing nothing more than going about the business of their lives, lives that had no direct bearing on yours. They weren't family members. You didn't generally have sex with them. You didn't generally work in the same office with them, either. Yet it was impossible not to see your lot in direct relation to theirs — impossible, therefore, not to feel defensive and even devastated when they did things you hadn't done, or simply did them differently (and now it was too late for you to go back and do them again).

4.

FTER WENDY HUNG up the phone with Daphne, she called Adam. She knew he'd be excited by the news—excited and horrified. She could already hear him going off: "No—tell me it's not true! Do you think it's too late to stage an intervention? . . ."

"Hey, Pope, what's up?" he said.

"You're not going to believe this," said Wendy, "but Daphne and Jonathan are getting married."

"Yeah, I got an inkling that was going on," Adam volunteered in a casual voice. "I actually talked to Daphne on the phone yesterday, and she said she had some big news but she wanted to tell you first."

"I didn't know you talked so often," said Wendy, startled by her husband's response.

"We don't," he said. "But 'cause of her mother and everything, she's really knowledgeable about home care and stuff—you know, her mom has someone living with them out in Michigan. So I just thought, if it comes to that with Dad, it would be good to know what the options are."

How could Wendy argue with such a noble and selfless pursuit? "Right," she muttered helplessly.

"But I agree," he continued, "the Jonathan news sucks. The guy is a complete schmuck. But what can you do? She loves him, I guess, and she probably wants to get married like every other woman on the planet. You know?"

Wendy was so shocked to find out that her husband and best friend were in regular contact that she couldn't think of anything else to say.

"Is something the matter?" said Adam.

"What are you talking about?" said Wendy, playing dumb. She prided herself on not being a jealous type. Besides, what was there to be jealous of? Daphne had just gotten engaged to Jonathan. And Daphne and Adam had known each other for as long as Wendy had known him — technically, five minutes longer.

Even so, she felt hurt. She couldn't justify it. She couldn't deny it, either. She'd wanted to be the one to tell Adam the news. She didn't necessarily like the idea of her husband and Daphne having an independent friendship, either. It made her feel excluded. Which, in turn, made her want to exclude Adam. "Listen, I've got another call," she told him. "Can I call you back later?"

"You sure you're okay?" asked Adam, sounding unconvinced. "You're not mad I talked to Daphne, are you?"

"Why would I be mad?" said Wendy.

"I mean, she said you were the one who gave her my cell number."

"It's fine. Really. But I have to go."

• • •

Wendy woke up the next morning feeling even more disoriented than she had the day before. In the subway to the city, she searched her brain for someone who would remind her who and where she was.

She landed on Sara Denato, reasoning that Sara, on account of her perpetual engagement, had the most incentive to find Daphne's news as upsetting as Wendy did. That said, spreading happy gossip wasn't like spreading gossip-gossip, Wendy told herself. Arriving at the office — and her conscience clear — she typed the following email:

In case you haven't already heard . . .
DAPHNE IS GETTING MARRIED!!!! (Yes, to Federal Prosecutor Man.) Also, did I mention they met FORTY-ONE DAYS AGO?? (Insane, I know.) XXW

Sara immediately wrote back:

Okay, I officially want to kill myself. It took me and Dolph forty-one days just to decide on a regular night for couples counseling—Mondays. Wow are we going to have a lot to talk about at our session tonight. . . .

Wendy felt better. Meanwhile, Sara must have emailed the news to Paige. That or Paige had already heard, maybe even before Wendy had. When Daphne and Wendy had been on the phone the night before, Wendy had assumed that she was the first among their mutual friends to learn the Big News. After the following email arrived, however, Wendy couldn't be sure:

Wendy,

My concerns about the celerity of the engagement notwithstanding—never mind my feelings on marriage generally!—should you and I (as Daphne's closest friends) be throwing her an engagement party? Just a thought. Also, I should admit that my thoughts ran to a joint engagement party / fund-raiser for Doctors Without Borders, the latter being, to my understanding, Daphne's favorite cause. Please let me know your feelings on such.

       Paige

Wendy was in no particular hurry to renew email contact with Paige. But she was equally wary of getting sucked into cohosting an engagement party with her. There was little doubt in Wendy's mind that such an event would quickly turn into an opportunity for Paige to guilt her into spending hundreds of dollars she didn't have, not only on medical help for victims of natural disasters, but on needlessly fancy party provisions, from monogrammed cocktail napkins to artisanally produced aged sheep's milk cheese from a monastery in the French Pyrénées. The list of demands would surely begin small and expand from there. At the same time, Wendy was concerned about appearing unsupportive of Daphne (and as cheap as she actually was).

Just then, a solution sprang into Wendy's head. She called back Daphne. "I meant to ask you on the phone before," Wendy began without introduction. "Do you want to go out for a celebratory drink tonight after work?" No doubt Daphne would be busy, just as she always was, Wendy thought. But at least now she could say she'd asked. (At least now she could tell Paige that she and Daphne were already busy making plans to celebrate.)

To Wendy's surprise, however, Daphne was both free and willing: "That's so *beyond* sweet of you!" she declared. "Let's see. I have therapy at five thirty. Then Snugs and I are having dinner at Babbo, but our reservation isn't until eight forty-five. Do you want to meet at seven fifteen, or something?"

The two women made plans to meet at a café/bar on Sixth Avenue. Wendy was then able to email Paige back:

Hi Paige. An interesting suggestion. I promise to give it some thought. In the meantime, am taking D out tonight to celebrate. Will be in touch, Wendy

That evening, as Wendy made her way up the avenue, she realized she was actually looking forward to seeing Daphne. It had been a long day at the office, and—it occurred suddenly to Wendy—she and Daphne hadn't gotten together on their own in weeks and weeks, and really not since Daphne had started dating Jonathan. Pulling open the door to the café, Wendy vowed to herself that she wouldn't mention the fact that Daphne and Adam were in regular touch. What was the point? It would only make her look insecure. She'd wait for Daphne to bring the matter up first, or she wouldn't discuss it at all.

To Wendy's surprise, Daphne was already there, seated at the bar, her BlackBerry pressed to her ear. As Wendy approached, Daphne raised her free palm in a gesture that seemed simultaneously designed to acknowledge Wendy's presence and beg her patience. Yet Daphne took her time getting off the phone. "Wait, you're joking!" she went on. And "Oh, my god. . . . Well, did you tell him to mind his own fucking business? . . . I'm sorry, that's just ridiculous. . . . I'm

sure. . . . But listen, Wendy's here. I should go. . . . Yeah, that's
true. . . . No . . . I didn't say that! . . . Well, whatever you
want to do . . . I mean, you could. . . . No, I totally
agree. . . . Okay, love you." (Presumably, it was Jonathan.) Finally, Daphne set her BlackBerry down on the bar and looked
up at Wendy, now seated on the stool next to her, pretending
to examine a cuticle. "Hiiiiiiiiiiiiiiiiiiiiii!" Daphne began.

Maybe it was strange to feel intimidated by someone you'd
known for fifteen-plus years. Then again, Wendy had never
seen Daphne look as "done" as she looked that night. She was
wearing knee-high black suede boots and a close-fitting, black
and white, botanical-print dress cinched at the waist with a
black patent leather belt. She was also sporting a four-carat
emerald-cut yellow diamond embellished with bilateral diamond baguettes — a ring so massive and effulgent that everything around it seemed dull, including Wendy. She couldn't
think what to say except — as Daphne thrust her knuckle
under Wendy's nose — "Wow. It's beautiful."

"Isn't it?" said Daphne. "I still can't believe Jonathan
picked it out himself."

Wendy glanced from Daphne's cynosure to the plain ham-
mered silver band she wore on her own fourth finger. (Adam's
freshman-year roommate ran a silversmith shop in Putney,
Vermont.) When she and Adam had gotten engaged, they'd
been in agreement that diamond mining was a nasty, exploit-
ative business, the products of which it was immoral to buy or
wear. Even antique diamonds, their crimes now relegated to
history, had seemed beyond redemption. Now Wendy couldn't
help but feel that she'd missed out on some elemental experience. "So, should we order drinks?" she said.

"Let's," said Daphne. . . .

"So, what have you been up to?" Daphne asked after they'd requested two mimosas. "I haven't seen you in, like, a thousand years!"

"You know, working, wasting time, still not getting pregnant while Adam's away all the time," Wendy told her.

"Sweetie!!!!!" Daphne tilted her head the way she always did.

Somehow, this time, Wendy felt repelled by Daphne's sympathy. "But let's not talk about me," she said quickly. "I want to hear more about the new Mrs. Sonnenberg!"

Daphne smiled sheepishly. "To be honest, I never thought I was the type to change my last name. But Daphne Sonnenberg *does* sound kind of cool. Doesn't it?" She wrinkled her nose.

"Very classy," said Wendy, who had never considered taking her husband's name. "But, then, so is Daphne Uberoff."

"I guess I was also thinking that if we have kids, it's easier for everyone if the parents have the same name, you know?"

"That's true," said Wendy, shifting in her seat.

Their drinks arrived. Wendy raised her champagne glass into the air and said, "Well, cheers. To you and Jonathan."

"You're the best friend a girl could have." Daphne held her own glass aloft to meet Wendy's. "But wait" — again the nose curled up — "we're not girls anymore, are we? Tell me the truth. Are we really old?"

"We're not that old," Wendy assured them both, before guzzling half her mimosa in a single gulp.

"Too old to wear white at a wedding?"

"Why not? It's your wedding. But wait, are you guys already planning?"

Daphne tucked a stray tendril behind her ear and smiled

again. "Well, we've talked about a few ideas. Jonathan's family belongs to Temple Emanu-El, which is right near the Pierre. But I don't know — I was thinking something more low-key than that. I mean, it's not like I'm a virgin of eighteen!" She laughed. "Anyway, it probably won't be for a while. I mean, we only met six weeks ago." She laughed again. Wendy was reassured to hear that Daphne was at least cognizant of the minuscule amount of time that had elapsed since she and Jonathan had met. But could she really be considering a synagogue wedding? "Meanwhile, you're the only one of us who's been married," Daphne continued. "So tell me what it's like." She leaned forward on her bar stool, her grin leering, her long black legs flapping beneath her like a scuba diver's fins. "Do married people still have sex? I mean, for fun?"

For a split second, Wendy found herself wondering if Adam had complained to Daphne during one of their phone calls about his and Wendy's lack of a spontaneous sex life. Wendy had friends with whom she talked about sex, sometimes graphically — Maura, for instance. (Deprivation seemed to make the subject that much more interesting to her.) But for whatever reason, Daphne had never been one of them. For all of Daphne's public displays of emotion, there was a way in which she kept her private life off-limits. Wendy supposed she ought to seize the opening. In light of the trouble she was having conceiving, however, she couldn't help but find Daphne's question tactless.

But then, it was Daphne's special night, Wendy reflected, and therefore not the right time to be raising petty objections. "Sometimes," she replied, trying to match Daphne's light tone. "Though, to be honest, not that often." Adam was right,

Wendy thought: she couldn't keep her mouth shut. "Speaking of my conjugal partner, I hear you and Adam have been talking about medical care for his father?"

Daphne touched Wendy's sleeve. "I just have to say, you have the greatest husband in the world. I mean, he loves his dad so much. It's so touching to watch. Anyway"—she sighed—"I've been trying to help him out where I can. Sometimes I think it just helps to talk, you know? I mean, I remember when my mother got sick. It was so surreal. Like you just can't believe that these towering giants who raised you are suddenly so weak and helpless!"

"I'm sure," Wendy said. But she wasn't sure at all, maybe never would be. Judy Murman had always seemed less like a towering anything than a tetchy child. "By the way, on an unrelated topic, I love your dress," Wendy went on. "Where'd you get it?"

"Oh, god—*this?!*" Daphne lifted the extra fabric on her hip as if Wendy had been admiring an old dishrag. "I got it, like, a million years ago at some Catherine Malandrino sample sale."

"Huh." Wendy filed away the information in case, at some later point, she wanted to emulate the effect. It was by studying Daphne that Wendy had always figured out what cut of jeans to wear, what color lip gloss, and whether to go with silver or gold jewelry (and how much). Yet Wendy lacked both the money and the motivation to be as stylish as Daphne was. (Somewhere deep down, Wendy thought she was above fashion—or was she too far beneath it ever to get a foothold?)

"Anyway," Daphne said, sighing again as she scooped an

enormous banana-shaped buttery-leather handbag off the floor—no doubt another back-of-the-closet find, Wendy thought, "I should really get going."

Wendy glanced at her watch: it was only 7:58. Had Daphne's Lateness Problem expanded to include a Leaving Early Problem, too? And how soon before she didn't appear at all? "I thought your reservation wasn't until eight forty-five," Wendy said, feeling hurt.

She felt relieved, too. At the sight of Daphne seated at the bar forty-five minutes before, a part of Wendy had worried that they'd run out of things to talk about; moreover, that at some point along the way, she and Daphne had lost the thread that had always sustained their conversations.

Daphne scrunched up her face apologetically. "I'm so sorry. It's actually at eight fifteen. I didn't realize." She touched Wendy's arm again. "Do you want to leave with me or—I know how you sometimes get freaked out sitting alone." What was Daphne trying to imply?

"It's fine," Wendy told her. "Go ahead. I'm going to finish my drink." She saw Daphne glance at her empty glass. "I mean, I might order another one," Wendy said, embarrassed to have been caught in a lie.

"Oh! Well, it was great to see you. And thank you *so* much for the mimosa. It was beyond delicious." Daphne kissed Wendy in the vicinity of both cheeks. Then she sashayed from the room, her ponytail swinging like the pendulum on a grandfather clock.

At the very least, Daphne could have *offered* to pay for her drink, Wendy thought as she watched the door close behind her. Wendy would have said no. At least, she liked to think she would have said no. Though, in truth, having just borne witness to the small fortune encapsulated on the fourth finger of Daphne's left hand, Wendy might have let her leave the tip.

Later that night, back home in Brooklyn, Wendy recalled suddenly that it was her mother's sixty-fifth birthday the next day. She went online and ordered a bouquet of roses, dahlias, and chrysanthemums with the cheesy yet somehow convincing name "Thinking of You." It was no lie: Wendy thought often of her mother. Some of those thoughts were negative, of course. But mostly she thought it was a shame they didn't get along.

She arrived at work the next morning to find a blinking red light on her phone. She hit the "voice mail" button and punched in her password. The first message was from Judy, thanking Wendy for thinking of her. "At the moment, I'm thinking I'm very old," she said. Wendy winced. Even though she didn't particularly like her mother, she hated to think of her as sad.

The second message was from Adam, asking her to call him as soon as possible. Wendy couldn't tell if the news was good or bad, and she dialed his number with trepidation.

When Adam answered, he started talking so fast that at first, Wendy didn't understand him. She had to ask him to slow down. "Sorry," he said. He sounded out of breath. "My dad! He woke up this morning! The nurse was changing his catheter bag, and his eyes suddenly opened. Then he started moving his hands. The doctors are saying they've never seen anything like it!"

"Oh, Potato, that's wonderful!" said Wendy. She hadn't

heard her husband sound so happy in months, maybe years. She was happy, too. Happy for Adam. Happy for Ron and Phyllis. Happy for herself. She didn't have to be all grown up yet, after all. Maybe Adam could come home now. And maybe now he'd finally realize how precious life was, Wendy thought—how precarious, too—and try harder to make things happen in his own.

"I just can't believe it," he said. "I mean, he's not talking much yet, but when I went in there this morning, I swear he looked right at me and said, 'Lazy ass.' My mother was screaming so loudly the nurses had to come in and ask her to quiet down."

"You're kidding," said Wendy, with a shudder of recognition.

On Saturday, Wendy caught the 11:00 AM Acela to Boston. Adam picked her up at the station, and they drove straight to Mass General.

Ron didn't say anything to her, but, this time, his eyes seemed to follow her as she made her way to his bedside. Phyllis sat beaming at her husband's side, his hand in hers, muttering, "It's a miracle," over and over again. Wendy thought of the otherwise forgotten holiday weekend when she'd walked into the Schwartzes' kitchen in search of orange juice and, to her embarrassment and awe, found her in-laws making out against the dishwasher.

Not surprisingly, for the rest of the weekend, high spirits abounded in the Schwartz household. Wendy and Adam even had sex in Adam's childhood bedroom, which had been converted only partially into a guest room. (His high school wrestling trophies still occupied the top shelf of the bookcase; Vonnegut paperbacks and SAT prep books filled the lower levels.) It was only day eight of Wendy's cycle. So it probably wasn't good for much, she figured. But it was nice to feel close again.

It was also nice to feel Adam's arms around her naked back.

At the end of the weekend, Adam followed Wendy down to Brooklyn. He said he had some business to take care of in New York. Wendy couldn't imagine what kind of business that was. But she didn't want to pry or to put him on the defensive. So she didn't ask him to elaborate. The plan was that the two of them would drive back up to Newton on Thursday morning in a rental car in time for Thanksgiving dinner.

Wendy had been away from their apartment for only two days, but she found waiting for them an unusually tall stack of mail. As she climbed the stairs, three steps behind Adam and Polly, she leafed through the pile. Since it was nearing Christmas, there were catalogues galore—one from a wine lovers' club, another from a purveyor of holiday decorations, yet another from Macy's announcing a "mattress event" (whatever that was; Wendy was fairly sure she'd never participated in one). To her exasperation, there was also another issue of *The New Yorker*. Wendy prided herself on not missing an issue, though she was currently five behind.

To her even greater distress, there was also a bill from Visa.

While Wendy waited for Adam to unlock the door, she debated whether to open the envelope now or to delay the unpleasantness for another time. The balance was nearing ten thousand dollars. The previous month, the finance charge alone had topped two hundred bucks. Wendy didn't see how they were ever going to pay it all back. She couldn't understand how their debt had grown so large, either, and she instinctively blamed Adam for its accretion. True, in late August, she'd spent a few thousand dollars on a new computer, but that had been a necessity, in addition to a tax write-off. (An electrical storm had blown out the hard drive of her old desktop.) As for her new Marc Jacobs peacoat and Sigerson Morrison boots, she'd felt guilty and terrible for weeks after buying them but had justified both purchases on the grounds that having quit therapy, she was saving them nearly six hundred bucks a month. What's more, having grown up with a single mother who couldn't afford to buy her designer clothes, Wendy felt she deserved them — even as she proudly regarded herself as antimaterialistic.

Meanwhile, Adam, while bringing in no money, continued to buy books, movies, and music for no purpose other than his own entertainment. Had he really needed a new set of speakers to attach to his iPod? "Special delivery from Uncle Visa," she said, entering the living room behind him. Adam turned around and fixed his hazel green eyes on her. He was still the cutest guy she'd ever been with, she thought. She secretly considered it a fluke that he'd agreed to marry her. She still felt unaccountably proud to be seen walking in the company of his Converse high-tops. She waved the bill in his face.

"A lovely homecoming gift," he said.

As Wendy forced the bill into his hand, an envelope she hadn't previously seen fluttered to the floor. It must have been caught inside the flap. She leaned over and lifted it off the floor. It was stamped "Certified Mail," and it read, "OPEN IMMEDIATELY — TIME SENSITIVE DOCUMENT." While Wendy ran her fingernail under the flap, she let her imagination run free regarding its contents: *Just call this number to claim your expense-paid seven-day Caribbean vacation—and also to receive a year's subscription to* Sucker's Rewards *at the special discount price of only one hundred thousand dollars a month. Send your credit card number today! Offer only valid in the lower fifty states.* . . . She unfolded the paper. The document was titled "Notice to Terminate Tenancy" and it was addressed to both Wendy and Adam:

> Dear Tenants,
>
> You are hereby notified that your tenancy of the premises is terminated on December 15, 2005 (last day of rental period) and on that day you will be required to surrender possession of the premises to the Landlord. Judicial proceedings may be instituted for your eviction if you do not surrender possession of these premises on or before the date above. . . .

Wendy couldn't believe what she was reading. If she understood correctly, she and Adam—never mind Barney and his metal chairs—were being thrown out of their apartment in less than four weeks. Last she'd checked, their landlord was a crabby old lady in a floral housecoat named Bedonna Rodriguez. According to the letter, however, the building was now owned not by a person but by an entity called Turnkey Holdings. No doubt the place would be torn down to make way for some shoddy condo development with rows of air conditioners bulging from its facade. Wendy had seen other houses on the block fall victim to the same fate. *Surely we have legal rights,* she thought. Then she recalled that their lease had expired the previous summer, and no one had asked them to sign a new one. Nor had they thought to ask for one. "Forget the Visa bill," she said, her eyes scrolling down the length of the document. "We're being thrown out of our apartment."

"What?" Adam grabbed the letter out of her hand.

"I can't believe it." Wendy shook her head in despair as she sank onto the sofa and covered her eyes with her palms.

"This is bullshit," said Adam, scanning the letter himself. "I'm calling a lawyer."

"Lawyers cost money we don't have."

"We'll find one who's willing to work on contingency. My dad's a lawyer. He'll help us." It was as if Adam had temporarily forgotten that his father had just woken up from a coma. "I mean, when he's better," he said.

"But they want us out by December fifteenth," said Wendy. "That's less than a month away. There's no time." It was at moments such as these that Wendy wished she had a husband who would at least impersonate the Man of the Family—that is, promise to find a new and better roof to cover their heads (and maybe even go back to work, if that was what it took).

But after a few moments' thought, all the Man of Wendy's Family could come up with was: "This place is a dump, anyway." He squatted before Polly, rolled her head in his hands, and said, "Come on, lil' girl, let's go out for some fresh air." He grabbed her leash, then his keys. Then he disappeared back outside.

Despite everything, Wendy couldn't wait for him to get back.

Wendy had never been crazy about their apartment. She held the puke green linoleum kitchen counters in special contempt.

But it had wood floors and decent light. It was relatively quiet. Plus, their bedroom looked out over a sweet urban garden.

Her attachment to the place increased exponentially after she began to comb through real estate ads for the first time in four years. Since she and Adam had last looked, prices seemed to have increased by 50 percent. A one-bedroom in Sunset Park, a working-class neighborhood to the south of the South Slope, now rented for what she and Adam were currently paying to live in their two-bedroom. Of course, she and Adam didn't technically need a second bedroom. Adam could always set up his study in the living room or bedroom. But what if Wendy finally got pregnant? Then what?

Wendy was at her office the next morning, pretending to edit an angry screed on the administration's domestic surveillance programs titled "Send Bush to Gitmo" — while actually scanning the "no fee" apartment postings on Craigslist — when the following email arrived:

Wen

So you're not going to believe this but it looks like you and I are going to be neighbors again after all these years!!! Yes Jonathan and I are moving to Brooklyn believe me I'm in shock too basically what happened is that we made this total low-ball bid on this brownstone in Cobble Hill right near Cobble Hill Park and we never thought they'd take it so we didn't even bother telling anyone about it but what do you know our broker called us yesterday and said that the other offer had fallen through (the people couldn't get a mortgage or something) and the owners were willing to accept ours!! Anyway the house needs some work (bathrooms kitchen etc.) but the proportions are amazing it's 23 feet wide with a 14 foot high ceiling in the parlor plus it has these completely gorgeous carved marble mantels in every room I just feel so incredibly blessed I only wish we could afford it (ha) but really we're going to be so poor in the next few years it's not even funny seriously if you see me on the West Side Highway at three a.m. wearing hot pants and a bra you'll know why Speaking of career stuff can't remember if I told you that Jonathan is going back to the private sector? In any case he's starting at Skadden in September in the white collar crime division (someone has to pay for the reno) Anyway hope you guys are well BTW am so beyond thrilled for Adam his father really is a hero xxoo Daf

p.s. Assume you're going back up to Boston for Turkey day? J and I are flying back to Michigan so he can finally yikes "meet the family" (wish me luck)

The fluorescent light over Wendy's cubicle was suddenly blinding to the point of intolerable. She leaned back in her desk chair and closed her eyes. She hated the way that Daphne omitted all traces of proper punctuation in her emails. "Wendy," someone was saying behind her head. She immediately recognized the voice as belonging to Lincoln. But in that moment, she felt indifferent to his authority. "It's not a good time," she said without turning around. She couldn't believe those words had come out of her mouth; what had she done?

"As Her Royal Highness wishes." Lincoln sniffed before walking away.

Maybe she would lose her job, too, Wendy thought, as she listened to Lincoln's Doc Martens fade into the background. Then she could feel even sorrier for herself than she already felt, if such an emotion was possible. Ever since Wendy had moved to the borough ten years earlier, she'd been fantasizing about buying one of its stately nineteenth-century row houses. And now Daphne, who'd been to Brooklyn maybe five times in ten years, was about to become the proud owner of one — even as she had the audacity to cry poor.

At the same time, Wendy loathed herself for feeling the way she did. Envy was a bulldozer emotion; it had a way of wiping out all other impulses in favor of a single picture of want. As she closed Daphne's message, Wendy tried to clear the slate. She told herself that she and Adam had a deeper and more meaningful relationship than Daphne and Jonathan would ever have, no matter how many square feet they occupied. Moreover, the puniness of her and Adam's bank account freed them of the disfiguring illness that lately seemed to have infiltrated even their left-leaning social circle: realestateitis. Wendy would go to dinner parties and find that there was only one conversation at the table that animated the guests other than the war in Iraq: the rapid appreciation of their New York City condos, co-ops, and town houses.

"Well, Katie bought her place in ninety-seven for four hundred thousand, and she just had it reappraised for one point six," they'd say. And "We're not feeling like quite as big suckers as we did when we bought the place, because the apartment over us just sold for three hundred thousand more than we paid, and it barely had plumbing!" And "The sad thing is, pretty soon the only people who are going to be able to afford this neighborhood are corporate lawyers and Wall Street people. I mean, it's great to see all the empty lots cleaned up. And it's definitely a lot safer at night. But it still makes me sad."

Wendy was sad too, heartbroken even. But there was no

need to lament your ceiling height — or even have the requisite "mixed feelings" over gentrification — when you didn't own the floor beneath it. Besides, compared with the borough's vast swaths of poverty and hopelessness, she and Adam were downright privileged, Wendy reminded herself. With his education and experience, Adam was sure to find a job as soon as he deigned to reenter the workforce. In the meantime, there was fruit in the fruit bowl, milk in the refrigerator, and a Marc Jacobs coat hanging on the coat tree (even if, technically, it hadn't yet been paid for).

And it was a luxury, Wendy knew, to work at a magazine of politics. (She could have been processing dry-cleaning tickets; she could have gotten hit by a bus.) There were also parents in the background who, at least on Adam's side, would never let them go hungry. Wendy assumed as much, even if, to her private chagrin, Phyllis and Ron had yet to offer them a down payment on an apartment of their own. That said, someday she and Adam might inherit the equivalent of one, possibly even more. Not that they'd ever discussed the matter. Even in the most intimate marriages, Wendy had learned, there were certain subjects that were taboo for a spouse ever to mention — i.e., when your parents die, how much do you think we'll get?

But Wendy's attempt to console herself failed. Because wherever you were on the socioeconomic spectrum, it never felt like you had enough. You still needed an extra million (or two or three) to become the person you were supposed to be, the person you saw others becoming. Just as those people who were ahead of you were clearly cheating you out of your rightful due in a ruthless zero-sum game. That was how the city increasingly made Wendy feel. She felt an unbridgeable chasm opening up between herself and Daphne. But it wasn't even about Jonathan — not directly. It was about money: stupid, magical, filthy, actually quite useful money.

When Wendy and Daphne were first starting out in the city after college, money hadn't seemed to matter. At least, it had been easier to pretend that it hadn't — back when they'd all occupied the same low-level media jobs, shared the same dingy tenement walk-ups, worn the same ripped jeans and holey sweaters, dated the same pretentious slackers. (Daphne's were always taller and better looking, but still.) It had been sex that merited fascination and envy. Sex and beauty. Money couldn't buy either one. It hadn't been any easier back then. Maybe it had even been harder. At the very least, it had taken more energy to get dressed in the morning, since every new day carried with it the promise of unforeseen frisson for which one naturally wanted to look one's best.

But it had been different. More nerve-racking. More exciting, too. Back then, you got the feeling that your luck could change at any moment. Now the parameters of your life felt already drawn, your epitaph lapidary.

It had also been easier to imagine then that Wendy and Daphne and their circle of friends were all actors in the same existential play in which the material world figured if at all as a mere backdrop to their anomie. That had been the fantasy. Only Daphne had ever come close to embodying it. Only Daphne had been light and floaty and fucked up in just the right way. Only Daphne had seemed sufficiently divorced from pedestrian needs. Only Daphne, with her skinny legs and runny eyeliner, had ever looked the part. (She always looked a little dazed and, at the same time, just this side of haughty.)

She'd acted the part, too. Only Daphne had had the nerve to get by without a job. Only Daphne had tried heroin. (When Wendy looked back, she thought of all the stupid things she'd *never* done.)

The irony was that it was Wendy—progeny of Columbia Presbyterian Hospital, graduate of Hunter High School, patron of the Peculiar Pub before she was eighteen—who was native to the city, and Daphne who hailed from the sticks. Yet, after college, it had been Daphne who had been Wendy's ticket around town. No one ever turned Daphne away from anything, even as Daphne herself often went under cover as one of her fabricated personae.

One time, she'd been "Donna," a "stripper in New Jersey."

Another time, at a book party they'd crashed at Pravda, a trendy Russian-themed bar in NoHo, Daphne had introduced herself to a group of suit-jacketed men as "Jackie," a "colorist" at a hair salon uptown.

To Wendy's amazement, none of them had called Daphne's bluff. "Huh," they'd said, and "Really," their eyes flickering behind their glasses like bulbs that hadn't been screwed in tightly enough. "And what's that like?"

"It's just a job." Daphne had shrugged. "You know."

"Just a job," the suited men had muttered, moving in closer, later staggering away as if wounded.

Afterward, Daphne had laughed and laughed. Doubled over, she'd asked Wendy, "Ohmygod, did you see the face of that guy with the beard? He was trying to act all respectful and politically correct, like I was going to be offended if he asked me what I was doing at a party for a fucking biography of J. P. Morgan!"

"That was too funny," Wendy had told her.

Too funny for me, she later thought. Looking back, it seemed to Wendy that all the best punch lines had belonged to Daphne. The joke hadn't ended there. It turned out that most of Wendy's friends, Daphne included, had upper-middle-class parents in the background who, one day, as their offspring approached thirty, had appeared as if from nowhere with down payments and extra sets of keys. Slowly, the talk had turned from William Burroughs's *Naked Lunch* to kitchen countertops on which to serve lunch (i.e., the merits of granite versus Corian). Until one day, all anyone seemed to care about (Wendy included, but still) was real estate and babies, the latter having become just another necessary acquisition—along with Oeuf cribs and Bugaboo strollers, Wüsthof knives and Waterworks showerheads—in the pursuit of the perfect bourgeois home.

Or was Wendy being unfair? Maybe her close friends were more complicated than that, Daphne included. Besides, until recently, Daphne's disastrous love life had still been her main preoccupation. And wasn't it Daphne's right to make a home? Or was there, just maybe, another way of doing so? Was acquisition necessarily synonymous with maturity? Wendy wrote back:

Daphne,
I'm in shock! A whole brownstone. Wow. Congratulations. Not sure Cobble Hill qualifies as neighboring, but it's a hell of a lot closer than Murray Hill. That said, looks like Adam and I are

going to be moving—not sure where to yet. We just got an eviction notice, if you can believe it. The place is a shit-hole, anyway, but it's still a huge pain in the ass having to look for a new apartment, especially with the holidays coming up. Anyway, that's great news for you guys. Please send some real estate luck this way (i.e., to your future homeless friends).

XW

p.s. I want to hear all about your "meet the parents" moment when you get back. Speaking of in-laws, yes, we're heading up to Newton, per usual. . . .

Normally, Wendy would have followed her email to Daphne with emails to all of their mutual friends, relaying this latest news flash from Daphne-ville (snide commentary included). In that moment, however, Wendy found herself wishing only to hide from the world. It seemed to Wendy that when she and Adam hadn't been looking—had been busy watching *Twilight Zone* reruns and checking their email and doing whatever else they did with their time—the rest of the educated population had been busy preparing for the future: taking out thirty-year mortgages and transferring savings into Roth IRAs. She imagined an exemplary couple peering out their sparkling clean double-sided Marvin window glass, heads shaking with pity and scorn, as she and Adam lugged a urine-stained mattress down the street in search of a bus shelter in which to spend the night.

Wendy arrived home from work to find Adam watching the *Lehrer NewsHour* on PBS. The death toll was rising in Iraq, and two talking heads were debating the merits of withdrawal. Wendy thought that despite Saddam Hussein's being a bad guy, invading Iraq had been a terrible idea that would cause a needless amount of suffering and set a harmful precedent in the world. Just prior to the invasion, she and her colleagues from *Barricade* had participated in a large antiwar demonstration on the East Side avenues of Manhattan. Wendy had carried a placard that read, "Just Say No to U.S. Imperialism." (Unsure where to buy really big cardboard, she'd asked a coworker to make her sign; otherwise, she might have opted for a slightly more subtle slogan.) Wendy had found the rally exhilarating, until the efforts of a certain horsebacked New York City police officer to contain the mob left her severely claustrophobic and doubtful that she had a future as a political activist.

Or was that just an excuse? Maybe it was impossible to process the fact of mass deaths, the three thousandth suicide bombing, the four thousandth improvised explosive device. Maybe she'd grown disillusioned after Bush was reelected. Maybe Iraq's descent into chaos seemed so preordained that she found it hard to continue to register shock and outrage. Whatever the case, Wendy's interest in the war had waned, while her personal concerns had risen to the forefront of her mind—even as she was aware that compared to the daily threat of being blown to smithereens, those concerns were hopelessly banal. So she'd stopped trying to justify them. Which in turn had given her permission to be bitter. "I suppose you already heard that Daphne and Jonathan bought a brownstone," she said, hanging up her coat.

"Nice for them," said Adam without looking up. It wasn't clear from his answer if he'd already heard or not—only that he was in a bad mood, too. Which, to Wendy, didn't seem entirely fair.

"Speaking of real estate," Wendy continued, "I went through all the listings, and there's nothing in our price range—not for a two-bedroom. At least not in the South Slope."

Adam didn't answer.

"So maybe it's time we talked about you going back to work." For the second time in one day, Wendy had shocked herself with her gall. Although the very words had been in her head all afternoon, she hadn't planned on uttering them out loud—hadn't felt it was her right, had feared they'd lead to a big argument or worse. (Every time she and Adam fought, Wendy worried they'd get divorced.) Her heart was now galloping at such an accelerated pace that it seemed possible it might come catapulting through her shirt.

Adam's eyes were still affixed to the screen. "I thought you agreed to support us for twelve months," he said.

Wendy sat down in a chair across from him, partially blocking the TV. "I did agree to support you," she said in as calm a voice as she could register. "But I didn't know we were going to get evicted. Also, would you mind turning off the TV for a second, since this is important?"

Adam eyed her coldly as he lifted the remote control off the coffee table and hit the power button. The talking heads stopped talking. Then he said, "My screenplay is important to me."

"What screenplay?" she wanted to cry out. But how could she do so without admitting that she'd spied on his computer? Besides, there was always the possibility that she'd looked at the wrong file, that just today he'd been busy writing the denouement. Though what dramatic event that would entail, she couldn't say. (The discovery of an untapped well of functional sperm on a distant planet?) So she said, "I don't see why you can't work on it at night, or in the mornings, or on the weekends."

Adam let out a long sigh. Then he said, "Wendy, don't you see what you're doing here? You're envious of Daphne's town house, so you're taking it out on me. Don't you realize that money isn't what make couples happy? Let's say I went to work at Goldman Sachs tomorrow, and we moved into some mansion in Brooklyn Heights with fireplaces and wainscoting. Do you really think you'd be happy? Don't you see you'd just be on to the next thing—upset because you didn't have a baby yet, or a fancy car, or whatever? You're never satisfied. That's just who you are. You felt deprived as a child, and there's nothing anyone can do to make it up to you. You could marry Bill Gates and still think you were getting fucked over."

Blood rushed to Wendy's face, and she gripped the side of her chair. Adam had touched on the truth, but—to her mind—distorted it beyond recognition. Which only made his accusations that much more maddening to her. "That is so fucking unfair," she shouted. "It's just a bullshit excuse for you not to have to do anything with your life! FUCK YOU." With that, Wendy got up and walked out of the room. She and Adam hadn't had that bad a fight in years. It was terrifying. It was a tiny bit exciting, too, if only because feeling estranged from your husband created tension that, after enough years together, wasn't always apparent.

It was also like walking around with an icicle attached to your back.

Wendy and Adam were still talking only intermittently when, three days later, they left for Thanksgiving. "We need to stop for gas," he'd say. "What time does your mother expect us?" she'd ask. "One or two," he'd answer. They passed the hours listening to National Public Radio. But Wendy found the patient, soft-spoken voices of the program hosts to be immensely grating. Between bathroom, snack, and gas stops; Polly's hourly need to relieve herself; and the near-standstill traffic on I-95 between the Bronx and New Haven, the trip seemed to go on forever. Secretly, Wendy felt bad she'd never learned to drive and therefore couldn't relieve Adam of some of the burden of getting them there. But she was still too mad at him to admit as much. Finally, at quarter to four, they pulled into the Schwartzes' circular driveway.

There was no sign of Ron, but Adam's older brother, Bill, was there with his wife, Susan, and their two charmless pigtailed daughters, Rachel, five, and Briana, seven. Wendy had never known what to make of her brother- and sister-in-law. Bill, who was a tax lawyer like his father, had gone to Tufts for college and Fordham for law school. But his demeanor and dress suggested a man who'd had no previous contact with urbanity. He arrived for dinner wearing belted jeans and white sneakers the size of small yachts. Susan, meanwhile, wore a permanent expression of exasperation on her thin lips. Before becoming a stay-at-home mom, she'd worked for the Massachusetts Office of Travel and Tourism. (It was hard to imagine her talking anyone into visiting the state.) She addressed both children by their first and middle names. "Briana Rose," she'd say, "will you please remove your elbows from the table?"

Phyllis must have sensed that something was wrong between Adam and Wendy. She spent the entire meal talking even faster and more relentlessly about nothing in particular than she normally did. "I couldn't remember what time I put the turkey in. Isn't that crazy? I don't know where my head is these days! Wendy, can I offer you more sweet potatoes? What a cute top you're wearing. Just the other day, I was thinking about that time you and Adam drove that U-Haul across country. I can still see you pulling into the driveway looking like you hadn't showered in a week! I have to admit, I never thought you'd make it. I was sure we'd be getting a call from Logan Airport. I remember telling Ron . . ." She chattered on and on.

After the meal, the entire family climbed into Bill's boat-sized Dodge Caravan and drove to Mass General, bearing flowers and fruit pie. Adam's father was now speaking several words at a time. Which was several more words than Wendy spoke to her husband the entire night.

Adam accompanied Wendy back down to the city that Saturday, ostensibly to help look for a new apartment. But on Sunday, when all the open houses were held, he claimed not to feel well and went back to sleep. So Wendy, trying not to feel any more exasperated than she already felt, set out alone in search of new digs.

The first place she saw had a bathtub in the kitchen; the second had been advertised as occupying the "garden floor" of a brownstone, but only the upper half of the apartment's two windows were aboveground.

At first glance, the third place Wendy visited — the top floor of an aluminum-sided frame house, five streets away from their current address — was scarcely an improvement over the first two. Proximity aside, it might as well have been located on a different planet. At one end of the block was a car wash, at the other a store that sold nothing but fire extinguishers. The concrete expanse of the Prospect Expressway was directly across the street; catty-corner to that was an entrance to the Brooklyn-Queens Expressway. Wendy had to assume that the sound of traffic filled the living room at all hours of the day and night. The stairwell smelled like kitty litter. And the brokers were charging a fee of 12 percent of the annual rent for the privilege — or was it punishment? — of living there.

But on second glance, the place was clean and spacious enough. It had a small alcove off the bedroom that, in a crunch, could be used as a nursery. The R station was right across the street, on Fourth Avenue. Most important, the rent was comparable to their current one. Figuring they were unlikely to do better, and concerned that some other desperate couple might come to the same dreary conclusion, Wendy called Adam.

He sounded as if he'd just woken up. Or maybe he was still asleep. But after listening to a brief description, he muttered, "It sounds fine — let's take it."

"Don't you want to come see it first?" asked Wendy.

"I trust you," said Adam.

"The bedroom is in back, but it might be loud, especially at night," said Wendy, wary of being held accountable if and when they couldn't sleep.

"We'll get used to it."

"And you realize it *directly* faces the expressway? I mean, you can practically see into the cars."

"Whatever. It's not about the view out the window."

"Then what's it about?"

Adam paused before proclaiming, "It's about being with the people who care for you. Unfortunately, certain people don't always realize that."

"Point taken," said Wendy.

But as she wrote a check for several thousand dollars and handed it to the broker, she wondered if she even agreed with the point that her husband had made.

5.

(LATE JANUARY)

WENDY WAS ON her computer at the office, perusing red carpet photos from the Golden
Globe Awards, when Lincoln's face appeared
over the burlap wall of her cubicle. This time,
there was no escaping his pockmarks. "Can I see you in my office?" he said.

Wendy's heart shrank to the size of a pea. *I'm getting fired,*
she thought with alarm—if not as much of it as she might
have imagined she'd feel—as she rose from her chair and followed him down the hall.

Lincoln's office was neat to the point of obsessive. The few
stacks of papers that lay on his desktop were lined up at perfect right angles. The only decoration was a framed 1981
campaign poster from the Parti Socialiste Français, featuring
a youthful-looking François Mitterand. "I don't know if
you've heard," he began, "but Shirley resigned last night. Or
rather, walked out."

"Really?" said Wendy, who had not heard.

Lincoln grimaced. "She was unhappy with what she perceived to be our lack of coverage of Hurricane Katrina. Apparently, we only ran twenty-seven articles on New Orleans last year versus a hundred and six on the war in Iraq. She saw it as evidence of a racial bias on the part of the magazine."

"Huh." Wendy nodded. What any of it had to do with her was still unclear. She and Shirley Mansard, who was the only African American on staff, as well as the only other female editor at a senior level, were cordial without being close. Which is to say that the mere sight of Shirley, her bearing regal to the point of despotic, struck fear in Wendy's heart and made her want to apologize for being white every time they ran into each other at the water cooler.

"We would have liked to bring in someone from outside," Lincoln went on. "But we don't have the money. So we're offering you the job of managing editor."

Wendy couldn't believe what she was hearing. She knew she ought to be insulted, but she wasn't. "Really?!" she squealed with all the excitement of a schoolgirl upon learning that she's won two free tickets to the Ice Capades at Madison Square Garden in a coloring contest. (In fact, precisely this thrilling thing had happened to Wendy when she was eight.) "Wow. That's great. I mean, not about Shirley leaving, but about the job. Really, I'm honored."

"But it's a large responsibility, Wendy," said Lincoln. "You can't come waltzing in here an hour late every morning. And you'll have to generate stories as well as edit them. Which means keeping up with the papers on a daily basis. And by papers I don't mean celebrity gossip Web sites." His eyes locked punitively upon hers.

"Of course," Wendy said, wincing.

"We can offer you a raise of five thousand dollars."

"Great."

"And you'll get Shirley's old office."

"Fantastic!" The raise was nice. But it was the prospect of having a door to close that excited Wendy most of all. Now even Lincoln would be forced to knock before entering.

Wendy was busy transferring the last of her Bic ballpoints into Shirley's old office—rollerballs fell outside the limits of the magazine's budget—when the first knock arrived. It was accompanied by, "I'm so sorry to bother you, but I just wanted to introduce myself. I'm Alyson? Oh, and that's with a Y. My parents got kind of creative when I was born." She laughed. Wendy didn't. It seemed that Lincoln had forgotten to tell her that in addition to a raise and a door to close, she'd also be receiving her own college intern to boss around. And not just any intern, but a New York University senior who seemed guaranteed to make Wendy feel old and irrelevant.

Her shiny hair was cut in an insouciant shag. Her high breasts flopped beneath some complicated jersey top with dolman sleeves. Her legs were so long that she appeared to be wearing stilts. That she was wearing ballet flats seemed, somehow, like the final insult. At five foot eleven—or whatever she was—she didn't need the extra height. "Nice to meet you, Alyson with a Y," Wendy said, smiling brightly. Now she'd have to worry about what she wore to work every morning, she thought unhappily.

"It's great to meet you, too," said Alyson. "And I just want to say, I'm so completely stoked to be working for my favorite magazine on the planet that I really don't mind what you give me to do. Like, if you want me to get your lunch for you or something, that's fine."

"I don't think that'll be necessary," Wendy said, laughing. "But you can do some research for me if you want. We have a little library here in the office, but it doesn't have all the periodicals we're interested in. For some stuff, I might ask you to go to the public library on Forty-second."

"Ohmygod, I would love to go to the library for you!" declared Alyson. "That's such a cute idea. Also, you should know that I'm very left-wing. I grew up privileged, I guess you could say, in Rye, but it really sickens me to know that my parents are getting tax breaks on their capital gains income while millions of hardworking families struggle to put food on their tables every day. Also, I'm really, really opposed to the war in Iraq. I mean, people are, like, dying over oil! It's so wrong."

Wendy was seized by a sudden desire not only to be chilly and ungrateful, but to come to the defense of the Bush administration, attack poor people for being lazy drug addicts, and possibly even advocate the expansion of America's military presence in the Middle East. She stopped herself by recalling the boredom and alienation that had accompanied her own college internship (at a travel magazine, where she'd done nothing but fact-check room rates). Besides, it wasn't Alyson's fault she had nice breasts. "Well, we're glad to have you here," said Wendy, attempting to rise above her base instinct — to kick the girl in the shins. Then she rolled her chair into her desk and hit the space bar on her recently reinstalled computer so Alyson would get the hint and leave.

"Ohmygod, you still use email?" she said, taking note of the software on Wendy's screen. "That's so adorable!"

"You don't use email?" asked Wendy, confused.

Alyson shrugged. "I guess I just text, really."

"You probably don't have a home phone, either."

She squinted quizzically at Wendy. "What do you mean by 'home phone'?"

"Never mind."

Finally, Alyson left Wendy to contemplate her various outmoded methods of communication in peace. But the pleasure proved short-lived. As the morning progressed, one after another of *Barricade*'s roster of middle-aged male editors — some, like Lincoln, with pockmarked skin; others with more superficial cosmetic defects like nose hairs that needed clipping and twenty-pound tires around their midriffs; all of them unattractive in some irredeemable way — began to poke their large heads through Wendy's door. Ostensibly, they came to congratulate her on her new position. *Actually* was another matter. "A well-deserved promotion, Wendy," they'd say while pivoting on one orthopedic lace-up to face the cubicle at which Alyson now sat, just outside Wendy's door. "And you must be —"

"Alyson."

Hand extended. "Welcome aboard, Alyson. I'm Ralph/Don/Ed ___."

"Nice to meet you Mr. ___!"

"Please — call me Ralph/Don/Ed. And let me just say, it's a pleasure to have some young blood around these parts for once. . . ."

Wendy felt as if she'd just charioted in from ancient Greece.

Glancing at her feet, she couldn't be sure that, beneath her boots and socks, her toes hadn't turned an even deeper shade of purple than Lois's.

Wendy arrived home from work that evening to find her husband playing his acoustic guitar. " 'He's sure got a lot of gall,' " came the yodel-like cry from the bedroom, " 'to be so useless and all. Muttering small talk at the wall while I'm in the hall. . . . ' " Wendy proceeded to the kitchen, only to find that the faucet wouldn't turn off. Standing over the sink, she didn't know which of the many sounds filling the apartment she found to be the most grating — the metallic hum of the highway traffic outside, the Bob Dylan impersonation coming through the wall, or the drip-drip in her face. There was nothing she could do about the first one. As for the second two, in the interest of preserving her marriage, she decided to tackle the faucet, stuffing a paper towel up the spigot. She knew it was a temporary solution. On the other hand, it was unlikely to cause ill will. And Wendy had begun the new year trying to be more supportive of Adam, if only because nagging and berating him to go back to work and have sex with her more often seemed to get her nowhere.

At the very least, they were getting along better now. Ron's accident seemed to have made Adam more sentimental about family, too. He'd attached a photograph of his nieces ice-skating in duck costumes to the door of their refrigerator. And the previous month, around the time that Wendy was ovulating, he'd consented to having intercourse twice in a forty-eight-hour period without first mocking her single-minded focus on reproduction.

Soon, Adam appeared in the kitchen, guitar in hand. "Hey, managing editor!" he said. (Wendy had called him that morning to tell him the good news.)

"Hey, Bobby," said Wendy.

"Bobby?" said Adam.

"Dylan."

"Oh." He laughed. "Just keeping the old fingers limber, you know?"

"Of course."

"So, how's the new job?"

"Great," Wendy told him. "Except Missing Linc forgot to tell me I was getting assigned a ridiculously beautiful NYU intern. I almost had a heart attack when I saw her."

"Cool!" said Adam, his eyebrows jumping.

"The worst part is — she's really nice. Though she did make fun of me for having a home phone."

"Oh, come on." Adam took Wendy into his arms and twirled her, his guitar behind her back. "You're the sexiest editor *Barricade's* ever had."

"What you mean is, I'm the only female editor at the magazine now, my competition being a bunch of middle-aged Marxists with visible butt cracks."

"Aw — you're too hard on yourself. Not to mention on the Marxists. They're people, too. Listen — what do you say we go celebrate tonight?"

"And blow some of my raise?"

"Exactly."

"I thought I'd send the extra money to Visa every month."

"Come on, you have to have fun sometimes."

Easy for you to say, Wendy thought but refrained from uttering out loud. Then again, Adam had a point, she thought: they hadn't been out to eat in weeks. What's more, leaving the house would get him to put his guitar away. "I guess we could take a car service to Blue Ribbon Sushi or something. There's nothing around here." Wendy couldn't stop herself from pointing that last fact out — and in doing so reminding Adam that she was still bitter about having to live on "No Prospect Avenue," as she'd recently dubbed the block.

Over the previous few months, she'd done her best to cheer the place up — painting the walls of the living room pale yellow, hanging wooden blinds, bringing home fresh flowers from the grocery store whenever she remembered. But nothing seemed to work. Home was supposed to be a retreat. The new apartment felt more like a highway rest stop. (Arriving home, Wendy always half-expected to find a food court at the top of the stairs, raising the tantalizing question: the Nachos BellGrande at Taco Bell or a slice of pizza from Sbarro?)

"There's always the White Castle on Thirty-second," offered Adam.

"Can you please not depress me!" Wendy was suddenly livid. That he could joke about such things!

"I don't see why you hate it here so much," said Adam.

"Because it's depressing," said Wendy.

"Maybe *you're* just depressed and taking it out on the neighborhood."

A part of Wendy longed to escalate the dispute — to tell Adam that if she was depressed, it was because he was depressing her. But again, she stopped herself. "What do you say we drop this conversation?" she asked.

"Fine with me," he answered.

"Good. I'm going to go get changed." As Wendy exited the kitchen, she called back to him, "How's your dad today?"

"Good, thanks," Adam called back. Ron was at home now, with a round-the-clock nurse attending to him. He and Adam spoke on the phone every day. From what Wendy could gather, the conversations meant a lot to both of them.

Wendy had also begun the new year trying to be more appreciative of Daphne's friendship, if only because she suspected that the resentment she increasingly felt toward her best friend had more to do with her coveting of Daphne's house, ring, and husband's earning power than it did with Daphne's arrogance, insensitivity, egocentrism, or insincerity. (Though the latter attributes were arguably at play as well.)

Renovations on Daphne's brownstone had begun the second week of January. The second week of February, Daphne called to invite Wendy to come see the progress. Wendy knew she'd be racked with jealousy. She was also curious to see the splendor in which Daphne would soon be living. And would Daphne take the living room in a midcentury modernist direction, with Saarinen womb chairs and brushed-steel tripod lamps with oversize white shades and maybe even a Warhol lithograph or two? Or would she veer in a more traditional vein, with Persian carpets, potted ferns, and burgundy leather club chairs with brass nail heads angled sportily against the hearth? And what about the kitchen? Would it feature country-style glass-front cabinetry or something sleeker and more opaque, perhaps with elongated horizontal pulls in brushed nickel, or maybe even no hardware at all? Wendy agreed to visit the following Saturday.

"I'm so happy you're coming!" Daphne declared. "I desperately need your help decorating. You're always so good at stuff like that."

"Please," protested Wendy, who knew for a fact that Daphne's statement was false. "I have no talent for anything visual." Even so—and even as Wendy reminded herself of Daphne's propensity for spewing utter flimflam—she felt flattered by the suggestion. It had always been like that, she thought resignedly: the grasping, aspiring side of her brain winning out over the level-headed one.

The day before Wendy was due to visit Daphne, which happened to be Valentine's Day, yet another unwelcome menstrual period greeted her in the salmon-colored ladies' room that *Barricade* shared with the Youth-net student exchange office down the hall. (On occasion, gorgeous Estonian teens could be spotted shuffling toward the elevator in skin-tight stone-washed jeans.) Wendy had been trying to conceive for twelve cycles. According to modern medical science, she was infertile. Devastated by the verdict, she teared up on her way back to her office. Just outside the door, Alyson tried to intercept her—something about not being able to locate the current issue of *Dissent*—but Wendy gave herself permission to be rude, if only this one time, and kept walking.

She shut the door behind her and sat down at her desk. On the upside, she thought, after work she and Sara were making their annual pilgrimage to the circus. One look at the lady who hung by her hair always filled Wendy with awe and wonder at the mysteries of the world. Still fighting off tears, she dialed the number of her new ob-gyn, Dr. Wendy Kung. (Wendy Murman's old ob-gyn, like her old therapist, had stopped accepting *Barricade's* bare-bones insurance policy, CarePlus Medical, after the company announced it would no longer reimburse for the removal of any cysts or growths unless they were already cancerous; but they couldn't be too cancerous, because that meant you were already going to die, so why bother trying to save you.) To Wendy's further agitation, however, Dr. Kung's secretary announced that Dr. Kung's next available appointment wasn't until late July.

Wendy could feel her internal stopwatch ticking even faster than usual. "It's actually an emergency," she told the woman. "I can feel some kind of hard mass in my pelvis."

Dr. Kung's secretary sighed testily before squeezing Wendy into Dr. Kung's schedule for Monday.

Wendy hung up the phone feeling more relieved than she did guilty. She found an email message from Gretchen waiting for her:

wen, thanxs for the sweet note! i know, it's RIDICULOUS that you still haven't met the twinnies. but, sadly, afraid it will have to wait another week, as i'm actually on a plane headed to new guinea. but let's definitely schedule something for when i get back. if you can stand take-out, maybe you could come over for dinner one night?? though if you want to see/meet the babes, it might have to be on the early side. though, to be honest, am not entirely sure what time they go to bed these days. to be even more honest, have been so busy at work lately that i've hardly seen the babes myself; all i can say is: THANK GOD for our nanny, dorothea. she just might be the greatest human being alive today. i'm dying for her to move in. actually, she's staying over six nights a week already, but i'd love for her to do sundays, too. unfortunately, she has her own family to look after. shit, am being told to shut off all electronic equipment. have a great week. luv u, g

It wasn't Gretchen's fault that Wendy still wasn't pregnant, Wendy reminded herself. It was also true that Gretchen had had a difficult time conceiving. Yet, Wendy found herself increasingly scandalized by Gretchen's blasé attitude toward parenting. Gretchen had planned on taking three months off after Lola and Liam were born. Three months had quickly turned into three weeks. Sara claimed to have seen her on her headset, cold-calling Goodwill ambassadors to the United Nations, while still in the delivery room. Or did Gretchen know something that Wendy didn't know? Were babies actually really boring and annoying, even babies who didn't cry all day long like Lucas Rose? Wendy sometimes wondered if she actually wanted children, or if she just wanted to keep up.

She wrote back:

New Guinea??? You definitely get around, my friend. Meanwhile, glad to hear things are going so well with the babies/babysitter. Call me when you get back to town and we'll make a plan. Am happy to come to your place. Also, I may need the name of your fertility doc. (The business of conception not happening on its own, alas.) Or maybe I should just steal one of your kids! (Just kidding.) XW

For dinner that evening, Adam made Wendy a hamburger in the shape of a heart. Wendy thought it was cute—sort of.

To Wendy's astonishment, a Valentine's Day gift arrived from her mother as well—an IOU for a night at the St. Regis hotel. The accompanying note read, "Dear Wendell. To make ends meet, my student and research assistant, Douglas Bondy, works as a bellhop here. So if thanks are due, please direct them to him. Mom. p.s. Perhaps you were unaware that you were conceived on the second floor??"

Wendy's first reaction—after her initial shock that her mother had bought her a Valentine's Day present—was irritation at her mother's over-crediting of Douglas Bondy. Her second reaction was horror at the reference to her own, sordid beginnings. Also, what were her hairy hippie parents doing in the St. Regis? Upon further reflection, however, she was overcome by gratitude for her mother's generosity. What had gotten into her?

The snow began to fall on Friday evening. It fell all night. To Wendy, gazing out her bedroom window the next morning, Brooklyn appeared to have been put to sleep under a giant down comforter. That, or Adam's screenplay's "high concept" had come true, and New York had fallen victim to a surprise nuclear attack. The glimpses of jutting steel aside, the view was almost pastoral. Even more disorientingly, the Prospect Expressway was quiet. Wendy considered canceling her trip to Daphne's house and spending the day hiding under the covers with a good book and pretending she was in Vermont. But she figured she might as well get the visit over with.

By late morning, the snow had stopped and the sun had come out, but it was still cold and windy. Crossing Fourth Avenue, Wendy felt as if she were being stabbed by hundreds of tiny daggers. At the same time, she found it invigorating to be outside, braving the elements; to have her thoughts dominated by nothing more complicated than the desire to keep warm and to move forward.

The R train, which was the only subway in close walking distance to Wendy's apartment, didn't stop anywhere near Daphne's new house. So Wendy got out at Court Street and trudged the rest of the way there through snow, ice, and sludge. Forty minutes later, her feet drenched, she arrived at Amity Street between Clinton and Henry.

Genteel and secluded in feel, the block was lined with four-story brick and brownstone town houses in the Greek Revival and Italianate styles. Before she left her own apartment, Wendy had written Daphne's address on a scrap of paper and stuck it in her coat pocket. As she struggled now to unfold the paper, her fingers numb, she thought of those prehistoric people whose remains were occasionally discovered in remote tundras buried beneath three feet of ice, but with their flesh and even their hair miraculously still attached to their bones. Finally, she managed to open the slip. The numbers had bled into one another. But from what Wendy could decipher, she was already standing out front.

Daphne and Jonathan's brownstone managed to be both charming and imposing. A high stoop with a decorative ironwork balustrade led to a pair of carved wood double doors that had been painted a shiny shade of red. The doors were flanked by rectangular pilasters etched with leaves. On the top step, a dwarf spruce fashioned like a smoke ring poked out of a gently oxidized stone urn. In the tiny front garden, an old-fashioned streetlamp, looking like something out of Charles Dickens's London, shot out of the snow. Someone had already shoveled both the stoop and the bluestone walkway that led to the lower entrance. On the parlor-floor level, cast-iron guard railings that matched both the balustrade and the areaway fence that separated the house from the sidewalk protected what appeared to be floor-to-ceiling windows. A work permit had been taped to the inside of the window closest to the door. *It's just a house,* Wendy reminded herself—*just a pile of bricks and beams*—as she climbed the stairs and buzzed a discreet bell tucked behind one of the pilasters.

Daphne came to the door in a bright pink velour hoodie and matching sweatpants, her feet ensconced in shearling slippers, her hair pinned up with a rhinestone-studded butterfly clip. (Only Daphne could make tacky look cute.) "Wen—you are such a HERO for coming out in this cold!" she declared. She threw her arms around Wendy. "I was sure you were going to cancel, and I was already so bummed out about it."

"Well, here I am," said Wendy.

"God, you must be SO frozen."

"It's cold out there. I won't lie to you."

Daphne was always so friendly that it made it hard ever to be mad at her, Wendy was thinking as she followed Daphne through a second set of antique doors and into a hallway illuminated by a brass chandelier. Wendy recalled the time in college when, for once, she'd been the bigger mess of the two. Wendy's first real boyfriend, a premed student from Mamaroneck named Evan, had broken up with her without explanation. Daphne had plied her with drinks, told her that men were jerks, and proposed that the two of them go to the movies "and forget about all [their] guy problems." Daphne had been so sweet, so reassuring. Wendy had felt so loved and protected. But an hour later, Daphne was suddenly putting on her coat and saying, "I totally forgot I said I'd meet Josh. Are you going to be okay if I go out for a few hours? I promise I'll be back soon." (Face squinched up.)

What could Wendy say? "I'll be fine," Wendy had told her. "You go have fun."

At the rear end of the hall was a graceful curving staircase with a polished mahogany banister and a thick red runner; to the left was a third set of double doors. "First, let me take your coat," Daphne said, arms outstretched.

"Oh, thanks," said Wendy, handing over her parka.

"Do you want sweatpants or anything?" Daphne asked while Wendy pried the first of two snow boots off her feet.

"I should be okay as long as I get these things off," Wendy said, tugging at the second. Finally, both boots came off. She set them down on a mat next to the interior doors, then made an admittedly exaggerated production out of shaking her feet, frozen though they were.

"Poor you," said Daphne, lips puffed out and down like a clown's.

"That's much better," said Wendy, lapping up the mixture of pity and attention that Daphne was currently lavishing on her.

"You really are such a good friend for coming over in this weather."

"Oh, please — let's see the house!"

"Weeelllll . . ." Daphne ushered Wendy through the third set of doors and into the parlor.

It was the most gorgeous construction site that Wendy had ever seen. There was paper all over the floor, and paint cans, rollers, and trays on top of that. But even unfinished, its plaster walls still covered with primer, the room — massive and sun speckled, its fourteen-foot ceiling decorated with lacy plaster-work—was a masterpiece. Two white marble fireplace mantels with scalloped edges and elaborately carved keystones jutted out of one wall. A humongous gilt mirror leaned against the other. A crystal chandelier descended from a plaster medallion on the ceiling like a sprig of perfectly ripe grapes.

"So here's our future living room!" Daphne announced brightly. "I was really hoping they'd be further along by now, but everyone says renovations always cost twice as much and take twice as long as you planned. So what can you do?" She sighed and shrugged at the same time, as if it wasn't actually that big a deal. (As if she had both time and money to spare.) "Anyway. I think we're going to go with this weird color in the front parlor called 'lobster bisque.' Beige just seemed kind of 'nineties.' And white seemed too boring. And there was no way Jonathan was going to go for actual pink. Also, we're getting this huge Rug Company rug from Jonathan's parents as a wedding present, and it has all these reds and oranges in it. So we needed something to match that. Obviously, the trim is going to be white. But, seriously"—she turned to Wendy, her nose crinkled—"does bisque sound really *fugly?*"

"First of all," Wendy said, feeling in that moment that honesty was the best policy, "let me just say that this place is insane. I mean, it's like a museum! The fireplaces. The mirrors. The ceiling. It's amazing."

"I love this room, too." Daphne smiled. "I just hope we're happy here."

"Why wouldn't you be happy?" asked Wendy, who thought she saw a hint of doubt pass across Daphne's face. But maybe she was only imagining it, wishing it were true. . . .

"Oh, I don't know." Daphne slapped the air. "Don't listen

to me. I'm just nervous about the paint color!" She laughed. "But, really, does bisque sound gross?"

Now it was Wendy's turn to shrug. "I don't know," she said. In fact, the color did sound a little garish to her. "I guess I'd have to see the shade. Do you have one of those color strips?"

"I think I have one upstairs," said Daphne. "But first, come see the kitchen." She took hold of Wendy's forearm. "Or, I should really say—the place where the kitchen might one day be!" She laughed again as she led Wendy to the back of the parlor, past what would surely be the dining room. (Daphne would probably furnish it with some ten-foot-long quasi-rustic monastery table, Wendy thought.) "Meanwhile, we're thinking of going with wheat-colored taffeta drapes for these back windows," Daphne continued.

"That could be nice," said Wendy, whose toes were finally beginning to thaw.

Daphne directed Wendy into a newly Sheetrocked area to the right of the dining room, where four or five Central American men were busy unloading what appeared to be a large wood-paneled refrigerator. "Hi, you guys!" Daphne lifted her hand at the men, who smiled and laughed, seeming to find the sight of her and Wendy amusing, before returning to the business of refrigerator installation. So far, only the island had been installed: a glossy white barge with elongated silver pulls and a white marble top. "So, here's the beginnings of the kitchen!" Daphne said, turning back to Wendy.

"Very sleek," said Wendy, hating herself for recognizing the designer (likely Poggenpohl, she decided). She ran her hand across the top of the island. It felt cold and smooth.

"To be honest, I was kind of reluctant at first to have the

island put in," said Daphne, "just because it looks so modern compared to the rest of the house. But our architect said we needed more storage. I mean, that's kind of the problem with these old town houses. They're so long and narrow that there really isn't room for a dining room and a full kitchen on the same floor. Anyway"—she shrugged—"I guess it's nice to have somewhere you can grab a bite without having to sit all the way down at the table. You know?"

"Right," said Wendy, who didn't see how sitting down at a table in a room that looked like the one at whose periphery she stood constituted any kind of effort.

"Also, I love these drawers. They're so quiet." Daphne pulled out the drawer closest to her right hand, then pushed it back in, an operation that was indeed silent and seamless. "Meanwhile, as you can see, the fridge has arrived. It's supposed to go over there." She pointed at the far corner. "And the stove will go in the middle there, next to the sink"—again, she pointed at an indistinct place on the opposite wall—"if it ever arrives." She laughed warily. "Our architect ordered it from Italy. Don't ask me why. And don't even get me started on the cabinets. They were supposed to be here, like, a month ago. Whatever." Daphne shook her head as she led Wendy back toward the main staircase. "Anyway, I want to show you the upstairs. We're 'staging,' so we're already living up there. Which is great, except we don't have a kitchen right now. Which kind of sucks."

"I'm sure," said Wendy.

Just outside the parlor door, in view of the stairs, Daphne came to a sudden halt and indicated that Wendy should do the same. "I'm sorry," she said, teeth gritted apologetically as she grabbed hold of Wendy's wrist with one hand and removed her slippers with the other. "Do you mind terribly taking your socks off before we go upstairs? It's just that, with all the construction dust and everything—"

"It's fine!" Wendy cut her off, taken aback not so much by Daphne's request as by the half-guilty, half-panicked look on Daphne's face. It was a look that suggested to Wendy that Daphne thought Wendy belonged to such an inferior social caste that the concept of tracking renovation detritus between floors of a brownstone was sure to be alien to her. Without further comment, she pulled off her socks and stuffed them into her empty boots. But inside, she simmered.

Shame and anger turned to covetousness, however, as Wendy's still-tender toes sank into the plush carpeting that lined the stairs. The feeling only grew more intense after she followed Daphne into the master bedroom, which had its own carved marble fireplace and had already been outfitted with a mahogany sleigh bed. For the picture before her was not just one of bricks and beams, or even marble and mahogany, but of a refuge—less from the noise and chaos "out there" as from the noise and chaos inside her own head that made her see both sides of every argument and wonder what she really believed and who she therefore was. Rationally, Wendy knew that a home was defined by its people, not its furnishings. Yet a part of her wanted to believe that if the sleigh beds were in place, the happy family would follow. (And that a higher thread count meant a hotter sex life.) Marcia used to say that marriages were "hard work." But Wendy had always suspected that there was a shortcut—that money (if only she and Adam had money!) would do some of the backbreaking labor for them.

At the same time, Wendy could neither understand nor justify her longing for the particular luxury that Daphne's house promised to deliver. Once, Wendy had prided herself on living simply. When had the basics ceased to be enough? And when had refrigerators and toilets, utilitarian by definition, become shiny objects to covet and pine for? (And was "using the facilities" really that much more pleasurable on a tankless, sensor-activated TOTO Neorest with an integrated Washlet seat featuring warm-water washing, automatic air dryer, and deodorizer—versus a plain old American Standard?)

"Are you sure you don't want these?"

Wendy had become so lost in her own thoughts that the sound of Daphne's voice startled her. Daphne was dangling a pair of woolen socks in her face. "That's okay," said Wendy, preferring in that moment to be a martyr to the cause of her own middle-classdom.

"Are you sure?" asked Daphne.

"I'm fine, really."

"Anyway, as I was saying, any time you ever want to stay here, please just let me know," Daphne went on. "I mean, it's embarrassing how much space we have! Right now we have two guest rooms on the third floor. I mean, at some point in the future, one of those might turn into a kid's room." Wendy could feel her blood pressure rising. "But for now, I swear, we could literally house a whole family up there!"

Why don't you? Wendy thought, knowing full well that were she to own a brownstone, she'd be unlikely to invite a homeless family to live in the top floor of it, either. That didn't mean she was above guilting others for failing to do so. And wasn't it Wendy's right under the circumstances to make Daphne feel just the tiniest bit bad about her good fortune? "Wow, you're lucky," she said faux-wistfully. "We can't even afford an apartment with a real second bedroom anymore."

"You should go work at a glossy magazine or something!" Daphne blurted out, her eyes flashing as if she'd just had a brainstorm. "Like at Condé Nast or Hearst or something. I'm sure they'd hire you in a minute. And they pay really well."

Maybe there was nothing offensive about Daphne's words in and of themselves. Yet in the context of her "mansion tour," Wendy found the suggestion inexcusable. She thought of the time when she and Daphne were in their twenties and trying on clothes in the dressing room of a Lower Broadway boutique. Wendy had been complaining about how she hated her knees. "Well, what about trying a skirt that falls *below* the knee?" Daphne had suggested. As if the idea had never occurred to Wendy. (As if that were the advice she'd been seeking.) What Daphne never seemed to understand was that Wendy liked to complain. Just as she wanted Daphne to listen and, where possible, commiserate, then refute her contentions with generic words of praise. So often, Daphne's advice sounded patronizing or, worse, downright insulting. "I could," Wendy finally answered in the most righteous tone of voice she could summon. "It's just that—I guess I care more about what's happening in the world than about the shopping habits of rich people. Which is basically what all those magazines are about. You know?"

If Daphne experienced the line as a personal dig, she didn't let on. "Well, that's your right," she said, shrugging. "Meanwhile, what's happening with Adam? Is he planning on going back to work soon?"

Wendy could feel her face growing warm. "He's still working on his screenplay," she answered quickly.

"Oh—that's cool!" said Daphne, nodding. But Wendy could tell that she didn't think it was cool at all.

Wendy didn't think it was cool, either. But in that moment, her frustration with Adam's employment situation seemed like her own private business. It hadn't always been that way. Once, Wendy had told Daphne everything. Ever since she and Jonathan had become an item, however, Wendy had found herself increasingly protective of both her husband and their marriage.

Wendy treated herself to a car service home. As she entered her apartment, the shabbiness of the living room was suddenly explained to her both by its lack of crown molding and by its low ceiling, so low that it seemed in danger of caving in. Or maybe it was Adam, seated in the middle of it, wearing an old Mets cap and watching the Cartoon Network, who seemed to be bringing the walls down around him. "How was Daphne's manse?" he asked. "Appropriately luxurious?"

No doubt he'd spent the afternoon smoking pot, Wendy thought. She sniffed twice in rapid succession. "It smells funny in here," she said, even though it didn't.

"What are you talking about?" Adam snapped back, clearly offended.

"Nothing. Sorry," said Wendy, guilty. It was Saturday, the "day of rest," she reminded herself. He wasn't hurting anyone by sitting there. She hadn't wanted to marry a corporate lawyer. Nor was it Adam's fault that Daphne had been insensitive to their real estate situation.

"You didn't answer my question," he said.

"Oh, right. Daphne's house. It was like Versailles in there," Wendy told him.

"I can't believe you bothered going all the way there in this snow."

"It's just snow."

"Maura called."

"Thanks."

Wendy went into the bedroom to call her back. But even with the door closed, she couldn't overcome the sensation that the place wasn't big enough to accommodate the two of them. "Will you meet me for lunch?" she asked Maura. "Please?"

"Wendy—there are four feet of snow out there!" Maura protested.

"I'll come to you."

"I don't eat lunch."

"You can have water."

"I'm not thirsty."

"I'm begging you. Please?! I really need to vent."

"It's not my fault you quit therapy."

"Look who's talking."

"That's different. Gloria told me I was finished."

Wendy paused before venturing, "I have to admit, I've never believed you."

There was a long silence at the other end of the line. Finally, Maura spoke: "Okay, so I lied."

"I knew it!" cried Wendy.

"She always wanted to talk about why I hadn't finished my dissertation. It got annoying after a while."

"Now you have to come meet me. It's your punishment."

"I'm working on my dissertation."

"Another *bald* lie."

After much sighing, Maura agreed to meet Wendy at a diner on Fourth Avenue that was near her rental studio. Maura hadn't won the real estate lottery, either. Nor was she particularly close to Daphne. All of which made Wendy think that Maura would be the ideal listener to her griping.

"So, I went to see Daphne's house this morning," Wendy began over scrambled eggs. "And it was totally insane. Seriously, it looked like a museum in there. But no, she was all upset because the cabinets hadn't arrived yet from Italy." She rolled her eyes. "Then she started bragging about how they have so much space upstairs they could house two extra families. I had to fight off the impulse to tell her she should. And then, when I said, 'You're lucky you can afford eleven extra bedrooms; we can't even afford two,' she suggested I leave my job and go to work at *Lucky* or something, writing captions about pants." Wendy tutted. "Like it's NEVER occurred to me that I might get paid better at a glossy magazine! So I said, 'Sorry, I'm not interested,' and she said, 'Well, what about Adam? Is he going back to work?' Like it's any of her damn business!" Wendy shook her head. "I'm sorry. I love Daphne. I always will. But her narcissism has really gotten out of control—basically, ever since she hooked up with Jonathan. It's like she can't see that other people don't all have the same financial profile as her." No sooner had Wendy concluded her monologue, however, than she felt mean and petty for having spoken so critically about her best friend.

Nor did Maura's response, surprising to Wendy in its temperateness, make her feel any better about the vitriol she'd just spewed. "That sounds aggravating, I agree," Maura said, sucking on the slice of lemon that had come with her tea.

"But, you know, the guy's rich. And the Uberoffs aren't exactly hurting for cash, either. I'm sure they helped, too. And, I mean — come on — it was never like Daphne pretended she was some big bohemian or something. I guess my point is, if I had dough like that, I'd probably buy a town house in Cobble fucking Hill, too. I'd probably order my kitchen cabinets from Italy, too. I mean, wouldn't you?"

"I guess," Wendy was forced to admit.

On Monday, Wendy left work early to go see Dr. Kung in her York Avenue office. She might as well have shown up an hour late. To fill the time as she waited for her name to be called, she read a brochure about pelvic floor disorder. (And did the pelvis have a ceiling, too? Wendy wondered. And, if so, how high was it? And was the floor parquet?) Finally, a nurse called her name and escorted her into Dr. Kung's inner chambers. It was another twenty minutes before Dr. Kung herself appeared — in four-inch-high red pumps and a white lab coat unbuttoned to reveal steep cleavage. "Nice to see you — Wendy," she said, reading off her clipboard. "You know, we have the same name."

"I know, it's funny," said Wendy, who didn't actually find it all that funny.

"Is your name short for anything?"

"Well, technically, Wendell. But no one calls me that. Just my mother."

"My name is short for Wenhui," offered Dr. Kung.

"Really," said Wendy, anxious to get on with it. In the past few years, all of her doctors had gotten strangely chatty. Wendy suspected they'd all attended the same workshop that stressed the importance of "people skills" in winning the trust of their patients.

"So, I understand you feel something hard in your pelvis?" asked Dr. Kung.

"Well, not exactly," conceded a now cringing Wendy. (Who knew that receptionists wrote down patients' complaints?) "I mean, I think it went away. But I can't get pregnant. And it's been twelve months. To be honest, that's kind of why I'm here."

Dr. Kung's scowl was unmistakable. It was clear she thought Wendy was wasting her time. "How often do you and your partner have sex?" she asked.

"Well, during the week I'm ovulating, at least three times every month," Wendy told her. It was a slight exaggeration, but still.

"What about the rest of the month?"

"What does it matter if I'm not ovulating then?"

"How do you know you're not ovulating?"

"Well, I take my temperature every morning. And I use those ovulation-predictor kits from the pharmacy."

"You think you know when you're ovulating," said Dr. Kung, in what struck Wendy as an unnecessarily superior voice. "But nobody knows for sure unless she comes in here every day of the month and gets an ultrasound."

"Well, I'm not saying I know the exact hour," said Wendy.

"And you're thirty-four?"

"I turned thirty-five at the end of last year."

"And how long is your cycle?"

"Usually around twenty-six days. Sometimes a few days shorter."

Dr. Kung scribbled something on her clipboard. Then she cleared her throat and said, "You have your period, what? Four, five days?"

"Something like that," said Wendy.

"As soon as your period is over, have sex every day until the fifteenth day of your cycle. Maybe even the sixteenth day, just to be sure. You'll be pregnant in three months."

"But I've been trying for twelve cycles!" cried Wendy, on the verge of tears again. She hadn't lied about having a hard mass in her pelvis only to be told that she wasn't having enough sex with her husband! She felt as if Dr. Kung wasn't taking her problem seriously. At the same time, she suspected that Dr. Kung was right. Only, Wendy didn't see what she could do to rectify the situation. She and Adam were too many years into marriage for the orgiastic marathon that Dr. Kung seemed to be advocating. Or was that just an excuse for the waning of passion between them (and Adam's obvious ambivalence about having kids)? "But what if there's something wrong with me?" she asked. "Or even with my husband?"

Dr. Kung sighed wearily. "You want his sperm tested?"

"Yes, please," said Wendy.

"Fine. You want your tubes tested also? It's a painful procedure."

"Yes, please," Wendy said again. She was already in agony, she figured; what was a little more of the same?

Dr. Kung was writing the second of two referrals, when she paused, glanced up at Wendy, and said, "Do you want some more advice?"

"Sure," said Wendy.

"Buy some nice underwear."

Had Dr. Kung spied Wendy's decomposing Hanes Her Ways on the companion chair in the corner? The thought was so excruciating that as Wendy exited the woman's office, she knew she'd be changing gynecologists yet again.

That evening, over carrots Vichy (James Beard, p. 207) and broiled ham steaks (Ibid., p. 121), Wendy told Adam about her visit to Dr. Kung's office, albeit in a slightly revisionist form. "So I saw Dr. Kung this morning," she began in a faux-breezy tone, "and she said there was probably nothing wrong and we probably just weren't having enough sex during the second week of my cycle. But just to be sure, as a first step, she said you should get your sperm tested."

"You want me to jerk off into a test tube?" Adam narrowed his eyes in amusement and — it seemed to Wendy — irritation, all in one.

"Paper cup," she said, wincing. "I mean, since it's easy to check —"

"Easy for you to say!"

"I just mean, it's not like it's painful or something — unlike the tube test that she wants me to get, which is supposed to be really unpleasant."

Adam laid down his fork. "Do we have to talk about this while I'm eating? Or, at least, attempting to eat." He reached for his water glass. Wendy didn't answer. For a few moments, they sat in silence. "I got my college girlfriend pregnant, you know," he announced, while inspecting a carrot in the overhead light.

"I know," said Wendy, "but it's possible that something

happened since then—like during that operation you had ten years ago." For months, she'd been itching to bring up the subject of Adam's hernia operation.

"They didn't cut off my balls, for god's sake!" He shook his head as he cut into his ham. He brought the meat to his mouth. Then he said, "If I agree to the test, can we stop talking about my groin?"

"I appreciate you doing this," said Wendy.

"I better not run into anyone I know," said Adam.

Why did he always have to make her feel like he was doing her a favor? It was his future too, his baby she was trying to conceive. Or was he just trying to inject some humor into a situation that wasn't necessarily funny? "I'm sure you won't," she told him. "The office is on some random street in the East Thirties."

"Are you sure I can't do it in the Bronx?" Wendy was about to volunteer to find Adam a more remote location, when he answered his own question: "Whatever. I'll wear a wig and sunglasses. By the way, if you don't mind me saying, this is the worst dinner I've ever eaten."

"Well, you can cook your own food tomorrow night," said Wendy, who wasn't sure if she should be insulted or agree.

"I will," said Adam, lowering a fork to the floor. "I got a treat for you, Polly."

Adam's dog, until just then resting peacefully at his feet, let out a high-pitched wail and bolted from the room.

"Screw both of you." Wendy began to laugh.

Adam laughed, too—so hard that he eventually fell off his chair. Then Wendy fell off hers. As the tears ran down her cheeks and she clutched her stomach, it occurred to her that she and Adam hadn't had such a good time in months, maybe years.

Adam's results came in first. As he learned in a phone call the following Monday and relayed to Wendy upon her return from the office that evening, his sperm numbered in the several hundred million per milliliter. "That's insane," Wendy said happily, "You're like a one-man sperm conglomerate!"

"Just call me Captain Stud," said Adam. He began to dance around their living room like a disco king, circa 1979. Wendy was again reminded of how adorable her husband could be. (She still longed to be his disco queen.)

Contrary to Paige Ryan's warnings of several months before, Wendy's fallopian tubes proved fully functional as well. Wendy knew she ought to feel relieved by this piece of news, too. And she was. But it also left her further frustrated: if there was nothing wrong with her, why was she still not pregnant? A part of her was tempted to lie to Adam and tell him there was bad news, if only so he wouldn't advocate further patience, as Dr. Kung had. (Wendy didn't know if she had any left in her.) Not that she and Adam were in any position to afford fertility treatments. If it came to that, Wendy figured, their best hope was Adam's parents. From what she gathered, however, the Schwartz family was already spending a small fortune on Ron's care. For all Wendy knew, they had nothing more to hand out. Never mind the fact that Adam would likely be too proud to ask them for help, and probably wouldn't give Wendy permission to do so, either.

Phyllis called Tuesday evening, and only Wendy was

home. (Adam had gone out for a beer with a college friend.) For several minutes, the two discussed Ron's prognosis. Then Phyllis said, "Anyway, how are you, my dear?"

While Wendy and her mother-in-law typically limited their conversation to trivial subjects, Wendy was aware of having spent a considerable amount of time that fall discussing Ron's medical condition. It seemed fair that Phyllis should reciprocate. The words were suddenly pouring out of her. "To be honest, not that well," Wendy told her. "I'm having trouble getting pregnant. It's been a year. And the doctors can't find anything wrong with either of us."

"My poor dear!" cried Phyllis. "Why didn't you tell me earlier?"

"I didn't want to bother you, with Ron sick and everything."

"Please — we'll be happy to do whatever we can. Just say the word. I need more grandchildren!"

Wendy felt a great wave of calmness and well-being washing over her. "Thanks, Phyllis," she said. "I really appreciate you saying that. We're not at that point yet. But if and when we get there, I'll let you know."

"Please do."

"Oh, and can you do me a favor in the meantime and not discuss this with Adam? I worry he'll be mad at me if he knows I told you."

"Of course!"

Wendy hung up the phone feeling greatly relieved. But relief was followed by embarrassment at the sudden loss of privacy, and anxiety that Adam would find out what she'd done. And why had she? Was she only after money or was she looking for comfort, too — comfort she'd been unable to find elsewhere? (Or was it just that she had to tell everyone everything, and Adam was right yet again?)

And why was it that Wendy spent so many of her waking hours worrying that her husband was mad at her, or was going to be mad at her soon?

6.

FROM WHAT DAPHNE had told Wendy, Jonathan had hoped to have the wedding ceremony at the conservative synagogue in Cobble Hill that he'd recently joined. But Daphne would have had to formally convert to Judaism, and there hadn't been time. Or maybe she wasn't so inclined. Wendy never found out the full story — Daphne had been cagey in her retelling of it — but the end result was that both ceremony and after-party had been slated for the Prospect Park boathouse, a graceful Beaux Arts structure built in 1905 to resemble a Venetian library. As wedding venues went, the boathouse was small. So fewer than a hundred people had been invited. The list, of course, included Wendy and Adam. On the evening of the event, he seemed for once more eager to leave the house than she did.

Wendy had called a car service to drive them there. But the driver didn't speak English and couldn't find the correct turn-off. They circled the park an extra time before locating it. By the time their battered Lincoln pulled into the driveway — fifteen minutes later than intended — Wendy was in a state of near panic. She'd been asked to read a Shakespeare sonnet at the beginning of the ceremony. She wondered if Daphne would ever forgive her if she didn't show up in time.

To Wendy's relief, the cantor was only just approaching the dais, which, on account of the unseasonably warm weather, had been moved outside to the boathouse's terrace, overlooking a lily pond. Two slender columns of folding chairs faced the dais. Wendy in her black basic and Adam, dressed for once in a suit, albeit a secondhand one in sky blue with a ludicrously wide lapel, sat down at the end of the second row. Moments later, the somber strains of Bach's Unaccompanied Cello Suite No. 1 in G Major began to sound behind them. Then the chuppah appeared, its birch poles entwined with gold leaves and, upon closer inspection, being supported by Daphne's younger brother, Will; two buff-looking men whom Wendy didn't recognize; and — was it possible? — Paige Ryan, dressed for the evening in a bright orange skirt suit with a peplum jacket.

"She looks like a giant yam," Adam muttered under his breath.

Wendy stifled a giggle despite her hurt. Never mind that Daphne had asked her to give a reading during the ceremony and a toast at the dinner following it. (Or that she would surely have complained about the weight and strain to her back.) Wendy couldn't bear the idea that Paige had been assigned a special role in the ceremony and, debatably, the most special role of all.

Next down the aisle was Jonathan, his arms linked with his parents'. By the look of it, Mr. Sonnenberg, tall and frail and leaning on a cane, was considerably older than Mrs. Sonnenberg, a small expensive-looking woman with gold jewelry and a silver-blond bob. As for Jonathan himself, he looked handsome, Wendy thought. But that evening, dressed in a black tuxedo embellished with a cream-and-blue prayer shawl and matching cream yarmulke, he exuded dignity above all else. He was standing so straight that he appeared to be leaning backward. Or, as Adam put it in a just-audible voice, "Exhibit A—stick up ass."

Wendy kicked him in the ankle. She was suddenly terrified that someone would hear him, even as she relished his running commentary. (It made the spectacle of Daphne and Jonathan's wedding a little less surreal.) Jonathan assumed his place under the chuppah, and his parents took their seats in the front row.

Daphne appeared soon after that, balanced on the arm of her jowly, red-in-the-face, yet still somehow debonair father, Richard. Wendy could have predicted that Daphne would make a beautiful bride. But the sight of her that evening in her white satin, delicately ruched column dress, her hair swept up and back, her eyes faraway, her skin opalescent, her curves the tiniest bit more supple than Wendy remembered them being, made the hair on Wendy's arms stand up. Age and experience had lent Daphne's face a certain angularity that, paradoxically, seemed to highlight her fragility. She looked as if she belonged to another species of woman—the kind who floated ten feet above the earth while the rest of womankind, Wendy included, toiled in the loam.

Daphne joined Jonathan under the chuppah, and the music stopped. "Friends," the cantor began in an oily voice, "welcome. Shalom. We are gathered here on this beautiful spring evening to witness and celebrate the marriage of two fine young people whom I've had the pleasure of getting to know in the last few months, Daphne Uberoff and Jonathan Sonnenberg."

"He's met them once," quipped Adam, prompting a second kick and a "Sh!" from Wendy.

A Hebrew prayer was followed by: "To begin, the bride and groom have selected readings to symbolize the love and respect they share for one another. First, Daphne's friend Wendy will read Shakespeare's Sonnet One Hundred Sixteen."

Her heart pounding—she hated public speaking of all kinds—Wendy stood up from her chair and walked to the podium. Gazing out at the crowd, she was amazed to discover that she recognized no more than a third of the guests. What's more, the third she knew included classmates of hers and Daphne's from college she hadn't seen in fifteen years. Wendy was reminded that Daphne had always had many more close friends than she let on. The crowd vanished from view as she unfolded the sheet of paper in her hand and began to read:

> *"Let me not to the marriage of true minds*
> *Admit impediments. Love is not love*
> *Which alters when it alteration finds,*
> *Or bends with the remover to remove:*
> *O, no! It is an ever-fixed mark,*
> *That looks on tempests and is never shaken; . . .*
> *It is the star to every wandering bark,*
> *Whose worth's unknown, although his height be taken.*
> *Love's not Time's fool, though rosy lips and cheeks*
> *Within his bending sickle's compass come; . . ."*

Relieved to be finished, Wendy walked back to her seat and sat down.

"Did it ever occur to you that 'bending sickle' is a redundancy?" asked Adam while the cantor introduced the second reader — Jonathan's brother, David. "I mean, all sickles are bent. So much for the Bard's mastery of the English language."

Wendy repressed another laugh as a shorter, slightly less good-looking version of Jonathan rose from his chair. "Song of Solomon Two," he began in an unexpectedly sonorous voice:

> *"Listen! My lover! Look! Here he comes, leaping across the mountains, bounding over the hills.*
>
> *My lover is like a gazelle or a young stag. Look! There he stands behind our wall, gazing through the windows, peering through the lattice.*
>
> *My lover spoke and said to me, 'Arise, my darling, my beautiful one, and come with me.*
>
> *See! The winter is past; the rains are over and gone.*
>
> *Flowers appear on the earth; the season of singing has come, the cooing of doves is heard in our land.*
>
> *The fig tree forms its early fruit; . . .' "*

As David Sonnenberg walked back to his seat, Wendy found her eyes suddenly wet and her lower lip quivering. It was the evocativeness of the verse. It was the gentle undulations of the chuppah over the bride and groom. It was the enthusiasm with which Daphne and Jonathan had inserted themselves into history and literature and religion. It was also the lack of irony implicit in their stillness, the firmness with which he gripped her hand, and the quiet pride in her smile as she gripped back. Embarrassed by her tears, Wendy turned away from Adam. She thought back to her own wedding party.

A few nights after they were married at City Hall, friends had gathered at a local Brooklyn dive. Wendy had worn a green floral dress that she'd bought in a thrift store. The hem had been coming undone. She hadn't bothered cutting the stray threads. The entertainment had consisted of their friend Howie performing Karen Carpenter hits on the ukulele. Someone had brought salsa and chips. The open bar had lasted two hours, and only the beer and soft drinks had been free. It had been everything that Wendy and Adam wanted—or, at least, everything that Adam had convinced Wendy that they wanted. Looking back, it was hard to differentiate between the two.

Looking back, Wendy was mystified as to why she and Adam had gone to such lengths to avoid having a traditional wedding. Surely the Schwartzes—who'd sat in a corner booth, looking confused if not unhappy—would have been amenable to helping foot the bill.

"Tell me you're not crying," said Adam. He elbowed Wendy in the ribs as the cantor began to sing.

"Maybe," said Wendy, suddenly wanting him to see her tears and realize she was a woman who believed in love; a woman who had been deprived. She turned back to him, blinking and sniffing to buttress her cause.

"You're not secretly in love with the groom or anything, are you?" he asked.

"It's a wedding. People cry."

"Meaning, if your eyes are dry, you're a stone-cold bastard like me?"

Wendy didn't answer. Wasn't it just like Daphne's life that she should manage to get married on the most beautiful night of the year? she was thinking as a delicious breeze fluttered her bangs and tickled her cheeks — a night so clear and lovely that even the city air seemed perfumed.

And every emotion was magnified by half.

After the cantor delivered an ingratiating homage to the intelligence and compassion of both the bride and the groom, as well as their respective love of literature and the law, he handed Jonathan and Daphne matching goblets filled with red wine and instructed them to drink. Which they did. Finally, it was time for the vows. "Do you, Jonathan, of your own free will and consent, take Daphne to be your wife, and do you promise to love, honor, and cherish her throughout life?" he asked.

"I do," Jonathan answered commandingly.

"And do you, Daphne, of your own free will and consent, take Jonathan to be your husband, and do you promise to love, honor, and cherish him throughout life?"

"I do," said Daphne, her voice even wispier than she was.

Then Jonathan reached into the inside pocket of his suit jacket and produced a thick platinum band, which he promptly slid onto Daphne's already iridescent left hand.

"O God, supremely blessed, supreme in might and glory," the cantor continued, "guide and bless this groom and bride standing here in the presence of God, the Guardian of the home, ready to enter into the bond of wedlock, answer in the fear of God, and in the hearing of those assembled." He placed the now-empty goblets on the floor wrapped in a colorful scarf. Daphne and Jonathan promptly shattered them beneath their feet. Then the crowd erupted in cheers, and Jonathan and Daphne came together, their lips and bodies joined as if two lifetimes weren't enough to contain the vastness of their ardor. *Daphne and Jonathan must be madly in love with each other.* The thought came to Wendy in the form of a revelation. All winter, she'd assumed there were ulterior motives at work in Daphne's heart. Now Daphne and Jonathan's love seemed as pure to her as any fig trees forming early fruit.

"Congratulations, Mrs. Sonnenberg. I'm Daphne's friend Wendy."

"Thank you."

"And this is my husband, Adam."

"Nice to meet you."

"Congratulations to you both."

"Thank you."

A nontraditional receiving line had been established just inside the doors to the boathouse. . . .

"Jonathan! Congratulations." (Wendy.)

"Glad you could make it." (Jonathan.)

"Congratulations." (Adam.)

"Thank you. Oh, and for the record, everything's free tonight. Free bar. Free dinner. Free entertainment. It's a socialists' utopia." (Jonathan, turning to Adam.)

"Give me a fucking break," Adam swore under his breath as Wendy elbowed him in the side and muttered, "Keep moving." (He kept moving.)

"Always a delight to see you, my dear." It was Daphne's father.

"Richard," said Wendy, air-kissing him on one cheek, then the other. He smelled like bourbon and Old Spice. "What a wonderful occasion. We're all so happy for Daphne. Also, thanks again for contributing to our special issue. Your defense of Hezbollah's charitable works definitely provoked debate!"

"Any time, my dear Cindy," he said, his eyes already focused over Wendy's shoulder.

When it came time to greet Daphne's mother, Wendy didn't know if she should shake her hand or lean over and attempt to hug her—not only because Claire Uberoff was confined to a wheelchair, but because the woman had never been particularly friendly to her. Insofar as Wendy was capable of *not* taking things personally, she'd learned not to be offended. Before her illness, Daphne's mother had been a well-respected hematologist at the university hospital. In the intervening years, far from turning adversity into challenge or finding that multiple sclerosis allowed her to see what was really important in life—as characters always seemed to do in TV movies—Claire Uberoff had grown angry and self-pitying. In the end, Wendy settled on a compromise lunge that involved shaking Claire's hand as she laid a tentative hand on her shrunken back. (All Wendy could feel was bone.) "Congratulations, Dr. Uberoff," she said, smiling as sincerely as she could. "This is such a happy day."

"Yes, it is," the woman answered stolidly.

Finally, there was the bride to greet. Daphne quickly swallowed Wendy into a bear hug.

"You look so beautiful," said Wendy.

"Thank you—and thank you for coming," said Daphne. "I'm just so happy you're here. My oldest friend! Or practically. And Adam!" Daphne abruptly released Wendy and took Wendy's husband in her arms.

"Congratulations, Mrs. Sonnenberg," he said, one side of his smile rising higher than the other.

"This is crazy, isn't it?" Wendy could have sworn she heard Daphne mumble in Adam's ear.

"It's not crazy at all," he mumbled back. "It's great."

Wendy had no idea what to make of their exchange. It seemed to reference some earlier conversation in which she'd had no part. It also seemed intimate in a way that surpassed the casual friendship she understood the two of them currently to have. What's more, Daphne and Adam's embrace seemed to last seconds longer than it needed to, and to be tighter, too. Or had Wendy imagined the whole tableau? Confused and agitated and suddenly craving a cigarette—and the illusion that she didn't need anyone or anything, nicotine excepted—Wendy walked back out onto the balcony.

There, she found a small group of teenage girls and older women lighting up. None of their faces were familiar to her. "I'm sorry," Wendy began. A pack of Parliaments soon appeared in her face, courtesy of a sullen-faced wraith in combat boots with eight-inch platform soles. Wendy thanked her. The girl grunted in reply.

Wendy was busy taking her first heady inhale, when Paige Ryan appeared in her purview. "Well, I guess you're still not pregnant!" she announced, loud enough for the entire wedding party to hear.

And I guess you're still a psychotic bitch, Wendy thought.

Adam appeared moments later. "Hey! I was wondering

what happened to you," he began in a judgmental voice. At least it sounded judgmental to Wendy. (Adam was the kind of pot smoker who considered smoking marijuana a wholesome and possibly even salubrious experience, whereas mass-produced cigarettes were clearly the devil's own calling cards.)

"What was that about with Daphne in the receiving line?" asked Wendy, in no mood to apologize.

"What was what about?" he said.

"I heard you whispering about how crazy *it* was. What's *it*?"

"Oh, that was nothing." Adam flung back his head. "It was just that Daphne really didn't want a big formal wedding. And Jonathan did. So she was just bugging a little about all the pomp and circumstance, so to speak."

"I thought you guys talked about having sick parents."

"We do."

"Among other topics, I guess."

"Oh, come on," said Adam. "You should be happy your husband gets along so well with your friends!"

"I'm thrilled," Wendy told him. "Ecstatic, even." She'd never heard herself sound so jealous. Then again, she'd never before had a reason to feel that way.

Sixteen circular tables covered with crisp white tablecloths had been set up in the hall. At the center of each table was a cylindrical glass vase crammed full of white tulips. Champagne in hand, Wendy found her place card at table three and sat down. To her relief, Adam's card was opposite hers. Somewhat less pleasingly, Paige's scripted name appeared two places from her own, while Pamela, Sara, and Gretchen, and their respective spouses (and spouse-equivalents) had all apparently been seated at another table. "Yo, Shakespeare Lady," began a short bald guy with popping eyes. "I'm Steve."

"Nice to meet you," said Wendy. "I'm Wendy."

"And this is my leading lady, Deb." He motioned at a scowling woman seated to his right.

"Nice to meet you, too," said Wendy.

The woman lifted the corners of her mouth in distant imitation of a smile, but said nothing.

"And I'm Wendy's husband, Adam," Adam called from across the table.

"Pleasure," said Steve, motioning with his chin while lifting a highball glass to his lips. "So check this out. Ever heard the story of how Jonathan dressed up as Aunt Jemima for Spring Fling? Fucker nearly got himself kicked off campus."

"You're kidding," said Wendy, thankful for any information that put the groom in a bad light.

"I'm guessing you two were in the same fraternity?" said Adam.

"You assume correctly," said Steve. "Delta Chi. Cornell University. Class of ninety-one. But the Sonnenbitch studied harder than me. Which is probably why I'm in wine distribution and he's a federal prosecutor. Now, who has more fun is another matter. Right, Deb?" He nudged his wife, who continued to stare peevishly at the wall.

"Aw — lawyers are a dime a dozen in New York," offered Adam.

"Nice of you to say," said Steve. "And your trade, if I may ask?"

"At the moment, I'm writing a comic screenplay about sperm and living off my wife."

At least he's honest in that regard, Wendy thought.

"Nice work. I toast you, my friend!" Steve raised his glass.

Next to appear was a forty-something guy with a pink complexion, graying temples, and deep creases around his slate blue eyes. He wasn't terrible looking, Wendy thought, but there was something puffy and almost misshapen about him. His shoulders seemed too narrow for his frame. Or maybe it was that his belly seemed to belong to a much larger man. He was wearing a sports jersey of some kind with a high V-neck and a numeral 9 emblazoned on the front of it, and an ill-fitting blazer over that. "Name's Jeremy," he offered in a grumbly English accent, his right hand darting into the air as he sat down in the empty seat next to Wendy's. (He had a Guinness in the left.)

"Name's Wendy," said Wendy. "Nice to meet you."

Paige's matching orange evening bag appeared before Paige did. She chucked it onto her bread plate. Then she yanked out her chair. "So, what's for dinner?" she said.

"Wait—let me guess," she answered her own question before anyone else had the chance to do so. "A choice of grilled Angus hanger steak or braised salmon in a tarragon-leek sauce, both served with julienned vegetables and potato au gratin." Her eyes combed the figure to her right. "And you must be Daphne and Jonathan's live-in carpenter."

"I do a bit of carpentry every now and then." Jeremy shrugged.

"But don't you live in Daphne's house?"

"I let the flat downstairs." He shrugged again.

"Paige Ryan," she said, holding out her hand. "I'm sorry to have to report that the bride has set us up."

"Lucky you," he said grimly, his own hand not quite extended.

"So can you hear them up there having sex?" It occurred suddenly to Wendy that Paige was wasted—and also that, for reasons of her own (her recent divorce, perhaps?), she, too, might be suffering through Daphne's wedding.

"Never heard anything," replied Jeremy, apparently unflappable. "Thick walls, I guess."

Paige finished off her single malt in a single sip, before looking away and declaring, "Anyway, you should know that I have certain unresolved hostility issues with regard to the opposite sex."

"I never would have guessed," Jeremy murmured into his beer.

It was dinnertime. Nearly true to Paige's prediction, the menu choice was filet mignon or halibut vertically piled with julienned zucchini and rosemary potatoes. (Wendy ordered the halibut, Adam the steak.) Table three was the table situated closest to the four-piece jazz band, which played standards throughout the meal. Which meant that it was hard to make conversation. Which was fine by Wendy, since she'd already run out of things to say to both Steve and Jeremy; Deb didn't talk, and Wendy had no particular inclination at that moment to speak to her husband or Paige.

While Wendy ate, she watched Daphne flitting between tables, throwing her arms around her guests or grasping their forearms conspiratorially and whispering in their ears, as if each were her nearest and dearest. And as if Wendy were one of a hundred-odd intimates, and yet the only one among them who had somehow failed to grasp this essential fact—that Wendy was no more important to Daphne than anyone else in the room.

The evidence was suddenly piling up: when Daphne finally made it over to Wendy's table, she addressed them as a group and stood between Jeremy and Paige. "Are you guys having fun? Is the food okay? I'm such a nervous hostess. I swear it's why I never throw parties!"

"Don't you worry your pretty little head," Steve assured her. "We're having a frigging blast."

"Juicy steak," added Adam.

"Only the best for you," said Daphne, winking.

Wendy smiled, but said nothing.

Richard Uberoff had never been accused of disliking the sound of his own voice. His wedding toast, the first to be delivered that night, failed to provide fodder for a counterargument. Beginning with a detailed disquisition on Voltaire's view of marriage, it perambulated its way through the centuries, stopping off at Hegel, Macaulay, and Tocqueville. By the time he reached Wittgenstein, Steve the Wine Distributor had taken off. "If you'll all excuse me," he'd announced in a stage whisper. "A line awaits me in the men's room—so to speak."

When he returned, Richard had only just reached 1970—and Daphne's arrival in the world. From there, he quickly segued to his feelings on fatherhood. It was another ten minutes before he returned to the subject of the bride. "Let no man say that Daphne Uberoff, when in possession of a need or want, has ever taken the opportunity to practice

forbearance. My dear son-in-law, I do hope you're listening!"
In twenty-eight minutes, there was no other mention of Jonathan Sonnenberg than that. Her feelings about the groom
notwithstanding, Wendy found it shocking and amazing
that Daphne's father hadn't taken more time to acknowledge the man who'd rescued his daughter from a life of pill
popping and mistress-hood. Then again, in Professor Uberoff's defense, he'd only met his son-in-law on one previous
occasion—namely, Thanksgiving. He also lived in Michigan,
was obsessed with his own reputation, and was quite possibly
unaware of Daphne's.

As Richard raised his glass, Wendy thought she saw a fleet-
ing expression of contempt pass across Daphne's face. What's
more, the look seemed to be directed at table three, if not at
Wendy. Glancing over the tulips, she could have sworn she
saw Adam roll his eyes in concert with Daphne. Was it possible that he was the intended recipient of her gaze? Or had
Wendy imagined this, too? (It was too late to say.) Daphne
was already approaching the microphone, where, with a great
display of mirth and gratitude, she embraced her father, albeit
remembering to turn her head for the benefit of the wedding
photographer.

Jonathan's father was next. In a shaky voice, he spoke of
the first time his son had beat him at squash. He also recalled
a camping trip for which eight-year-old Jonathan—thank
goodness—had remembered to bring a compass. If it was a
far shorter toast than Richard Uberoff's, it was also less than
scintillating. A third of the way in, a restive murmur of conversation spread through the room. It didn't subside until Mr.
Sonnenberg had finished speaking.

Finally, it was Wendy's turn, the turn that Wendy had

spent the entire previous month dreading. Prior to the wedding, she'd composed a list of talking points. Each referenced an amusing anecdote that, in lightly roasting Daphne's egotism, revealed both her affinity for friendship and her unrivaled desirability to the opposite sex — while studiously avoiding the subject of her recent past. As Wendy stood up from her chair and approached the lectern, however, the list seemed suddenly beside the point. Alcohol, combined with Daphne's suspicious behavior toward Adam, had left Wendy feeling strangely emboldened, even excited. As if a marvelous, unforeseen opportunity had come her way, an opportunity she couldn't afford to pass up. She kept the list folded in her left hand and angled the microphone toward her with her right.

"I'm Daphne's friend Wendy." She began to improvise. "I hate public speaking. So I'm going to keep this short. Daphne and I went to college together. Back then, Daphne changed majors as often as she changed boyfriends. First, there was Comparative Literature — and Josh. Then there was Government — and Craig. Then there was Film Studies — and Andy. The list goes on. And on. But it always seemed to me that Daphne's main field of expertise was herself." A sprinkling of giggles greeted Wendy's ears, goading her on. "Not only is she the most entertaining and insightful relayer of her own emotional highs and lows that I've ever met, but Daphne's life has always been a little more exciting and dramatic than the average person's." Wendy paused. "I guess my main worry about Daphne becoming a happy married lady is that she's going to get just as boring as the rest of us." More chuckling. "On the upside, I suspect she'll be less likely to wake me and my husband up at two in the morning, threatening to jump off the Brooklyn Bridge. Because, really, what is there to say when you've gone domestic with a good and *available*"—Wendy paused to accentuate the novelty of this concept—"guy?" She raised her voice an octave in imitation of Daphne. " 'You won't believe the latest—Jonathan and I roasted a chicken and rented a movie!' For once, I think I'll be within my rights to say, 'I'm sleeping, Daphne. Can we talk about this in the morning?' "

The crowd—if not Daphne herself—erupted in guffaws. (A quick glance in Daphne's direction revealed only an amused smile. Or was it bemused?) Had Wendy gone too far? As the laughter died down, Wendy felt suddenly panicked at the thought that Daphne would be furious at her. "But, really," she went on, "over the years, Daphne has been a warm and wonderful friend who's made life more interesting, more stylish, and generally more fun. Please join me in raising a glass on behalf of my old and dear friend Daphne and my new friend Jonathan. Some people say there's no such thing as love at first sight. But Daphne and Jonathan have proven us all wrong." Wendy paused, unable to stop herself. "That, or they were both desperate." She paused again. "Just kidding!"

There was more laughter, but this time it struck Wendy as being more embarrassed than joyful. Had she proven herself, once and for all, to be a despicable human being? She raised her glass. The crowd raised theirs. "Daphne, Jonathan—congratulations. I'm so happy for you guys."

As the crowd applauded, Wendy walked over to table one, where Daphne received her hug with the same jocular expression with which she'd embraced her father. But was this, too, a performance? Despite the liberties she'd taken, Wendy returned to table three telling herself that her toast had been in the spirit of lighthearted fun — even as, on some deeper level, she was aware that it contained the seed of a withering critique.

The collective verdict seemed to confirm the latter.

"Ouch," said Adam.

"Yo — they ought to call you 'maid of dishonor,'" said Steve.

"I'm just glad we're not friends," quipped Paige.

Steve's wife, Deb, continued to add nothing to the conversation, while Jeremy appeared to be reading an English football magazine in his lap.

Reaching for her chardonnay, Wendy felt suddenly, unpleasantly sober.

Wendy spent the remainder of the evening regretting her toast. She was still angry at Adam. But she needed his support more and was therefore willing to overlook his trespasses — at least for the moment. "Do you think Daphne hates me now?" she asked, as the jazz band struck up Cole Porter's "I Get a Kick Out of You," and Jonathan and Daphne began their "first dance."

"She'll get over it," said Adam, not exactly reassuring Wendy.

Yet another drink later, Wendy joined Sara and Gretchen and their respective dates on the dance floor. (Pamela and Todd had jogged home to co-breastfeed Lucas; Adam was too cool to dance in public.) The band was now playing a saxophone-embellished version of the hip-hop single "Hot in Here." For a few delirious minutes, Wendy allowed the music to transport her to a realm of pure rhythm, a realm diminished only by the incongruous sight of Jeremy twirling a rigid but ecstatic-looking Paige across the floor.

Meanwhile, Sara's fiancé, Dolph, dressed in an emerald blue Prada suit and lavender tie and with his hair slicked back like a chipmunk's, had embarked on a series of crotch-centered gyrations performed with one arm bent backward behind his head and the other extended out in front of him. Within minutes, he'd attracted a circle of cheering spectators. Minutes after that, Sara could be seen bent over, her arm across her stomach. "Are you okay?" Wendy yelled over the music. (For a split second, the thought occurred to her that Sara might be dying of embarrassment.)

"Not really," Sara yelled back.

"Do you want me to take you to the ladies' room?"

"Yes, please."

Leaning over the toilet bowl, Sara revealed she was pregnant with Dolph's baby.

"Oh, Sara, that's wonderful news!" Wendy said, as instantly glassy-eyed as she was amazed and impressed. Apparently, Sara and Dolph had heterosexual sex, after all.

"I know you've been trying," Sara offered between gags.

"Don't worry about me right now," said Wendy, reaching for Sara's hair. "Worry about your dinner."

"I think I'm going to be sick," she said. And she was.

It was left to Wendy to clean her up, then fetch Dolph — no easy task, not only because Wendy had to break through his now extensive fan base to reach him, but also because he was in perpetual motion. Finally, she managed to grab hold of his sleeve. "Sara's sick!" she bellowed over the music. (Nelly had been replaced by ABBA.)

"Oh, Christ—not again," he said, eyes rolling, as he followed Wendy off the dance floor. "I know she can't help it, but the woman really does have impeccable timing. 'Dancing Queen' is only my FAVORITE SONG EVER."

"Maybe they can play it again?" suggested Wendy.

"Maybe," said Dolph. "Anyway, where's the patient?"

After reuniting the expectant parents, Wendy headed back to the bar. Scanning the wedding party as she waited to be served, she realized that Daphne and Jonathan had already left the premises—without saying good-bye. That was their right, she told herself. They had a honeymoon to get to. They couldn't be expected to bid a special farewell to all ninety-two guests.

Gretchen appeared before Wendy at the same time as her Bud Lite.

"Sara just told me her big news," said Wendy, assuming that Gretchen had already heard.

"Don't be too jealous," said Gretchen—to Wendy's embarrassment. "Dolph still won't marry her."

"But he'll have sex with her," said Wendy. "Who knew?"

"Do you want to know a secret?" Gretchen lifted her Red Bull to her lips. "Rob and I have had sex exactly *once* since the twins were born."

"How old are they again?"

"Eight months."

"Once is better than never?"

"I guess."

"But wait—didn't you and Rob go on your honeymoon a few months ago?"

"I didn't tell anyone at the time, but I ended up flying home early for work. Or actually, I flew to Geneva for a meeting. That was a fake tan." Gretchen smiled guiltily.

"Hm," said Wendy, trying not to sound shocked.

"Do you want to know another secret?" Gretchen leaned into Wendy's ear. "I can't stand Jonathan."

"Here's another secret—you're not the only one," Wendy muttered back.

"Honestly?" Gretchen continued. "When Daphne asked me to sign the katubah—which is also a joke, since I've been to synagogue, like, once in the past twenty years, but whatever, anyway—I almost said no. I mean, I seriously didn't know if I wanted my name on that piece of paper. But what was I going to say?"

"I'm sure I would have done the same thing," said Wendy, flinching yet again—this time to hear that Daphne had wanted Gretchen's signature and not Wendy's on the frameable parchment document that confirmed Daphne and Jonathan's marriage under Jewish law.

"Oh, shit, I have to take this call—it's Angelina Jolie en route to Namibia," said Gretchen, pulling her headset out of her clutch and fastening it around her ear. "Gretchen Daubner, UNICEF," she trumpeted on her way out to the balcony.

Every decent wedding can claim at least one scandal. On that score, Daphne and Jonathan's nuptials failed to disappoint. At the end of the night, Steve the Wine Distributor had to be rescued off the lake, where he was discovered semi–passed out in a gondola alongside the scowling teenage cousin of

Daphne's who'd given Wendy a cigarette. Reportedly, both parties were half naked and too drunk to row back to shore.

Wendy left the party fairly inebriated herself, if still sober enough to recognize her bad mood. Her only solace was the thought that the tale of Steve and the Sullen Teen was so outrageous as to render her toast of less questionable taste.

Adam, on the other hand, seemed to think the evening had been a riot. "How funny was that gondola thing," he chuckled in the car home.

"Really funny," Wendy said blankly.

7.

URING THE WEDDING, Wendy had noticed that Daphne looked slightly more filled out than her usual skeletal self. She'd chalked up the weight gain to Daphne's having, for once, a reliable dinner partner. As Wendy learned in an email upon Daphne and Jonathan's return from their honeymoon at the Four Seasons resort on the Caribbean island of Nevis, however, there was another explanation entirely:

W we're back! Nevis beyond amazing and also really relaxing but first I'm so thrilled that you made it to our wedding I hope you and A had an okay time?? Also, your toast was *beyond* hilarious (God, was I really that needy a friend back in the day? Yikes)

Anyway I didn't tell you earlier because of the wedding and everything else going on but—drum roll—I'm preggers!! (Twenty-four weeks on Thursday insane I know) Anyway can't wait for you to join me in the motherhood mind f-ck (I know you're going to get there soon if you haven't already)

Meanwhile recently realized that I *still* haven't seen your
new place! (Pathetic I know) Let me know what your schedule
looks like next week and we'll make a date (while I still have
the energy to haul my suddenly HUGE butt around ha) XXD

Wendy turned her gaze out the window, at the endless
stream of cars on the Prospect Expressway. In that moment, it
seemed to her that she was the only person in the world who
wasn't headed somewhere. She tried to recall Marcia's words
about all of us being on "his or her own journey." But they
sounded hollow—like so much self-help-book hokum. Besides, from what Wendy could tell, everyone was on the same
journey: to the maternity ward at Methodist Hospital, if not
Mount Sinai or St. Luke's–Roosevelt. Wendy couldn't walk
outside her door anymore, not even on No Prospect Avenue,
without being accosted by reproduction in action. Everywhere
she went, everywhere she looked, there were double strollers
and swollen bellies, snack catchers and sippy cups. People
spoke of Calcutta as the epicenter of the overpopulation problem. As far as Wendy could tell, however, Brownstone Brooklyn was equally to blame.

But it wasn't just that she felt left behind. It was that
Wendy and Adam had been together for more than eight
years—and trying to conceive for well over one—while
Daphne and Jonathan had only just met. Wendy knew it
wasn't a race to the finish line. After all, wasn't the finish line
death? Yet she couldn't help but feel that, considering how
long she and Adam had been together, it had been their
right—Wendy's right—to go first.

And why did good things always seem to happen to the
quicksilvers of this world? No doubt Daphne's pregnancy

had been some kind of "early accident." Maybe the trick was to stop trying, Wendy thought. Only, once you'd started trying, how did you stop? Was it even possible to try not to try?

Wendy got up from her desk chair, walked the three steps necessary to reach her bed, and climbed under the covers. But even the sensation of warmth and enclosure failed to comfort her as it usually did. Her body had become her enemy. It seemed to be willfully defying her, laughing in the face of her designs for it. She thought of her early adolescence, when the sudden appearance of breasts and hair in strange places had made her feel similarly outraged.

She also felt hurt by how long it had taken Daphne to tell her the news. By "wedding and everything," Daphne seemed to be implying that she'd been too busy planning the Big Day to find time to inform Wendy. But in the space of twenty-three weeks had Daphne really not identified a single free moment? Wendy suspected that Daphne's silence had mostly to do with her not wanting anyone to think that Jonathan was only marrying her because he had to. But even if he was, after all that she and Wendy had been through together, could Daphne really be concerned about keeping up appearances in front of her?

Or was Wendy being punished for speaking out of turn—not just at the wedding? Wendy thought guiltily of the many catty conversations and exchanges she'd had over the years about Daphne with their mutual friends, some under the guise of concern, others blatantly bitchy. Had something Wendy had said gotten back to Daphne?

Or might there have been a charitable motive behind the delay? Maybe Daphne had put off telling Wendy because she'd known the news would only upset and frustrate her further. Which, of course, it had. Not only was Wendy still not pregnant, but the now almost ritualized disappointment that accompanied the sanguineous arrival of her menstrual period each month had taken all the romance out of the venture. Now it was just a science experiment that never worked. Now Wendy and Adam hardly ever had sex anymore, not even during the right time of the month. And on the few occasions they did, he just lay there on his back or side, letting Wendy do all the work.

Wendy was entertaining the distasteful idea that in the intervening weeks Daphne had confided in another, better friend (Paige? Sara?), when Adam appeared in the doorway. "What's up with you?" he said.

"Nothing," Wendy said as neutrally as she could. She knew how crazy it drove him when she got morose over their reproductive problems.

"Nothing?" he asked, cockeyed. "You just felt like climbing into bed at three in the afternoon and staring at the wall?"

Wendy didn't answer.

"Don't tell me you got your period again," he said.

He never knew when to let her be, Wendy thought. She felt as if the two of them were trapped on some transatlantic flight that was stuck on the tarmac, going nowhere yet unable to separate, trapped between two time zones, one already in the past, the other still in the future. "I didn't get my period," she told him. "Okay?" Wendy knew as soon as she'd said it that she should have kept her mouth shut. Her voice had grown shaky. Adam was bound to notice. He noticed everything.

"Well, then, another of your thirty-five-year-old women friends is pregnant — who is it now?" he asked.

"Daphne," said Wendy, swallowing hard.

"Oh, Christ!" said Adam, sounding suddenly distressed

himself. "I knew this was going to happen." Knew *what* was going to happen? That Daphne would get pregnant? That Wendy would be upset when she heard the news? His meaning unclear, he shook his head and walked out of the room.

The sky was the same color as the ever-growing mountain of newspapers in the hallway outside Wendy and Adam's apartment, waiting to be recycled. In short, it wasn't much of a day for a walk in the park. Plus, the park wasn't even nearby anymore. So Wendy, desperate to clear her head, took the subway to the Brooklyn Museum.

Walking through the Ancient Egyptian wing, contemplating the blank stares of the mummy cases and pharaoh statuary, she wondered if being in a bad mood was a modern invention. After all, here lay dead people who, judging from the facial expressions of their sculptural stand-ins, seemed completely fine, even mellow, about the biggest tragedy of all: their own mortality. And what if it turned out that all the skeptics were wrong, and you really did get to go somewhere new and exciting when you died? Cheered by this possibility, Wendy composed a reply email to Daphne with the goal of sounding gracious and supportive. Upon her arrival home, she typed it up:

D, Pregnant? What??? Thrilled for you, of course. That's great news. Can't believe you're gonna be a momma. When is baby due? Please send my regards/congrats to Jonathan, as well. Xxoo W

Fake excitement. Fake casualness. Fake, fake, fake. That was what had become of their friendship, Wendy thought as she clicked "send." But what other choice did she have? Getting along in the world seemed to require the endless peddling of palaver: of "You look great" and "Have a nice day" and "I'm so happy for you." It was like air. Or food. Or shelter. No one could get on without it. Yet no one meant a word of it. Or did they? Were other people simply bigger-hearted than Wendy was? And was it even possible to be happy for someone else's success when you hadn't achieved it yourself?

That night, Wendy discovered she was fast approaching her fertile peak. She wished her ovaries had chosen another time to release their inmate. But since they hadn't, she was determined to regain Adam's affections—even though the two had barely spoken since the morning, Wendy's frustration with biology seemingly deadlocked with his frustration with her. Or was there another explanation? Adam was already in bed, reading the 1974 true crime bestseller about the Charles Manson murders, *Helter Skelter,* his body turned toward the door. Wendy curled up against his back and slid an arm around his waist. But he made no acknowledgment of her presence, not even after she let her hand slip below his navel.

It was only after she began to burrow her fingers beneath the waistband of his boxer shorts that he finally spoke. "What—are you ovulating?" he said.

"Why does it matter?" said Wendy, wincing, even as she continued to prod.

"Why does it matter?" Adam laughed as he repeated her question. Then he rolled onto his back, forcing Wendy's right hand into retreat. "Because it's the only thing that matters to you anymore. I'm just incidental to the whole process."

"That's not true," she said.

"Of course it's true. It's the only time of the month you want to do it. God forbid you were ever just 'in the mood.' " His book now resting on his chest, Adam made quotes in the air.

The charge wounded Wendy, not only because she wanted to believe she was the kind of person who would never have married someone who used air quotes, but because to articulate their lack of a spontaneous sex life was to make it real and therefore of consequence. (It was easier to pretend that it wasn't.) "Well, look who's talking!" she cried. "You never want to do it, either."

"Well, then, we're even," said Adam.

"I'm in the mood now," said Wendy.

"Well, I'm not—sorry." Adam rolled back over onto his side and reopened his book.

But she was ovulating, damn it! And it only happened twelve or thirteen times a year. Why couldn't he understand that time was of the essence? That time was running out? Again, Wendy pressed up against her husband. For several minutes, they lay together like that, him reading and her waiting. And waiting some more. But for how much longer? She felt suddenly frantic and about to burst through her skin with her frustrated desires. Reproductive? Sexual? Material? She could no longer differentiate between the three. All she knew was that she wanted and wasn't getting. She could feel Adam's toes pressing conciliatorily into her own, but she quickly moved them away. She wasn't ready to make up. Besides, it wasn't his feet she needed. Believing in that moment that a surprise attack was her best strategy, Wendy disappeared under the covers.

But Adam was prepared. He had his defenses up, his anti-artillery loaded and cocked. "LEAVE ME ALONE!" he bellowed while pushing her face away from his crotch. "HAVE YOU GONE INSANE?" He scooted over to the edge of the bed.

Wendy emerged from beneath the covers equally livid. That Adam would dare withhold from her! He was her husband, damn it! (Sperm, she felt, was the least he owed her; he wasn't good for much else these days.) "FINE!" she yelled. "IF YOU DON'T WANT TO HAVE A BABY—FINE!" She felt humiliated, too—humiliated and, at the same time, fascinated by her humiliation: when had she become this terrifying succubus?

"YOU'RE RIGHT," Adam yelled back. "I DON'T WANT TO HAVE A BABY. I'M SICK OF THE WHOLE GODDAMN SUBJECT." He beat his chest like Tarzan. "I want to be appreciated for being me. You treat me like I'm a stud farm—not a human being."

"That's not true!" Wendy protested.

"That's how it feels!"

"I'm frustrated."

"Life is frustrating."

"It's been a year and a half and I'm still not pregnant."

"There's nothing wrong with you or me. It just hasn't happened yet. Why can't you live with that?"

"Why does everything get to be your decision?"

"My decision?" Adam scoffed. "Last time I checked, you were the one forcing us to have sex on a schedule."

"I feel like a failure," Wendy told him. "You can't understand that."

"A failure? You mean, if you were a better person, you'd

be pregnant by now? It's not a reflection of your character that you're not pregnant yet."

"It feels like one. It's all I think about." Wendy had never heard herself sound so pathetic. At the same time, it came as a relief to admit, finally, to the lack of poetry—or politics—in her head.

"Well, maybe you should go back to therapy," said Adam.

"We can't afford it," said Wendy. "Because you don't work."

"Oh, now you want me to pay for your therapy?!"

"No, I want you to help pay for our *life!*" Wendy also felt relieved to be admitting to her discontent over her husband's chronic unemployment—relieved and riled and depressed.

Adam shook his head contemptuously. Then he rolled back onto his side, flipped off his reading light, and pulled the covers over his shoulders and neck, victorious in his celibacy—at least for the moment.

"Did I tell you I'm going to this prenatal yoga class every Saturday?" Daphne was saying to Wendy over the phone a few days later. "It's a total nightmare. I can't even do downward-facing dog!"

"It takes a lot of arm strength," said Wendy.

"Also, do you know what Kegels are?" Daphne went on. "The teacher is, like, *obsessed* with them. She's like"—Daphne made her voice unpleasantly nasal—"People, if there's one thing you, take away from this class—please, I'm begging you—practice your Kegels: in the subway, waiting in line at the post office, on hold with your medical insurer. Whenever you find yourself with five minutes to spare, take the time to work your vaginal muscles. You won't regret it. Imagine you're in an elevator. First stop — the pelvic floor." Daphne reclaimed her normal speaking voice. "Of course, I can't even do one. You're supposed to hold your muscles down there tight for, like, five beats and then release them again — apparently so you won't pee all over yourself every time you sneeze. Whatever. I'll just wear diapers if I have to."

"Oh, please," said Wendy, who — was this terrible? — didn't mind the idea of Daphne's being incontinent. "I'm sure she's exaggerating."

"Maybe. Anyway, the only part of the class I can deal with is at the end, when you get to doze off under one of those Peruvian blankets while they play that hippie flute music with the tweeting birds. To be honest, the blankets smell like BO — clearly, no one's ever washed them — but by that point, I'm so exhausted I don't even care. Though I could do without that bullshit at the very end where you have to sit with your hands pressed together in prayer and everyone mutters 'Numismaya' — or whatever it is — in those really sanctimonious voices —"

"I think it's *Namaste,*" interjected Wendy.

"Whatever. It sounds like some special branch of stamp collecting." Daphne snorted at her joke. "Anyway, I swear I always leave there feeling like I've accidentally joined some brainwashed cult. It's why I've always hated yoga."

"I know what you mean," said Wendy, who, although she'd attended plenty of yoga classes in her lifetime, suspected that she didn't, had no idea, might never.

• • •

(Late June)

Adam had tried to discourage Wendy from throwing a baby shower for Daphne. "You're just going to get all depressed and upset and tell me everyone has a baby or is pregnant but you," he'd told her, his voice a mix of anger and exasperation.

What he couldn't understand was that it was the right thing to do—the kind of thing you did for your oldest friend who was seven and a half months pregnant with her first child, even if it meant showing off both your shabby apartment and your barren womb. Because not to do so would have felt like an admission of defeat. And because playing host was still preferable to having to attend someone else's shower for Daphne as a mere guest.

The buzzer began to ring at twenty to three. Sara arrived first, followed by Jenny Kenar, Audrey Lennon, Pamela, Gretchen, Jenn Gilmore, Courtney Kleesak, Hannah Dingo, and a woman Wendy didn't recognize (Daphne's cousin Alyssa?). All of them were accompanied by progeny under the age of four, most of them already born and squalling, a few in utero and still silent. The majority of the women harked back to Daphne's college days. Prior to Daphne's wedding, Wendy hadn't seen some of them in fifteen years. In several cases (Courtney Kleesak and Jenny Gilmore, in particular), Wendy would have been happy to extend that number to thirty. But that afternoon she was committed to being a model hostess. "So great to see you!" she greeted her friends and enemies alike. And "Hello there, little guy!" And "You can put your presents in that pile in the living room." And "You can leave your stroller in the hall, if you want—whatever's easier for you."

Adam had gone to Shea Stadium to watch the Mets play the Phillies.

Polly was spending the afternoon with a neighbor because Daphne had announced that she'd developed an early-midlife allergy to dogs.

Assuming Paige wasn't on her way — to Wendy's surprise, there was no sign of her — Daphne was, of course, the last to arrive. She was dressed for the occasion in a red-and-white paisley-printed wrap dress, all the better to show off her perfectly compact bump. "Ohmygod, all my favorite people in one room!" she cried, in an almost plaintive tone, at the sight of her ten best friends fanned out across the foyer. "Thank you all so much for being here. And Wen, it was so sweet of you to throw me a party. I'm forever in your debt." She embraced Wendy.

"It's my pleasure," said Wendy, for whom the acknowledgment felt like small but real consolation for not having a bump of her own.

In time, the gaggle migrated to the living room, where they organized themselves in a circle with Daphne at the head. "Your place is so cute," Courtney Kleesak said to Wendy, her eyes combing the apartment. "I swear my grandmother had that exact kitchen table — with the Formica and everything — in her nursing home." Back in college, Courtney had been the secretary of what Wendy thought of as the "officious brunettes" sorority. Following the birth of her son, Miles, a beady-eyed six-month-old who sat squirming in her lap, she'd reduced her job at the Department of Health, where she monitored mosquito spraying, to just three days a week. "Thanks," said Wendy.

"And I guess you don't have any problem getting onto the BQE." Courtney smiled smarmily.

"I guess not." Wendy smiled back.

"Daphne, you seriously make me sick," began Jenn Gilmore, a petite blonde with a barely there upper lip. "You've gained, like, no weight." To Wendy's recollection, Jenn had been in a bad mood since freshman orientation week. (Wendy recalled endless complaints on the subjects of her chemistry finals and her menstrual cramps.) Now visibly pregnant with her second—a two-year-old girl with short bangs and a sulky expression stood clutching her leg—Jenn reportedly planned to take time off from her job as a child psychologist at a private elementary school in Brooklyn Heights.

"That's so not true," Daphne protested. "I'm a total whale! I swear my doctor put me on a diet."

"Oh, please—"

"Please, yourself. Look at you!"

"I was just so relieved to finally be pregnant that I didn't care how fat and ugly I got," offered Gretchen, who wasn't remotely fat, either. "As you can probably tell." Just then, Lola began to bawl. Or was it Liam? Though Gretchen's twins were now almost ten months old, this was the first time Wendy had seen them—and she couldn't tell them apart. She also couldn't believe how cute they were. Bald and rotund, they both looked like miniature versions of Winston Churchill; apparently, Dorothea was feeding them well. "Shit! What do I do?" Gretchen cried. With panicked glances at her neighbors, as she lifted her squalling infant into her arms.

"Sorry," said Courtney, turning to Gretchen with a pained

expression, "but would you mind watching your language? I just don't want Miles exposed—"

"Sorry—I wasn't thinking."

"It's fine."

"Do you think she's hungry?" asked Gretchen. "Ohmygod, I think I forgot formula!"

"This is the longest Gretch has ever been left alone with the twins since they were born," Sara explained to the group.

"Thanks, Sar," said Gretchen. "Let's see how you do with a newborn, especially as a single mother."

"Nice—right?" said Sara.

"Please, you're going to be great!" said Pamela, slapping at the air. "To be honest, there's not much to do in the beginning. It's mostly just a lot of sitting around and feeling incredibly blessed."

Wendy thought she saw Gretchen roll her eyes.

A bottle was soon conjured for Lola, who fell silent as she sucked. As if to demonstrate her disapproval (of plastics), Courtney took the opportunity to unhook her bra, revealing an elephantine pink breast, which she proffered in Miles's face. Only, Miles kept turning away at the sight of it. "What's the matter, Bunny Wabby?" she asked in a saccharine voice. "Mommy's got lots of nice booby milk for you!" But still, he refused. Her voice quickly assumed a venomous edge. "Sweetie, why won't you EAT?!!!!" Finally, Miles took her nipple in his mouth and began to nurse halfheartedly. A look of beatification came over Courtney's face.

Just then, Lucas Rose, seemingly (and blessedly) unconscious in his car seat until moments before, began to howl. As Pamela lifted him into her arms, Wendy plotted her escape. "So, who wants something cold to drink?" she asked. "I have wine, beer, juice, water, homemade sangria. . . ."

Everyone, it seemed, wanted water. (Everyone was either pregnant or nursing or boring.) And why did no one else seem bothered by the pitch of Lucas's wailing? While Lucas carried on, Wendy's shower guests continued to chat. "My husband is, like, the king of swaddling," they said. And "My lactation consultant wants me to pump for four minutes after every feeding." And "How long does she go between feedings?" And "When are you due again?" And "How often does he spit up?" And "Well, I know this woman who was in labor for four days and then her spleen ruptured." And "That's so amazing you were able to run a marathon three months after giving birth!"

And "The problem with the Bugaboos is that they're really hard to fold up." And "The Pregos have that extra storage compartment under the seat." And "The McLarens are really light—they're great if you take the subway." And "I honestly don't understand how the poop gets on her back." And "Do you know how the schools are around there?" And "They make these special cups for inverted nipples." And "Have you tried Mylicon for gas?" And "I hear they have great nursing bras at Boing Boing." And "They sell pump accessories there, too."

And "They say it should be the consistency of pea soup." And "If you don't go fifteen minutes on each breast, he won't get the hind-milk." And "She completely flipped out after the birth. I mean, it was a total Brooke Shields situation." And "I've heard iffy things about that Montessori." And "Lead paint is no joke. Seriously. You should really get a professional cleaning after the reno is done. I know this girl who got lead poisoning. Finn used to play with her. She was always punching him in the face."

And "Wait—did you guys hear about Molly Wengert??? You know she's pregnant with twins, right? Well, apparently, the doctor threatened to hospitalize her and put her on a feeding tube if she didn't start eating. One of the fetuses is totally underweight and at risk for brain damage, and she's being a total anorexic freak about the whole thing and refusing to eat. . . ."

As Wendy went about filling her guests' drink orders, she recalled a time when all anyone talked about was getting into college, then getting hired, then getting married, now making babies—always without any recognition that anything of significance had happened before, or would ever happen again. (*What about illness, death, and divorce?* she thought hopefully.)

Wendy also thought back to fifth grade. As unathletic as she was overdeveloped, she'd always been picked last for kickball. She'd always been the last one left standing against the wall, wishing she could disappear into the gym lockers. She didn't feel so different now. After handing out two final seltzers, she sat down on the arm of the sofa.

"Believe me, I never meant to be pregnant while we were renovating," Daphne was telling the assembled guests. "I mean, we'd only been engaged for, like, two weeks when I found out. Poor Jonathan." She laughed.

"At least you were engaged," Sara said bitterly.

"You guys are so getting married before the baby is born!" declared Daphne.

"Yeah, sure," said Sara.

"Anyway, back to what I was saying," Daphne went on. "If any of you are thinking of getting pregnant again, or even for the first time" — her eyes latched uninvited onto Wendy's — "I'm now totally convinced it's all about sleeping as much as you can — obviously, after you've done it!" She laughed. "But seriously? I swear I slept ten hours the night I conceived. I mean, it makes sense if you think about it. If you're lying down, the sperm don't spend the trip fighting gravity. Right?" Her nose wrinkled, she scanned the crowd for affirmation. "Or is that just completely retarded?"

"I can't remember the last time I got eight hours of sleep," moaned Jenn Gilmore, turning to her daughter, who was in the process of unfastening her sandal strap. "Thanks to this little tyrant, who makes my life a living hell. Speaking of which, would you PLEASE, for the hundredth time, STOP THAT?" She slapped the girl's hand away. The girl began to cry.

Lucas was still whimpering.

Just then, Miles abruptly withdrew from his mother's breast and, his face a fiery shade of red, joined the chorus of discontent. "What's the matter with my perfect little angel boy?!" said Courtney, her lips puckered like a fish's. She answered her own question while holding his ass to her nose. "Did you do another poopie poop? You are such a stinky boy today!" She turned to Wendy with an ingratiating smile. "Sorry — do you mind if I change him in your bedroom?" She paused. "I assume you have a bedroom somewhere in here!"

"No, I sleep on the kitchen floor," said Wendy.

Courtney looked horrified.

"It was a joke. The bedroom is at the end of the hall."

"Oh." Courtney's lips formed a perfect O.

Wendy imagined fitting a rubber stopper into the rictus.

"Anyway, I should really get started on this pile," Daphne announced, another twenty minutes into the party. "I can't believe how much stuff you guys got me. It's insane!" The first thing she unwrapped was a pale yellow snowsuit with a matching pom-pom hat. (Daphne had decided to let the sex of the baby be a surprise.) "Ooooooooooooohhh," she cried in an avian-like decrescendo. "Alyssa, this is *too* cute."

"I know next winter seems far off," said Daphne's cousin, if that was who she was. "But I swear, the first six months fly by. And you're going to need something to keep babe-ala warm."

Next up was a silver spoon, followed by a Gymini activity blanket, a camouflage-print diaper bag, a magic swaddling blanket, a teddy bear, a Danish modern rattle, a "baby plush toy" in the shape of a hippo, and a pair of soft leather booties with contrasting dinosaur cutouts on the toes. A fresh round of "oooooohs" accompanied each item's unfurling. After Daphne unwrapped a second activity blanket, Wendy heard herself blurting out, "So, did you all hear about that American guy in Baghdad who was decapitated yesterday?"

A muffled chorus of "I knows" and "It's awfuls" rose and fell around her. Even Lucas Rose seemed to take a break from his incessant mewling.

It was Pamela who broke the hush. "It really is terrible over there," she said, shaking her head. "Worse, even, than when I was over there last year." (Reluctant to abandon her production team, Pamela, though six months pregnant and suffering from preeclampsia, had managed to sneak in a quick trip to Baghdad before giving birth to the Unhappiest Baby on the Block.)

Only Daphne looked unfazed. Daphne had never had a problem blocking out the rest of the world, Wendy thought. "Wen — these cookies are amazing," she said, her mouth full.

"Oh, thanks," said Wendy, gratified to think that Daphne had noticed the effort she'd gone to. "Believe it or not, I got the recipe off the back of the chocolate chip bag."

"Oh, my god, you are so *already* in training for parents' bake sales at PS Three twenty-one!!" Daphne shrieked back at her.

Wendy felt as if she'd been kicked in the stomach. It was the word *training* that hurt the most. It was too close to what she imagined to be the truth. Which was that she could only practice because the real thing remained out of reach. She folded an arm over her ribcage and angled her shoulders around her breasts. "I just like making cookies." She shrugged. She tried to smile, too, but her jaw muscles wouldn't budge. "So, who needs a refill?" she asked, standing up. She didn't wait for an answer. "I do," she muttered to herself. "Badly." By then, she was already halfway to the kitchen.

As Wendy banged a bag of ice against the side of the sink, she tried to determine if her upset was of her own making. No, she decided. It had been thoughtless of Daphne, first to brag about the ease with which she'd conceived, and second to tease Wendy about her cookie-making skills. Then again, maybe

Daphne was unaware of the extent to which Wendy's failure to become pregnant had caused her to suffer, Wendy thought. (Maybe her pride on the matter had led her to downplay her frustration.) Half-convinced of the latter—and newly determined to be a good friend—Wendy left the kitchen, a freshly poured glass of sangria in hand.

"Wen, come sit down!" Daphne called to her as she reentered the living room. "You're working too hard. It's making me feel bad!" She had a giant stuffed giraffe in her lap.

"Working? Try drinking," Wendy said with a quick laugh, while reclaiming her seat on the arm of the sofa. "So, have you guys decided on names yet?" she asked. Wendy had narrowed her own list of favorite baby names down to four: Maeve and Flora for a girl, and Ezekiel ("Zeke") and Otis for a boy. She wasn't entirely satisfied with any of the contenders, however. None of them possessed the right combination of familiarity and uniqueness. Maybe none of them ever would.

Daphne smiled coyly. "Well, we've been bouncing a few ideas around, but we're keeping our favorites a secret."

Another secret, Wendy thought. How many more of them were there?

"Speaking of nothing, what the hell happened to Paige?" asked Sara.

"Unfortunately, she had another engagement," said Daphne, frowning like a little girl whose ice-cream cone had just eaten the pavement.

"Did you guys hear about Paige and Brad Glom?" said Courtney with a conspirational smile.

"No—what?" said Hannah Dingo.

"Well, you know how he finally married his girlfriend of, like, twenty years? Apparently, Paige made some totally offensive toast at the rehearsal dinner about how she'd totally roped him into it. Also, Paige outed her as a former l-e-s-b-i-a-n." She glanced at Miles, presumably to make sure he hadn't learned to spell yet. "Apparently, Brad's no longer speaking to Paige."

"You're kidding!" came the squeals and laughs. And "No way!" and "That's hilarious!"

Wendy cringed. Had her wedding toast been discussed in similarly derogatory terms?

"Ohmygod, Audrey," said Jenn Gilmore. "Do you remember that time in college you got a black eye playing Greek League softball and Paige slipped you the number of a battered-women's shelter—under the guise of being *concerned?*"

"God—don't remind me," said Audrey, rolling her eyes.

There was more giggling.

"Yeah, but, you know, Brad kind of screwed Paige over with the yoga girl," Daphne interjected. It occurred suddenly to Wendy that Daphne never said a bad word about anybody. Could it be that she was the only loyal one among them? "I mean, it was pretty obvious Paige was in love with him all those years," Daphne continued while unwrapping a deep-pile-velour receiving blanket. She rubbed it against her cheek. "Could this be any softer? Hannah, you are too sweet!"

"Danny and I got the same one as a gift when Zola was born, and I swear she spent half the day rolling around on that thing," said Hannah.

Next up was a humongous silver box with cascading blue ribbons. "It's just a little something," said Courtney, who—was it possible?—was nursing Miles again.

Daphne untied the package, opened the box, and lifted out

a large wicker basket topped with confetti. Reaching into the fluff, she emerged moments later with a pair of miniature red-and-white-striped pants, which were attached to a rope cord in the manner of a clothesline with plain wooden clips. *"How* cute are these?" said Daphne. She began to pull the cord, but it extended farther than her arm allowed. So she stood up and began to walk backward toward the door, rope in hand. In the process, she revealed a matching red-and-white-striped sweatshirt. Daphne kept walking, and the tiny outfits kept coming, one after another after another, some decorated with stripes, others with lollipops and teddy bears and little lambs. There must have been a dozen of them. The gaggle gasped and ohmygodded. "Courtney, I can't BE-LIEEEEEEEEEVE you!!" Daphne squealed. "This is just *BEYOND!* I mean, this is, like, the most insane present EVER. And on top of the Diaper Genie I registered for? It's too much. . . ."

The dull ache that had settled in Wendy's temples during the earlier part of the afternoon had now given way to a pounding headache. She felt a burning sensation behind her eyes. Then she noticed that her present rested on top of what was left of the pile. On account of the money and effort she'd put into organizing the shower, Wendy had felt justified in buying Daphne a token gift. In light of Courtney's extravagance, however, she was seized by a familiar fear of looking cheap. "Wait, give that to me," she said, lunging for the package. "I think I left the price tag on." Wendy pried the present out of Daphne's hand. Then, yet again, she fled the room.

•   •   •

This time, Wendy walked past the kitchen and into the bedroom, past the bed on which she and Adam had failed to create a human life, and into the bathroom. She locked the door and sat down on the toilet. Through the shower window, she could hear the relentless whine of highway traffic. How many cars there were, she thought—and how many people inside them, each with their own stories of heartache and triumph and disappointment. And how random it was that she'd been assigned this life. Half-imagining she was Daphne and half-believing her own excuse, Wendy began to loosen the tissue on her gift, carefully unfastening the tape so she could seal it back up.

The baby "sleep sack" she uncovered looked even less substantial than she remembered it being. Lifting it by its minuscule shoulders, Wendy thought back to the infant who might have filled it, the infant she could have had while still in college. Back then, it had never even occurred to her to go through with the pregnancy. It was ironic to think about now, ironic without being sad. It was too many years later for that. She'd only just started the spring semester of her senior year. By the time she missed her period, she and Evan Suarez had already broken up. After all this time, it was mostly Daphne's absence in the aftermath that had stayed with her. Wendy had asked Daphne to come to the clinic with her—she'd trusted no one else with the information that she was pregnant—but Daphne had been having one of her periodic "migraines." Wendy still recalled the pity in the nurses' eyes when she'd asked them if they had the phone number of a taxi service, the shame she'd felt at being there alone.

Why couldn't Daphne just have taken two Tylenol?

Wendy now wondered. And what if the truth was that Daphne couldn't bear for anyone else to be the center of attention—not just the one with all the luck, but the one with all the pain, too? She pictured Daphne in the Wonder Woman costume she'd worn for Halloween that fall, pretending to be embarrassed about how short her short-shorts were. ("I feel like the whole world is staring at my butt!" Wendy recalled Daphne saying.) She longed suddenly for revenge.

She knew it was an immature impulse. The right thing to do was to wait for another day, when the two were alone and Wendy was feeling calmer. Then, in an open, nonaccusatory way, she'd share her hurt feelings with Daphne, remembering to begin all her sentences with "I," as opposed to "You," as in, "You're a duplicitous megalomaniac." Marcia used to encourage Wendy to "own" her negative emotions. As if they were handbags or cars or pets. But it seemed to Wendy that Marcia had missed the point: there was no use in acting responsibly toward people when your goal was to punish and humiliate them.

Just then, Wendy noticed a black pen lying on the windowsill. No doubt Adam had been doing Sudoku, his favorite new time waster. Maybe she would write something on the sleep sack, she thought. Only, what? Wendy lifted the pen off the sill and lowered herself onto the bath mat. Then she closed the toilet seat and laid the sleep sack on top of it. Her heart was beating madly, and she hardly knew what she was doing as she scrawled the words VANITY PROJECT in capital letters across the front of the garment. A dim voice in her head said, "Wendy—you're going insane." Not unconvinced by her own genius, she ignored it and rewrapped the present.

• • •

Wendy entered the living room to find Daphne saying, "He is too adorable," about yet another teddy bear with a grosgrain ribbon tied around its neck. She'd finally exhausted the pile of presents. Wendy placed her gift at Daphne's feet and once again claimed her seat on the arm of the sofa. It seemed to her as if twenty minutes passed—though it was probably only two—before Daphne lifted the package into her lap. "It's just a little something," Wendy told her, just as Courtney had.

"Wen, you really didn't have to get me anything," Daphne said. She began to unstick the tape that Wendy had only just refastened. She lifted the sleep sack into the air. "Oohh," she started to say. Then she fell silent, her face frozen midway between a smile and the vacant stare of the stricken.

"Are you okay, Daf?" asked Sara.

Blood rushed to Wendy's cheeks.

Daphne slowly refolded the sleep sack and placed it back in its tissue paper. Then she began to breathe in an exaggerated fashion, her jaw extended, her mouth ajar. "So let me get this straight," she began in a tremulous voice. "Just because you're Little Miss Political-Action-Career-Woman and I'm not, that gives you the right to mock the greatest achievement of my adult life?"

Wendy felt as if she'd walked onto the stage of the wrong play, only to find her lines useless. She wanted to yell, "How do you think I feel being the only one here without a baby?" But it occurred to her suddenly that what she'd done was more heinous than anything Daphne was guilty of. "It was just a stupid joke," she mumbled instead.

"Hilarious," said Daphne in a scathing voice. She turned to the rest of them. "In case you're wondering what happened, my old and supposedly dear friend Wendy has taken it upon herself to inscribe the phrase 'vanity project' on the sleep suit she intends my infant son or daughter to wear."

There were murmurs of confusion and disapproval.

"That is so psycho," muttered Courtney.

Daphne repeated the phrase in a caustic tone. Then she let loose a withering laugh. But whatever had amused her didn't last long. Her eyes were as slender as crescent moons when she turned back to Wendy and asked, "So — what? — is that supposed to be some kind of critique of my personality? Like you think I do everything I do just to flatter myself — is that it? Or is it just that I'm not allowed to have children because you can't get pregnant?"

Wendy felt like crawling under the Indian bedspread that doubled as the sofa slipcover (and upon which Daphne currently sat). What if Daphne was right? she wondered. What if Wendy was just jealous? And what if Daphne really did have a debilitating migraine that day back in college? As Wendy stared into her best friend's twisted face, she began to doubt the content of her own rage as well. In truth, the feeling Daphne increasingly elicited was older than their friendship — the feeling that no matter how far Wendy came, she'd never catch up. She'd always be racing to board a train that had already left the station. In her mind's eye, she could see the passengers in the back car, their noses pressed to the glass and resembling pigs' snouts, their mouths stretched wide with laughter, their hands waving good-bye. *See you later, if you ever get there,* she heard them calling to her.

Wendy doubted she ever *would* get there. That was her

fear, and her fear had become real to her. Once, she'd seen life as a wonderful absurdity. Now the race to excel and to acquire had become all-consuming. Even humor had fallen out of her repertoire. "Really—I didn't mean anything by it," she offered helplessly.

Without explanation, Daphne rose from her seat and strode toward the kitchen. Moments later, she reappeared with Wendy's two-pound bag of flour pressed to her perfect breasts. Wendy had meant to put the flour back in the cupboard before her guests arrived—she'd used it to make the cookies—but hadn't found the time. "Honestly?" Daphne began again in a shrill voice while waddling back toward Wendy. "For fifteen fucking years I've been putting up with your hostility. And not just putting up with it, but trying to make you happy, when I haven't been busy tiptoeing around you, worried I was going to say the wrong thing and insult you. Your insecurity has been, like, a full-time job. And what's my reward? You gave the most obnoxious wedding toast in the history of wedding toasts. I'm sorry to have *burdened* you with my problems all these years. I thought we were the kind of friends who could tell each other everything, but I guess not. I also thought you'd be happy for me when things finally started going well in my life. But you've been a complete *cunt* to me ever since I met Jonathan"—in her peripheral vision, Wendy could see Courtney covering Miles's ears—"and you know what? I've had it! FUCK"—she paused for effect—"YOU! Fuck your stupid baby shower. And fuck your chocolate chip cookies." Daphne took another step toward Wendy. Then she overturned the flour bag on Wendy's head, momentarily blinding her to all reality but the mushroom cloud that swirled around her head like a nimbus of scorn.

•   •   •

Wendy could only barely make out the identities of the women who rushed to Daphne's aid. Not that Wendy could entirely blame them. Daphne was the one carrying innocent life, while Wendy's belly was filled with nothing more sacred than sangria. Plus, Daphne had begun to weep, while Wendy stood motionless and quiet and, for the moment at least, unable to form an intelligent thought.

"Daffie, it's going to be all right," Wendy heard Jenny Kenar(?) saying.

"Do you want some water?" asked Hannah Dingo(?).

"Daphne, we're taking you home," announced Courtney. (There was no mistaking her snarl.)

"Okay," Daphne choked out between sobs.

Finally, the mushroom cloud began to dissipate, and Wendy's guests again became recognizable to her. Daphne was already halfway to the door, her slender arms looped through Alyssa's and Courtney's. The latter held Miles against her hip as if he were a designer handbag and stared backward at Wendy as if she were a suspected mugger. Jenny Kenar, Jenn Gilmore, Hannah, and Audrey stuffed Daphne's presents into shopping bags. Pamela, Gretchen, and Sara and their respective offspring lingered between the hall and the living room, looking uncomfortable. Naturally, Lucas had begun to cry again. "Do you want help cleaning up?" asked Pamela, clearly the most traumatized of the bunch, if only because conflict was alien to her.

"It's fine, really," Wendy told her. "You should all go home."

"Are you sure?"

"I'm sure." Wendy was thinking that she needed water. Flour had become affixed to the roof of her mouth.

She was also thinking that she couldn't wait for everyone to leave, especially the babies. Somehow, with their googly eyes and utter incomprehension, they made her the most ashamed of all.

8.

To Wendy's surprise, after she cleaned up the apartment, then herself in the shower, the flour pouring off her head in creamy rivulets, she felt okay — not great, by any means, but not terrible, either. Not as bad as she might have thought she'd feel. She felt like a pariah, of course. At the same time there was a certain relief in having disgraced herself and in having given up all claims to respectability or decorousness. It was so exhausting trying to get along with everyone all the time.

Wendy felt relieved, as well, to think she'd never again have to admire Daphne's house, husband, or appearance; never have to tell her how unbelievably adorable her newborn was sure to be, either. In retrospect, it struck Wendy that their friendship might have ended years earlier had Wendy not felt obligated to stick around. In light of Daphne's recent outburst, however, that sense of duty had fallen away; there was no need to feel responsible for someone who hated your guts.

It was the sight of Adam walking in the door at six o'clock that once again filled Wendy with doubt and shame. "How was the game?" she said, before he could ask her about the shower.

"Great," he said. "Delgado hit a two-run homer in the ninth and won it for New York. How was the babyfest?"

Wendy knew there was no point in keeping what had happened a secret. Adam would find out eventually. "Actually, it ended early," she told him. "Though not before Daphne dumped a bag of flour on my head and told me I'd spent the past fifteen years doing my best to ruin her life."

"Whaaaaaaaaaaat?!" cried Adam. *Was there ever a man whom gossip excited more?* Wendy thought irritably.

Then again, even Wendy had to admit that their blowup was a story made for retelling. She could already hear her guests regaling their other friends: *You won't believe what happened at Daphne Uberoff's baby shower....* "I gave her a baby sleep sack with the phrase 'vanity project' written across the chest," said Wendy. "It was a joke, but Daphne didn't find it funny."

Adam squinted in disbelief. "You wrote that, or it already came written on it?"

"I wrote it."

"Daphne's finally straightened her life out and found a little happiness in the world, and you're accusing her of being a hideous narcissist? Are you out of your frigging mind?"

Wendy was willing to believe that what she'd done was hostile bordering on inexcusable. But she hadn't told Adam so he'd make her feel even worse. She'd already been "floured." What further punishment did he have in mind for her? Fitting her into stocks in the town square? "No—apparently just a terrible person," she answered. "Never mind the thousands of hours of my life I've spent listening to Daphne go on about her problems and generally trying to be a supportive friend to someone who rarely if ever asks me a single thing about myself."

"Woooo—calm down," said Adam. "I'm just trying to understand what happened."

"What's it to you?" asked Wendy.

"It isn't anything to me! I just think it's a little ridiculous to throw a party for someone and then use the opportunity to insult the person. I mean, either you decide to be friends with her or you decide not to. It's like you want it both ways."

Wendy felt her temper flaring. But she'd already alienated her best friend; she figured she'd leave her husband for another day. "I don't want anything both ways," she said as evenly as she could. "I just want to stop talking about this, not least because it's not really any of your business."

"Fine," said Adam.

Just because you're close friends now with Daphne doesn't mean I have to be, anymore."

"I thought you wanted to drop the subject?"

"I do," said Wendy. Daphne and Adam's receiving-line exchange had crept back to the surface of her consciousness.

Wendy was still puzzled by what had happened to make her husband feel the need to defend Daphne at every turn.

Wendy wasn't sure what reaction to expect from their mutual friends—whether they'd shun her for her behavior or feel compelled to take a side (presumably Daphne's). A part of Wendy was hurt that no one had come to her defense after Daphne opened her gift. (What she'd written wasn't *that* bad, was it?) At the very least, Wendy figured, she still had Maura as a friend. That said, Maura had recently vanished to Mexico to "do research," even though, the last time Wendy checked, Maura's dissertation was on the Scottish Enlightenment.

A few days after being "floured," Wendy received the following email from Gretchen:

wen,

just wanted to see how you were doing. i'm sorry about how the shower ended on sunday. if it seemed like daphne overreacted, i think secretly she's really nervous about having a baby. can't say i entirely blame her, since motherhood basically ruined my life, and i'd rather feed starving children in africa than my own in brooklyn. there, i said it. does that make me a bad person? please don't answer that. but, seriously, i'd be institutionalized if it weren't for dorothea. . . . meanwhile, i'm sure d's big film news—assume you heard by now?—will go far to boost her mood and confidence. to be even more honest, i'm feeling a little envious myself. can't remember the last time someone threw money at me for doing basically NOTHING. (maybe never?) but, then, i work in the non-profit sector, so I'm not supposed to care about stuff like that. (yeah, sure.)

xoxog

p.s. remind me—are you guys headed anywhere fun in august??

Wendy appreciated Gretchen's show of support. She also appreciated Gretchen's honesty regarding both her failure as a parent and her envy of Daphne's good fortune. As for the basis of Gretchen's envy, Wendy knew that for the sake of her mental health, she ought to refrain from asking her to elaborate. But curiosity won out over self-protection, as it usually did. Wendy wrote back:

> Dear Gretch, Thanks for writing. I'm sorry too about what happened at the shower, but I think Daphne and I were headed for a split one way or another. Granted, I could have made that happen in a more grown-up fashion. Anyway, it's a little late now. . . . Meanwhile, I'm sorry to hear you're not enjoying motherhood more. Though it's probably good for me to hear it isn't all just a collection of "Kodak moments." Finally, no, I didn't hear about D's "film news." Pray tell. XW

Gretchen promptly replied:

> basically, this three-page treatment d wrote got optioned for a half million dollars by some division of warner brothers. as far as I know, it's about two best friends who are really competitive and try to seduce each other's husbands. (am hoping/assuming she was *not* thinking of the two of us, since—yuck— I'm so *not interested* in sleeping with jonathan! though if rob reciprocated d's advances, am not sure i'd be entirely surprised, since it's NOT LIKE WE HAVE SEX ANYMORE.) anyway, daphne is apparently going to be writing the screenplay, too. so she'll get even more $ if the movie is ever made. in short, it doesn't look like the uberoff-sonnenbergs are going to be hurting for cash anytime soon. not that they were before. not sure if you know that the sonnenberg elders own a renowned collection of old master paintings, including several rembrandts?? . . .

After Wendy finished reading Gretchen's second email, whatever embarrassment she'd been harboring over her behavior at Daphne's baby shower was instantly erased. Her only regret was that she hadn't also written "My Mother Is an Evil Shrew" in giant capitals on the back of the sleep sack. Envy was only part of it. Wendy felt exploited, too. There was no doubt in her mind that Daphne had had her and Adam in mind when she'd written up her film treatment. And that she could attach them to such a sleazy, gratuitous, and, most of all, presumptuous plot!

Wendy was exiting out of her email program when Alyson the Extraordinarily Attractive Intern appeared in her doorway. The expanse of leg between the top of her cowboy boots and the hem of her purple shorts seemed to encompass several football fields' worth of creamy, veinless skin. "I'm so sorry to bother you?" she said.

"What's up?" said Wendy, reminding herself that it wasn't Alyson who'd dumped a bag of flour on her head, then sold a movie treatment mocking her marriage.

"I think the office is on fire?"

"What?!" Wendy breathed in. It did smell a little like smoke, she thought. But if there was a fire, wouldn't the alarms be going off? Though, now that she thought about it, she didn't remember ever having seen any. . . .

Wendy stood up from her desk and walked out the door of her office and into the hall, Alyson tagging behind. She glanced from left to right, then left again — just as a curling plume of white smoke wafted out the door to the kitchen. "Holy hell," she said to Alyson. Then she bolted down the hall, yelling, "FIRE — EVERYBODY GET OUT!!" An assemblage of terrible haircuts and unkempt facial hair began to appear over cubicle walls and from inside office doors. "EVERYONE GET TO THE STAIRS!" Wendy cried.

Within fifteen minutes, the offices of *Barricade* were essentially wiped out. All eighteen staff members got out in time, but mostly because all one hundred sixteen pounds of Alyson the Intern had thought to run to the reception area, swoop all one hundred eight pounds of Lois into her arms, and carry the old woman piggyback-style down six flights of stairs. By the time the two of them spilled out onto the street, it was awash in sirens and flashing lights. At the sight of Lois and Alyson, Wendy found herself bursting into tears and consuming both in an enormous bear hug. Alyson cried, too. Lois remained predictably stoic. "You'd think Nagasaki was burning," she grumbled at no one in particular, causing both Wendy and Alyson to burst into hysterical laughter. That was how Alyson became Wendy's new best (young) friend.

Alyson also became the office hero. At an emergency staff meeting that evening at the all-white apartment on Union Square that Lincoln shared with his choreographer partner, Randall, the Misanthrope Himself took the opportunity to praise her "commendable work in rescuing the last surviving member of the Stevenson campaign."

Not that Lois would admit to any such gratitude. "As if I need to live through another year of the Nixon administration," she muttered—to much giggling.

After the meeting, Lincoln offered Alyson the job of "assistant to the executive editor" upon her graduation from NYU, the following January. And she gladly accepted, though not before reminding him that *Barricade* was her "favorite magazine ever." The assumption was that by then, the magazine would have a new office. In the meantime, they were all going to have to work from home.

Also in the meantime, early suggestions on the part of certain *Barricade* staff members that a right-wing conspiracy may have loomed behind the conflagration soon gave way to the mundane truth: the fire had been started by the broken coffee machine. What's more, the one working alarm, which was located in the elevator bank, had no batteries in it. All the local newspapers and news channels carried the story. Just as all of Wendy's friends called or emailed over the next twenty-four hours to find out if Wendy was okay. Wendy's mother called, too.

"Wendell — I'm so relieved to hear your voice," said Judy, in a shaky voice when Wendy finally rang her back the next day. "I was up all night worrying about you!"

"You were worried about me?" said Wendy in disbelief.

"Of course I was worried!"

"Oh, sorry — Lincoln had us all over to his house. I should have called you back when I got home, but it was really late. Also, I guess I didn't think you were the worrying type — at least, not about me."

"I'm not made of stone!" cried Judy, "Truth to tell, I was worried about Adam, too. He must have been beside himself."

"Actually, he was pretty mellow about the whole thing," Wendy told her. "He mostly thought it was cool that I got to yell 'Fire!' in a crowded building."

Judy cleared her throat imperiously. "Wendell, I think you need to seriously interrogate your desire to mock that husband of yours," she said, sounding like her old self. "He's a good man, and it's time you realized it."

Not surprisingly, the only "friend" who didn't check in was Daphne. Not that Wendy expected her to do so. It was rather that the fire confirmed for her what she already knew but didn't yet have proof of—namely, that her friendship with Daphne was officially over.

Wendy didn't miss Daphne so much as, without her ever-looming presence, she felt disoriented. For almost sixteen years, she'd been anticipating Daphne's reaction to everything that happened in the world—everything Wendy said and did, too. And now, in a single day, that "early-detection system" had been rendered defunct. Contrary to Wendy's fears, their mutual friends didn't abandon her. But Gretchen's email aside, they remained scrupulous about not bringing up Daphne. Wendy wondered if she would even hear about it when, presumably by the end of the summer, Daphne gave birth. Wendy also wondered what name Daphne and Jonathan would choose for him or her. Would they go with something trendy like Milo or Tallulah? Or would they opt for an unassailable classic like William or Elizabeth? And why did Wendy still care?

Her sense of the world being upside down was only enhanced by the fact that, for the first time in a decade, she found herself working at home. Adam seemed as disoriented by his and Wendy's new proximity as Wendy was. First thing each morning (which, for him, meant ten thirty), he took to disappearing with his laptop to his favorite coffee shop. He didn't return until practically dinner. Wendy was waiting for the right moment to remind him that his twelve months of spousal support were now up. In the meantime, Adam made plans to return to Newton for a few weeks in early August to hang out with his father, who was making slow but steady progress. He didn't invite Wendy to come along.

The evening before Adam's departure, Wendy and Alyson went out for drinks. Wendy ended up telling her all about her fight with Daphne. "Maybe you guys need to sit down and, like, talk?" suggested Alyson, who also took the time to teach Wendy how to text. Maybe that was why, to Wendy's astonishment, she found herself volunteering to pick up the tab.

The story might have ended there—in a stalemate marriage and a lost friendship—if Paige hadn't contacted Wendy an hour after Adam had left on the train, to see if the two of them could meet up later that day. "It's sort of important," said Paige.

Wendy couldn't imagine what Paige so urgently needed to discuss with her, but she suspected it had something to do with her falling-out with Daphne. Paige was probably trying to broker some kind of peace deal, Wendy figured. She had no conscious interest in reconciling with Daphne. At the same time, she was intrigued by Paige's intentions. Maybe also, Wendy was hoping that Paige might reveal how Daphne was feeling about their breakup. (Sad? Relieved? Indifferent?) Wendy couldn't help but be curious. She was also eager to hear more about Paige's unlikely new relationship with Daphne's handyman/tenant, Jeremy. Because as much gossip as Wendy consumed, it was never enough. There was still another story with the potential to bring color and humor to her mostly monochrome days (and reflect positively on her own less-than-ideal personal situation). It was also true that Paige's absence from Daphne's shower had left Wendy feeling more sympathetic toward her. Childless herself, Paige had perhaps felt similarly ill-equipped to handle the scrum of mothers and babies. Wendy told her she'd be happy to meet her at Guerrilla Coffee, on the western edge of Park Slope, at one.

It was hot and humid and hazy outside—the kind of August day when the sun feels like a vise clamping down on your back. Wendy emerged from the subway feeling as if her dress had melded with her flesh. She found Paige seated at a café table in back. Amid a sea of shorts and tank tops, she wasn't hard to miss—in her linen suit and two-tone Chanel slingbacks. "Paige!" Wendy called and waved to her across the room. "I'm just getting a coffee." She motioned at the counter.

Paige waved back, before returning to her *Wall Street Journal* "Weekend Journal."

In time, Wendy joined her at the table, paper cup in hand. "You look so nice!" she said, thinking she might as well get the conversation off to a friendly start. "Are you going somewhere afterward?"

Paige smiled unctuously as she laid down her newspaper. "As a matter of fact, I'm headed to a matinee performance of *Aida*. Truth be told, Broadway musicals aren't really my thing, but the proceeds go to the Spinal Bifida Association."

"Oh—cool!" Wendy nodded. "Well, maybe it will be fun?"

"Perhaps, but that's not really the point," Paige snapped back.

"Right," said Wendy. "Meanwhile, how's it going with Jeremy?"

"How's *what* going?" asked Paige, her head cocked and brow furrowed, as if she hadn't understood the question.

"Your relationship," answered Wendy, who was instantly reminded of one of the many things that drove her crazy about Paige—namely, her refusal to disseminate anything more than superficial information about herself, even as she systematically mined others for their darkest secrets.

"Oh." Paige tilted her head backward. "Well, since you ask, yes, we're having a very nice time together." Again, she assumed a tight-lipped smile.

"Well, that's great," said Wendy.

"Unfortunately, I'm not here to talk about Jeremy and myself," said Paige, flaring her nostrils and lowering her chin. As if she had the misfortune in this world of having been anointed an emissary of those concerns that others would prefer to overlook but that Paige, in good conscience, couldn't bring herself to ignore. "Let me begin by thanking you for meeting me on such short notice," she went on. "Please understand, as well, that this is very awkward for me." Wendy was stumped. Was Paige having trouble getting pregnant herself? Was she secretly hankering to become a left-wing journalist? "But my conscience is telling me that I need to say something. So"—she took a deep breath through her nose—"as you may or may not know, Jeremy does a certain amount of handyman-type work around Daphne and Jonathan's house. Last week he was hanging some blinds in Daphne's home office upstairs. She'd left her laptop out. The screen saver was most likely on, since Daphne hadn't occupied the room in what Jeremy estimated to be at least a half hour and possibly as much as an hour. However, as he climbed a chair to better reach the window, he knocked up against her desk. The desktop on her computer popped back into focus—"

"What's this all about?" Wendy couldn't stop herself from interrupting. When Paige felt she had something important to relay—as she apparently did now—she talked incredibly slowly. Wendy found herself (a) having trouble concentrating on the trajectory of Paige's narrative, and (b) growing crazy with impatience.

"Please! Let me finish," Paige barked and scowled, as if Wendy had just broken the Eleventh Commandment: Though Shalt Not Interrupt Paige Ryan. She sighed punitively before continuing: "I want to preface what I'm going to say next by attesting to the fact that Jeremy is not, by nature, a nosy person. Far from it. In fact, he goes out of his way, I would say, to mind his own business. I also want to add that I have not discussed what I'm about to tell you with Daphne. Not yet, at least. After careful consideration, I decided that the prudent thing to do was to approach you first—"

"PAIGE!" Wendy yelled. She couldn't take it anymore. It was as if her request had accomplished nothing more than to further retard the pace of Paige's speechifying. "PLEASE! I'm begging you. Where is this going? I have laundry to do."

Paige shot Wendy a fiery look before she announced, "As I was SAYING, the email literally appeared before Jeremy's eyes."

"What email?" asked Wendy.

"I'm about to tell you," said Paige, jaw clenched. "There was an email opened on Daphne's computer, and it was to your husband." She glared at Wendy so intensely that Wendy almost jumped backward in her seat.

"So?" said Wendy, bristling at the implication of impropriety even as it hit an exposed nerve. "They're friends. Why shouldn't they email?"

Paige took another exaggerated breath through her nose. "There was an email from Daphne to your husband alluding to the fact that Daphne's unborn child does not genetically belong to her husband, Jonathan."

"What?" said Wendy, squinting in confusion.

Her neck elongated, Paige reached her right hand across the table and placed it on Wendy's forearm. "I'm sorry to have to be the one telling you this."

"Telling me what?!" Wendy could feel her heartbeat accelerating.

"The email indirectly alluded to the fact that the baby's father is your husband, Adam."

Wendy's head had begun to spin. Or was it the room? All the laptops and coffee mugs and muffin wrappers appeared suddenly to be sailing through the air. "Indirectly alluded?! What the hell does that mean?" She shook Paige's hand off her arm.

"Just what I said," said Paige.

"You said nothing," Wendy shot back.

"Don't shoot the messenger, Wendy."

"Messenger? Messenger of what? Either tell me what the email said or I'm leaving!"

Paige looked away. "I'm afraid I'm not at liberty to reveal any more than I already have."

"You show up here to tell me my husband's impregnated my former best friend, but you can't go into details," cried Wendy. "This is officially *insane!!*"

Paige let her lids close halfway over her eyes, as if she could hardly stand to bear witness to her own truth-telling and sighed wearily. *"Living in fear that J is going to find out that Peanut isn't his,"* she began in a blank tone. *"Then what? Just feel like running away now. What are we going to do?"* Her recitation complete, she clasped her hands in her lap and cast her eyes downward, the faintest hint of a smile on her lips. Or had Wendy dreamt that last detail up?

Wendy felt that at any moment, her head might lift off from her body. She couldn't be sure that her heart was still in her chest. Her eyes filled with tears. She couldn't hide their dampness. Again, Paige reached a hand across the table. This time, Wendy lacked the energy to fight her off. "I got divorced, Wendy," Paige offered in a newly oily tone. "It's not that bad."

"Who said anything about divorce?" said Wendy, wiping her nose with the back of her hand.

"Wendy, your former best friend is having a baby with your husband. Do you really plan on staying with him?"

"You don't know that for sure," said Wendy, but her voice trembled as she spoke. (Her voice belied her conviction that Paige Ryan was a pathological liar who couldn't be trusted not to poison her coffee.) "And would you please stop calling me *Wendy?*"

"As you like," said Paige. Apparently miffed, she abruptly removed her hand from Wendy's arm.

Her limbs returned to her, Wendy took the opportunity to flee the premises. "I have to go," she said, rising from her chair and hooking her bag over her shoulder. "Have fun at *Aida.*"

•   •   •

243

The sun seemed even fiercer than it had twenty minutes earlier. It bounced off the parked cars and store windows, skew-
ing Wendy's vision. All the passersby on the sidewalk looked
like gargoyles. She stepped off the curb without realizing it
was there, jolting her insides. Of the many swirling thoughts
that occupied Wendy's head, the most dominant one was that
she needed to reach Adam — to have him remind her that
Paige Ryan was not her friend, never had been. She dialed his
cell phone as she walked. But it rang straight to voice mail.
She called again. He still wasn't picking up. Wary of leaving
Paige's accusation in a message — and thinking Adam might
already have arrived in Newton — Wendy dialed her in-laws'
house.

But Phyllis seemed confused by Wendy's question.
"Adam?" she said.

"Isn't he coming to stay with you?" asked Wendy.

"Yes, but we're not expecting him until the ninth!" Wendy
was baffled. Had she misheard him? Had he made other
plans for the weekend? Her brain began searching for innocent explanations, but all it came up with was nefarious ones.
Meanwhile, Phyllis had begun to conjure nightmares of her
own. "God, you don't think something happened to him," she
said with a little gasp.

Wendy could hear the panic building in her mother-in-law's
voice. She wished she'd never called. She barely had the energy
to deal with her own upset and confusion, let alone someone
else's. At the same time, she felt a sudden, overwhelming urge
to surrender the last remaining shard of her privacy to this
woman who had been like a second mother to her for the past
eight years. Or so she liked to imagine. "I think he's having an
affair," she choked out. "There's no other explanation."

"What?!" cried Phyllis.

"I think Adam's sleeping with my friend Daphne — or, I guess I should say, former friend."

"The girl who's always having affairs with married men?!"

"She's married now herself."

"Wendy, that doesn't sound like something my Adam would do."

It was her mother-in-law's use of "my" that took Wendy aback, made her think she'd overstepped (and now it was too late to retreat, too late ever to undo the damage). "I know it doesn't," she said, still determined to make her case. "But a friend of Daphne's just told me — a friend told me that Daphne is pregnant by Adam."

"What?!" screeched Phyllis, sounding, in truth, not entirely unhappy at the possibility.

"I don't have any proof," said Wendy, realizing that, for better or worse, she only had one mother after all.

"Well, Wendy, you've left me thoroughly shaken!" declared Phyllis.

"I'm sorry," said Wendy, her eyes again filling with tears — this time at the thought that she was losing everyone who'd ever cared about her. "I didn't mean to upset you."

"I know you didn't. I'm sorry for you, too. I just don't know what to believe right now."

"To be honest, I don't, either."

"If you hear from Adam before we do, will you please tell him to call home?" asked Phyllis.

"Of course," said Wendy.

She must have been gripping the phone too tightly. Her hand and ear were aching when she hung up.

* * *

By coincidence, Wendy found herself standing in front of the
old dive where she and Adam had had their wedding party
almost five years before. She walked in and took a seat at the
bar. At the very least, the place presented respite from the sun;
it was so dark in there that it might as well have been night-
time. Wendy ordered a screwdriver—it seemed like the kind
of drink you ordered when your marriage was uncovered to
be a sham—and looked around her. A handful of winos sat
slumped over their stools, their creased faces obscured in
shadow. One glanced curiously in her direction but, to her
relief, said nothing.

As Wendy waited for her drink, she caught sight of the
booth where she and Adam had huddled into the early hours
of that night. Its vinyl upholstery was peeling. The wood table
was all scratched up. It was a far cry from the Prospect Park
boathouse. Even so, Wendy recalled the evening as being romantic in its own way, romantic because she and Adam had
held hands beneath the table as they waited for the songs to
play whose identifying letters and number they'd punched
into the jukebox—back when songs meant everything, were
more important than money or status, summed up their
shared ironic take on the world as an exercise in futility, if
occasionally an amusing, bittersweet one. Now Wendy wasn't
sure what—or whom—to believe.

If Paige was to be trusted, there was a way in which Wendy
felt flattered to think that Beautiful Daphne Sonnenberg née
Uberoff found her husband that desirable and had gone to
such lengths to disguise the fact. It meant that on some level,
Daphne must have been jealous of Wendy, a novel and deli-

cious concept. Wendy also found it titillating to imagine herself embroiled in such High Drama: who would have thought that Boring Reliable Wendy Murman would ever occupy one of the points in a love triangle? The spurned woman as opposed to the "other woman," but still. A player. A leading character.

But it was not a play. That was the problem. It was real life. Just as, if Paige was to be believed, there was real life—flesh, blood, toenails, eyeballs—growing inside Daphne; real life that derived its genetic coding from Adam, life that should have been growing inside Wendy. It was this part of the story that she found intolerable: not just the vile image of Daphne opening her legs to a heaving, overly grateful Adam (so Wendy imagined), but the fact that a human being was to be born whom Wendy would be unable to hate, since babies were by nature innocent, none of them having asked to be put here, yet who would serve as an endless, agonizing reminder of Adam and Daphne's betrayal—a reminder that in all likelihood would outlive Wendy. The earth didn't seem large enough to accommodate both of them.

At the same time, Wendy remained in doubt regarding the veracity of Paige's story. Even if Adam had been secretly pining for Daphne all these years, Wendy still had trouble imagining that Daphne felt the same way about him. She tried to avail herself of the notion that Adam was virile or dynamic in some way she'd never noticed—or had stopped noticing, this many years into marriage—but she wasn't convinced. Adam's attributes aside, he was still short and unemployed, and Daphne had always favored tall guys with fancy careers—even if, admittedly, she had a soft spot for married men.

But how, then, to explain Daphne's movie treatment? And now Adam's disappearance? There were too many coincidences, and all of them led to one shocking conclusion. As Wendy exited the bar, she called Adam's phone yet again. He still wasn't picking up.

Wendy had been holding in her tears for more than an hour when she finally closed the door to her apartment behind her. The place was stiflingly hot, but she barely noticed. She threw herself facedown on the bed and wept. When she'd exhausted her supply of tears, she splashed cool water on her face, made coffee (the thought of food disgusted her), and tried to think rationally about her next move. But she couldn't come up with anything. The future stretched out before her like a giant question mark laid flat and crushed.

All she could see in her mind's eye was Daphne: her delicately chewed nails, her long sinewy thighs, her pert little breasts, her pale and lovely face. She heard her giggling, too, as she roughed up Adam's hair, then her quiet moans beneath him, as he thrust himself inside her with everything he had (and everything he'd kept from Wendy); then, after the act, the two of them talking about her in the slow drawl of the faux-concerned. "I just feel so baaaaaaaaad," Daphne would say, head tilted per usual. "I mean, Wendy's a really, really old friend of mine."

"Hey — listen — it's no one's fault," Adam would reassure her in a soft voice, while tucking a stray lock of hair behind her ear. "I mean, this whole thing took us by surprise. Neither of us was looking for it. It just happened. And it's bigger than both of us. I've never felt this way about anyone." He'd grab her by the forearms. "Daphne. Look at me. I'm in love with you."

Wendy knew that, if Paige was to be believed, it was Adam who had broken his vows and therefore Adam who had ultimately betrayed her. Yet as the afternoon progressed, Wendy couldn't help but feel that it was Daphne who deserved the brunt of her rage — Daphne who was carrying *her* child and had therefore robbed her of something sacred, Daphne whose very existence felt like an insult. (As the afternoon progressed, doubt regarding Paige's story fell away.)

At the same time, Wendy felt a driving need to confront Daphne in person — to hear her admit to her crimes and beg for Wendy's forgiveness, and also to tell Daphne what she really thought of her (and what she now wished she'd said to her at the shower). That wasn't all. Wendy had never been involved in a physical altercation in her life, but now she imagined punching Daphne in the face, knocking her to the ground, making her bleed — just as Wendy had been bleeding, month after month after month. Daphne had always been the drama queen. Now it was Wendy's turn. She felt like a teakettle approaching boiling point. She grabbed her keys, wallet, and sunglasses off the kitchen countertop. Then, for the second time that afternoon, she headed out.

The temperature had cooled, but the stairwell to the subway still stank of piss. "Spare a quarter?" asked the same homeless man who Wendy used to see in the 9th Street station. For a brief moment, she imagined he'd followed her there. And that he knew everything — where she was headed and why. Generally speaking, Wendy was too cheap to give money to beggars. But that afternoon, paranoia trumped parsimony. She stuffed a dollar into the man's cup. "God bless you," he muttered. Wendy kept walking.

As the R train crept along its route, she rehearsed her lines: "You're a deceitful, conniving *predator* who can't be happy unless you've ruined someone else's life. . . ."

Daphne and Jonathan's mansion was apparently all "done." The windows had been cleaned; the work permit notice had been removed. The flowerpot at the top of the stoop overflowed with impatiens and vinca, the latter cascading down the side of the pot like tears down a cheek. Climbing the stoop, Wendy was beset with a familiar sense of discomfort. As if she didn't belong there or anywhere else. But those were her old fears talking, Wendy told herself. She'd earned the right to go anywhere she wanted. It was Daphne who had trespassed.

She rang the bell and waited. She half-expected Adam to come to the door in his boxers, saying, "Oh, hey, Pope, what's up? Daf and I are just eating some take-out, if you want to join us. . . ." But no one answered. She rang again. Still there was no answer. Wendy idly turned the knob. To her surprise, the door clicked open.

Stepping inside, she was reminded of how magnificent the house was. The hallway had been painted a beautiful shade of robin's egg blue, the plasterwork trim a creamy white. To the left of the parlor doors a pewter vase filled with lush violet hydrangea blossoms sat atop an ebonized wood console. The polished mahogany banister glistened in the late-afternoon light. "Daphne! It's Wendy," she yelled in a voice that sounded hoarse and unfamiliar to her. Who had she become? Wendy wondered. "I'd like to talk to you." But there was no answer. It struck Wendy how quiet the house was. Her heart thumping, she climbed the stairs to the second floor. Every few steps, she paused to listen for signs of life. Still she heard nothing.

Arriving on the second-floor landing, Wendy noticed that the door to the master bedroom was ajar. Her heart beating even faster, she peeked inside. A pristine white spread lay smoothed over the four corners of Daphne and Jonathan's gleaming sleigh bed. Against the headboard, propped up in descending order like the animals on Noah's ark, was a procession of fluffy white pillows. To the right of the bed, pale yellow taffeta curtains pooled on honey-colored wide plank floors. To the left was a cherrywood dresser topped with wedding and family photos in sterling silver frames. All the people in the pictures looked so elegant and peaceful, Wendy thought, with admiration and fury.

Just then, she made out the muted rush of a running faucet. Her heart began to race. "Daphne!" she called. But again, there was no answer. She walked down the hall and tapped on the door behind which the noise seemed to be coming from. Receiving no reply, she slowly turned the knob.

It was the most sumptuous bathroom Wendy had ever seen. At the far end was a porcelain bathtub with claw feet; to the right, an all-glass shower stall with a marble interior; to the left were matching marble his-and-hers sinks with polished nickel legs and hardware. A steady stream of water poured out of the far one. On the white tiled floor between the sinks lay the most beautiful fixture of all: Daphne.

Her jaw was slack, her eyes were closed, her hair was everywhere. Her pregnant belly, its navel stretched flat, poked out of an old lace camisole top. Her head rested on one bare, outstretched arm. A small orange plastic vial with a white label had rolled under the sink closest to her head, its cap and contents missing. "Oh, my god," Wendy said, gasping. The original Valley Girl standard had finally met its match. "Oh, my god," she said again, all her old fears about Daphne finally confirmed — now that Wendy no longer cared.

But why now? Had Daphne's conscience acted up? Had she told Jonathan that the baby wasn't his? Had he told her to get out? And what did Adam have to do with any of it? (Why wasn't he here by her side?) Wendy bent down and felt for Daphne's pulse. She was alive. But for how much longer?

Wendy knew she had to think fast. But her brain was pulling her in two directions. She figured she could tiptoe back down the hall and stairs and close the door behind her most likely without anyone having seen her come in and without anyone ever knowing she'd been there (and with Daphne getting the punishment she deserved, the punishment she'd willed on herself). How much easier life would be if Daphne was dead, Wendy thought. Adam would be too devastated and ashamed to attend the funeral, but Wendy would sit politely in the back row. Everyone would agree it was a terrible tragedy. Wendy would have her husband back.

Only, what about the baby — the baby who Wendy wanted not to exist but who, in that moment, she couldn't help but think deserved a better fate than to die at the hands of its own maker, a prisoner of its own invention? And what about Daphne herself? Did her crime really deserve death? And would Wendy be able to live with herself if she left Daphne there to drift away? For almost sixteen years, Wendy had played the role of Daphne's protector. Could she really abandon that role now — now that Daphne was actually in need?

And yet, what had Daphne ever done for her? Wendy thought. Gotten her into a few exclusive parties. Filled the silence with her tireless chatter, her incessant use of the word *beyond*. Provided a distraction from Wendy's own problems — until Daphne became her biggest problem of all. Then again, until Daphne, Wendy had never really been close to anyone — not in the way she'd been close to Daphne. Daphne had always been so self-obsessed that, in some strange way, she'd taught Wendy what it meant to love.

Daphne also had an uncanny way of making Wendy feel empty and hopeless inside.

Every muscle in her body wanted to run. Instead, she pulled out her phone and dialed 911. . . .

After Wendy hung up, she knelt on the floor beside Daphne — held her hand and smoothed the hair off her forehead and told her she was going to be okay. And wondered how she could possibly be rooting for the woman she hated more than anyone else on earth to pull through. Maybe it was because, lying there, Daphne had never looked so dull, really — and so human after all.

EMS arrived six minutes later, complete with wailing sirens. Wendy ran to the front door. Brawny men in blue shirts were striding up the staircase, two steps at a time, when Jonathan appeared. "What the hell is going on?!" he said, his eyes shifting from Wendy to the men.

It was the only time she'd ever seen him looking undone. One of his shirttails was untucked. His eyes were red. Was it possible he'd been crying? Drinking? It also struck Wendy that Jonathan had never looked so handsome. "Daphne's sick," she said.

"What?!" he said, racing up the stairs.

From downstairs, Wendy could hear him moaning, "Daphne. Daphne. What have you done?"

Jonathan didn't ask Wendy to ride in the ambulance with him, but he didn't object, either, when she climbed in next to him. She felt it was the right thing to do, the kind of thing you did for your oldest friend in the event of her overdosing on tranquilizers while eight and a half months pregnant with your husband's child. She was also curious: to know what had precipitated Daphne's suicide attempt, and what had happened between her and Adam, and if she and her baby were going to live. Wendy was worried, too—not just about Daphne, but that the answers she sought would be buried with Daphne and her unborn child.

Long Island College Hospital was at the end of the next block, so the trip there took less than two minutes. The ambulance arrived at the emergency entrance, and a second crew whisked away Daphne's gurney, leaving Wendy and Jonathan to join the throngs of the worried, bored, and suffering. LICH wasn't one of the fancy New York hospitals—there were no soaring marble lobbies, no wings named after Wall Street moguls—but the emergency room had a partial view of the skyline and a fresh coat of paint. Children fidgeted. Adults talked on phones or paced. Others held bandages to their heads. Wendy and Jonathan sat down next to each other in the least-populated corner of the room. She longed to ask him what he knew, but she didn't have the nerve, couldn't find the right opening. An hour went by. Or maybe it was two. It was Jonathan who finally broke the silence. (Maybe he got curious, too.) "I thought you and Daphne didn't speak anymore," he said.

"We hadn't been," Wendy told him. "But I came over to

make up." Who was to say it hadn't been her intention all along?

"Interesting timing," said Jonathan.

"She told you about the baby, didn't she?" said Wendy, unable to stop herself, her heart in her throat.

"Yeah, she told me," he said.

"If you don't mind me asking, do you know where the father is?" It was now after eight and—it occurred suddenly to Wendy—she still hadn't heard a word from Adam.

"I don't give a *fuck* where he is," declared Jonathan. "The guy is a scumbag."

"At least you're not married to him," Wendy said with a laugh.

"What?" said Jonathan, his chiseled face twisted.

"We *are* talking about my husband, right?"

Jonathan let out a scalding laugh of his own. "No, that would be Mitchell Kroker Reporting Live from the Fucking Capital."

Wendy felt her stomach falling out of her body. "Mitch is the father?"

"Some kind of reunion deal. Maybe because we'd just gotten engaged. Had to go fuck things up, you know?" Jonathan shook his head in anger and bewilderment.

Wendy had never felt so relieved. Or so confused. Or like a bigger fool. How could she have gotten things so wrong? Was the world that much of a tease? Were we all stumbling around like Plato's cave dwellers, mistakenly believing that the sun rose this morning, when it had actually imploded a hundred million years before? "I'm so sorry," she began—just as a harried-looking doctor appeared before them.

"Are you the family of Daphne Sonnenberg?" she asked.

"I'm her husband," said Jonathan, standing up. Wendy stood up, too.

"She's going to be okay," said the woman.

Receiving this latest dramatic dispatch from Daphne-ville, Jonathan collapsed against Wendy and began silently to sob. He smelled like lavender and scotch. For a brief moment, Wendy imagined having sex with him, being his wife, padding around their Cobble Hill brownstone in shearling slippers, her hair pulled up in a rhinestone-studded butterfly clip. Then she recalled his comment about the Palestinians' being nomads and doubted that their marriage would work. "But we're not sure about the baby yet," the doctor went on. "She'll be going in for a cesarean in a few minutes." She turned to Jonathan. "If you'd like to be there with her—"

"That's okay," he said, pulling away from Wendy, his palm raised. "I'll wait here."

"I'm happy to go in with her," said Wendy, glancing from Jonathan to the doctor and back again.

"Whatever you want," he said, shrugging.

In fact, it was precisely what Wendy wanted. Maybe she was hoping to become a hero in Daphne's mind and compensate for what she'd done at her baby shower. Or maybe she just wanted to be the first of Daphne's friends to hear the "real story." (Wendy's personal investment aside, there had never been gossip quite like this, at least not in their shared social circle; under different circumstances, Wendy would already have been excited to tell Adam.) Or maybe, despite everything, Wendy still felt responsible for solving Daphne's problems.

•   •   •

It was a boy. Wendy heard the obstetrician say as much. Not that Daphne was aware of that fact. She was still unconscious. Maybe it was better that way. From what Wendy could gather, the baby wasn't in good shape when he came out. Not that she could see much from where she stood, behind a white curtain next to Daphne's head. But they gave him oxygen and who knew what else. Two minutes later, he uttered his first cry, and it was a piercing one. Two minutes after that, he was whisked out of the operating room for further examination.

Daphne came to in the recovery room forty-five minutes later. Wendy had followed her there, too. "Wendy," Daphne said slowly, blinking into the fluorescent light and looking stunned on multiple levels. "What are you doing here?"

Daphne's question immediately put Wendy on the defensive. (And here she'd just saved the woman's life! It was so typical, Wendy thought. She wondered why she'd bothered.) "I found you in the bathroom," she said, looking away. "I happened to stop by."

Daphne let out a long sigh and grimaced. Was it possible she was annoyed at Wendy for having rescued her? That she'd actually wanted to die? "And the baby?" she asked, visibly swallowing.

"He's in the nursery, being examined," Wendy told her.

"It's a he?" Her voice went up a few notes.

"Yes."

Daphne closed her eyes and sighed again. After a few moments, she began to speak, in a slightly slurred voice. "Jonathan and I had a fight. I told him the baby was Mitch's, and he said our marriage was over. I didn't know what to do. I didn't want to be alone again. . . ." She trailed off, as if lost in the past. After ten seconds, she resumed her monologue. "It was right after Jonathan and I got engaged. I was so happy to have him in my life, but I was still in love with Mitch. Or maybe I wasn't quite ready to let him go. Or give up being bad. Or maybe unconsciously I thought that if I got pregnant, he'd finally leave Cheryl. Or maybe I just wanted to be sure of what I was leaving behind. I can't even remember now. It seems like so long ago. It was just one night. Not even that, really. I didn't tell Jonathan, and I didn't even think about it until the twenty-week sonogram dated the baby two weeks earlier than I thought."

A few moments of silence passed between the two women, during which time it occurred to Wendy that (a) Daphne had attended not just her shower but her wedding with the knowledge that she was pregnant with another man's child; (b) she was an even better actress than Wendy had ever given her credit for being; and (c) the inscription on the sleep sack that Wendy had given Daphne at her shower was, above all, beside the point. "I'm sorry again about the shower gift," Wendy said. Then she paused, waiting for Daphne to apologize, too—at the very least for dumping a bag of flour on her head.

But it was still the same Daphne. (Apparently, a suicide attempt only went so far in changing a person's character.) "Don't worry about it, but thanks" was all she said, making eye contact for the first time, dim smile attached. "Anyway, I made this baby happen. I must have wanted it in some way. And I lived through tonight. And now I'm going to try and be a good mother, with or without Jonathan." She bit her lip and looked away, toward the door. "By any chance do you know where he is?"

"He's in the waiting room," said Wendy. "We came to the hospital together."

"He is?" Daphne turned back to Wendy, her eyes brighter than before.

At that same moment, a nurse wheeled in what looked like a clear plastic refrigerator produce bin and parked it next to Daphne. With a certain amount of difficulty, Daphne shifted her body to the side of the bed and peered over the edge. Wendy looked, too.

Lying in the bassinet, swaddled in a hospital-issue flannel blanket with mauve and turquoise stripes, was an astonishingly small, perfectly formed infant. His eyes blinked open and shut. His tiny tongue shot out of his tiny mouth with its rosebud lips before disappearing back inside. With his shiny black hair, dimpled chin, and vaguely entitled expression, he looked uncannily like Jonathan Sonnenberg. Daphne must have been thinking the same thing. She didn't say anything for a few minutes. Then she touched her finger to his cheek and whispered, "He's beautiful." And the joy and relief on her face were so exquisite as to be contagious.

"He *is* beautiful," said Wendy, choking up herself—and somehow relieved as well to think the baby was Jonathan's. Things were the way they were supposed to be. The sun would rise tomorrow after all. Corn muffins were still cake under another name.

"Would you mind getting Jonathan?" asked Daphne.

"Of course," said Wendy, who practically ran into the waiting room to retrieve him. (For the first time in memory, her pride at having helped facilitate a happy ending trumped her envy of another's good fortune.) "Daphne needs to see you," she announced breathlessly.

Clearly prepared for the worst, Jonathan grimaced before he stood up. He retucked his shirt into his pants. Then he followed Wendy back to Daphne's room.

Daphne had the baby in her arms now. Jonathan must have known what she and Wendy already knew from the moment he saw the child's face. Without any questions, he walked over to the bed and transferred the infant into his own arms. After a minute or two of cradling him—and presumably inspecting his genitalia—he announced, "Alexander Sonnenberg, welcome to the free world." And his voice cracked at the end of the sentence. Then he carefully laid the baby back in his bassinet, reached for Daphne, fell against her breast, and, once again, began to sob—this time audibly.

It was at that moment that Wendy realized she was no longer needed. (She'd already delivered her lines; it was time to walk off stage.) Without saying good-bye, she slipped out of Daphne's room, then out of the hospital and onto the street.

It was after midnight. The air had turned clear and breezy. Tomorrow would probably be a nice day, Wendy thought as she set off down Amity in search of a cab. Probably cooler and less humid. She barely glanced at Jonathan and Daphne's brownstone as she passed the front gate. She knew she wouldn't be back there any time soon. She'd seen too much now; knew too much, too; was destined to remind Daphne of a past she'd have to learn to forget if she wanted her marriage to survive.

Which was actually fine by Wendy. She was tired of being the person she'd always been around Daphne, anyway—the person who couldn't stop comparing herself to others when she wasn't busy trying to please them. It seemed clear to her now that trying to keep up meant never getting anywhere, missing everything. What's more, Daphne would forever be in her debt. Not that Wendy was keeping score, anymore. Still, it was a good feeling to have, the kind of feeling she could live with without ever having to lay eyes on Daphne's pretty face again.

Wendy eventually found a taxi on Clinton. On the way home, she checked her cell phone. There was one message—from Adam. She must have been in the operating room when he called. He sounded furious. "Thank you for fucking up my trip," he said. "It was Dad's birthday today. I was going to surprise him. I told you that. But no, you had to call my mother and get her all freaked out that I'd gone missing. She practically had the FBI out looking for me when I got there. It's like you can only think about yourself these days." He paused. "To be honest, I think we need to talk when I get home." He paused again. "To be even more honest, I've been thinking about getting my own place. Maybe we need some time apart. Anyway, we can talk about it when I get home."

Wendy realized suddenly that, far from cheating on her with Daphne, Adam had merely been confessing to her his desire to leave his marriage. Just as Daphne must have been sharing her own personal drama with Adam. That was all their relationship had been: an impromptu (if occasionally flirtatious) support group for troubled spouses.

The strange thing was: absorbing this potentially devastating piece of news, Wendy's first emotion was fascination. To think she'd become the kind of paranoid hysteric who had driven away her husband for no reason! She was like Anna

261

Karenina, she thought, only Adam didn't make much of a Vronsky. He wasn't that handsome or charming. He was definitely not a count. Also, Anna wasn't always nagging Vronsky to get a job. (Wendy wasn't planning on throwing herself in front of a train, either.)

Her second emotion was terror. What would become of her? Wendy wondered. Would she grow old alone? But fear mingled with a sense of relief. Somewhere along the way, Wendy had stopped finding Adam's T-shirt collection ironic, never mind amusing. The same went for both his unemployment and his failure to tell her he loved or missed her without prompting. And even though he hadn't cheated after all, he'd still acted like a jerk, she decided. Somewhere deep inside, Wendy still felt love for her husband. But she suspected that she mostly loved the memory of their being young together—though, if she was being honest with herself, she hadn't been all that happy in her twenties.

Opening the door to their apartment—and finding Adam's dirty socks balled up under the coffee table and resembling two dead mice—Wendy was reminded that she hadn't been particularly happy living on No Prospect Avenue, either. Now, at least, she'd have an excuse to move.

It was another two days—blurry ones; *Barricade* had found a new home in an old sweatshop in Chinatown, and everyone was busy unpacking—before Wendy realized she'd missed her period. Was it possible? There had been that one time while half asleep before work. . . . She took a pregnancy test, and two pink lines appeared side by side like two old friends. Or maybe two new friends. Tears quickly filled her eyes, because what she'd wanted for so long had finally happened, and also because her dream of creating the perfect family — the family she herself had never known — was apparently not to be.

On the other hand, she'd have a beautiful baby of her own. And she couldn't imagine not giving him or her all the nurturing and selflessness she had to offer, however little of them there was. (She couldn't imagine not bringing her baby to the circus to see the lady who hung from her hair.)

After Wendy dried her eyes, she started to laugh. And laugh and cry some more. Then she called her mother.

"It's about time," said Judy, sounding simultaneously irritable and elated. "Please congratulate Adam for me."

Wendy took a deep breath. "Adam doesn't know yet, and, to be honest, it might be a while before I tell him. We split up."

There was silence on the other end of the phone. Finally, Judy spoke: "Well, I know how you feel. I've always said that men were overrated."

"Thanks, Mom," said Wendy, tearing up yet again.

Wendy also called her friends. Everyone was thrilled for her. Or so they claimed. Though Wendy suspected that Maura, recently returned from Mexico, had taken this latest dispatch from "Wendy-ville" harder than she let on. "I'm so happy for you," she said, but her voice was thin and wan and not entirely convincing.

postscript

FTER FINALLY ADMITTING to herself that she was never going to finish her dissertation, Maura quit academia and moved full-time to Tulum, where she became a receptionist at a yoga retreat and fell in love with a mariachi singer.

Paige and Jeremy married and moved to London, where Paige launched her own highly successful hedge fund, and, even though they didn't need a second income, never stopped berating Jeremy for being a lazy drunk who lived off her largesse. (Either he didn't notice or didn't mind.)

Pamela became executive producer of *24 Hours*. She left Todd for a lesbian documentary filmmaker named Lori. Being a perfect husband, Todd took the whole thing well. He and Pamela shared custody of Lucas, who had to be enrolled in a special preschool for geniuses, having stopped crying at two and mastered algebra at three.

Four months after the birth of baby Jude, Dolph finally agreed to marry Sara, though not before admitting he had a crush on her older brother.

To all her friends' astonishment, Gretchen got pregnant again. She and Rob moved to a four-bedroom colonial in Summit, New Jersey, whereupon she threw out her headset and became a full-time mom (and got really depressed).

Alyson rose through the ranks at *Barricade,* becoming the youngest senior editor in the magazine's history. To enhance her income, she modeled part-time.

Ron Schwartz eventually made a full recovery. He officially retired from the tax law business and, along with Phyllis, moved to Sarasota, Florida.

After a paternity test confirmed that Daphne's baby was indeed Jonathan's, the two entered couples counseling with a certain Morgan Weintraub, PhD, who'd been recommended by Carol. Their marriage grew stronger. Two years after the birth of Alexander, they had a daughter named Daisy. Daphne and Jonathan also acquired more real estate—namely, a "cottage" in Sag Harbor, which happened to have six bedrooms and an in-ground gunite pool. To Wendy's relief, Daphne's screenplay got stuck in turnaround. By all appearances, it was unlikely ever to be made into a movie.

Meanwhile, Adam and Wendy embarked on a trial separation. Adam stayed in Brooklyn, while Wendy (with, later, her infant daughter, Lila) moved back into her mother's rent-controlled apartment on the Upper West Side of Manhattan. Conceived as temporary, the arrangement proved so copacetic that it went on and on. Three was a much better number for a family, Wendy found. It made everything less claustrophobic. You didn't have to pretend you didn't need each other at all because you needed each other so much. It also meant that Wendy had free babysitting. To Wendy's surprise and delight, Judy proved a loving and patient grandmother. It was also

Judy who, drawing on her experience with Jack the candle maker, had come to Wendy's emotional aid during her breakup with Adam.

Wendy did her best to keep Phyllis in her life, as well. Although the two never regained the closeness they once shared, Wendy made a point of sending her ex-mother-in-law regular email updates on Lila's progress.

Adam took care of Lila two afternoons and one overnight per week. He also got a job copyediting at a new online business magazine.

Tired of "preaching to the converted" and newly inspired to help others, Wendy left her job at *Barricade* and went back to grad school to become a social worker. To help pay the bills, she worked part-time in a Legal Aid office. There, she met and began dating a workaholic lawyer named Charlie, who was also divorced with a child. The two—and sometimes four—had a good time together. But Wendy's heart was never in it.

After a couple of years apart, she realized she missed Adam. Or maybe it was that she loved the sight of him and Lila together—the way he carted her around on his shoulders and snuggled her to sleep and made silly faces that made her laugh. It dawned on Wendy that she longed to reunite their family. The two started dating again—or, really, for the first time. They went out to dinner and the movies. They met for lunch in the park with Lila. Wherever possible, they avoided mention of Daphne. On Wendy's thirty-eighth birthday, Adam surprised her with an antique garnet ring. Garnet was a semi-precious—not a precious—stone, Wendy couldn't help but note. But she appreciated the gesture.

As for Wendy and Daphne, each December, they traded

holiday cards featuring photographs of their respective children. Every so often, one or the other emailed to suggest they get together for a playdate. "I'm dying to see you," Daphne would write.

"I know, it's been too long," Wendy would write back.

But when it came time to pin down a date, both would feign prior commitments.

One Saturday, several years after the night of Alex's birth, they ran into each other at the Children's Museum in Soho. They swapped small talk, and Alexander — now a handsome, hyperactive preschooler — immediately made off with Lila's security blanket, sending Lila into hysterics. To Wendy's shock, Daphne appeared to have gained a considerable amount of weight. Was it possible? Yes, Wendy thought: she was definitely heavier around the hips and thighs.

As Wendy pushed her stroller up Greene Street, she looked down at Lila and smiled. It wasn't just that Daphne had gotten fat. Wendy could never have imagined how much pleasure and confidence she'd reap from motherhood. She wondered if Daphne had reaped those things, too. It occurred to Wendy that Daphne's birthday was coming up the following week. Maybe she'd send her a card. She might even invite her out to lunch. . . .

ACKNOWLEDGMENTS

Special thanks to Maria Massie and Judy Clain, and also to Sally Singer, Cressida Leyshon, Jessica Palmieri, and Lucy D. Rosenfeld.

BACK BAY · READERS' PICK

READING GROUP GUIDE

I'm So Happy for You

a novel

Lucinda Rosenfeld

How to dump a friend

Lucinda Rosenfeld discusses how she came to write *I'm So Happy for You*

In 2001, I wrote a humorous essay for the *New York Times Magazine* called "How to Dump a Friend." I had a lot of fun with the assignment. Plus, my first novel, *What She Saw . . .* —an exhaustive account of all the boys and men in one young woman's life—had recently been published. It occurred to me that friendship in general, and more specifically female friendship and the competitive feelings it often engenders, was a fascinating, complex, and underexplored topic. This was true in literature but also in film and TV. I was as big a fan of the HBO series *Sex and the City* as anyone in my peer group. Yet the way in which the four leads interacted never rang entirely true to me. Talk of men and relationships dominated their conversation, whereas in my own friendship circle—I couldn't help noticing—we spoke as much about one another as we did about our boyfriends or (now mostly) husbands. Some of that talk was catty; some was concerned.

It took me several more years to figure out how to build a novel around the topic of friendship. The "problem" with constructing a narrative around friends (versus, say, lovers) is that, without sex and the promise of marriage, reproduction, etc., the stakes aren't intrinsically high. In romance, breaking up is understood to be a shattering event that throws the future into question. In friendship, it's a small setback, a minor irritation. If you don't like hanging out with someone, don't hang out with him/her anymore is the accepted wisdom. And yet, when I looked at my own life, I saw that friendship had been the source of both tremendous joy and profound hurt as friends had abandoned me, or I them.

In 2004, I got another assignment—this one from *New York* magazine—to write an essay about friend poaching. That became "Our Mutual Friend: How to Steal Friends and Influence People." I began to think about how friends, even best friends, rarely exist in a vacuum but are instead part of a larger clique whose dynamics are themselves always in flux. At one point I aspired to write a novel about a group of women à la Mary McCarthy's *The Group,* but it soon became apparent to me that, if friendship was my main topic, I would do better with two main characters. Eventually, I landed on Wendy and Daphne. Neither one is me, but I see parts of myself in both of them. I'm the insecure obsessive in Wendy, but I'm also the self-centered drama queen in Daphne. At various moments in my life, I've also been the steady "boring" one (Wendy), and the unstable, flaky one (Daphne). I've even been the glib, carefree Daphne who seemingly appears later in the novel. One of my goals in writing *I'm So Happy for You* was to make both main characters simultaneously problematic and sympathetic. If you come away loathing one or both of them, I haven't done my job.

Questions and topics for discussion

1. Wendy's desperation to have a baby has turned her and Adam's sex life into a "military operation." Do you think Wendy's militant determination is justified, or is she putting an unnecessary amount of stress on her marriage?

2. In the opening chapter, after Daphne stops answering her phone, is Wendy right to show up uninvited at Daphne's apartment? Would you do the same thing if a friend of yours were in a situation like Daphne's?

3. Wendy is not exactly ecstatic when things start to go well in Daphne's life. How do Daphne's sudden successes reflect on Wendy's self-image? If Wendy were happier, would she be happier for Daphne?

4. Do you think that the irony implied by the book's title can be applied to all friendships?

5. Regarding Wendy's work for *Barricade,* do you find her

actions and obsessions to be in keeping or in conflict with the political bent of her job?

6. Daphne, in her friendship with Wendy, has always been the "beautiful one." How does physical appearance affect the dynamic between them? Between friends in general?

7. In friendship as in love, one person may "fake it" for the sake of the other. When is it worth it to stretch or omit the truth in regard to a friend? In what ways do Daphne and Wendy cross that line?

8. The two men Daphne goes after don't seem like obvious choices. Why do you think she's drawn to Mitch Kroker and Jonathan Sonnenberg?

9. At first glance, Adam and Daphne seem like unlikely co-conspirators. What's your take on their alliance?

10. Wendy has a fraught relationship with her mother, Judy. What do you think of the role her mother plays in Wendy's life?

11. Did you relate more easily to Wendy or to Daphne? (Or both? Neither?) How so?

12. How does money (having it, wanting it, needing it) shape the novel? Do you think Wendy is justified in wanting Adam to go back to work? Would money solve their problems?

13. Wendy reads one of Shakespeare's sonnets at Daphne's wedding. In light of the story, what do you think of the lines "Love is not love / Which alters when it alteration finds"?

14. How do friendship "breakups" differ from romantic ones?

15. Name some of the essential differences between friendships among women and friendships among men.

16. Wendy has a fierce yet tacit antagonism with Paige Ryan. When Paige tells Wendy that Daphne's baby belongs to Adam, should Wendy believe her without first talking to Adam? Would you have believed Paige?

17. In the hospital, when Daphne admits to having cheated on Jonathan, does she seem genuinely sorry about the choices she's made? Should she be?

18. At the end of the novel, (mostly) everyone winds up in a place far different from where she or he started. Do you think Wendy and Daphne will be happy? Will they be happy — at long last — for each other?

19. What other books about friendship do you find particularly true to life? Did *I'm So Happy for You* remind you of any of them?

Lucinda Rosenfeld's friendship reading list

Aristotle (384–322 BC), *Nicomachean Ethics*
    In this classical text, Aristotle takes the position that true friendship, unlike friendship based on utility or pleasure, is defined by a mutual desire for goodness. Aristotle writes: *Only the friendship of those who are good, and similar in their goodness, is perfect. For these people each alike wish good for the other qua good, and they are good in themselves. And it is those who desire the good of their friends for the friends' sake that are most truly friends, because each loves the other for what he is, and not for any incidental quality.* Whether there are any friendships that *actually* live up to this description is open for debate!

Jane Austen, *Emma* (1815)
    Austen's books generally revolve around sisters. But in this beloved novel, charming "socialite" Emma Woodhouse gets overinvolved in the romantic life of her penniless friend Harriet Smith — to both comic and disastrous effect.

Honoré de Balzac, *Cousin Pons* (1848)
    Part two in the series known as Poor Relations, this brilliant, biting novel concerns a pitiful old theater conductor

7

whose relatives and neighbors slowly destroy his life. The only one who remains true to poor Pons is his best friend and roommate, a wistful German pianist named Schmucke. And yet even Pons and Schmucke have their tensions. A warning: the ending is so dark it's almost painful to read.

Fyodor Dostoyevsky, *The Gambler* (1867)

This autobiographically inspired novel ostensibly concerns a young tutor whose employment by a once-rich general and love of an elusive woman lead him to gamble, but it also contains some choice passages on friendship. One example: *Yes, most men love to see their best friend in abasement; for generally it is on such abasement that friendship is founded. All thinking persons know that ancient truth.*

Evelyn Waugh, *Brideshead Revisited* (1945)

The English class system is on full display in this searing, satiric portrait of two university friends, one rich and dissolute, the other poor and aspiring. The Masterpiece Theater version with Jeremy Irons as Charles and Anthony Andrews as the opium-addled Sebastian (1981) is — dare I say? — almost better than the book.

Mary McCarthy, *The Group* (1963)

This sprawling novel follows the lives of eight Vassar graduates in the 1930s as they grapple with marriage, Marxism, and the specter of their vanishing careers. This reader wished that McCarthy had devoted more time to chronicling the women's interactions with one another, but a highly memorable scene involving a diaphragm fitting nearly compensates for the lack.

Margaret Atwood, *Cat's Eye* (1988)

The cruelty of young girls is the subject of this disturbing psychological novel in which the narrator, now a middle-aged artist, reflects back on her unconventional childhood and the abuse she suffered at the hands of her sadistic "best friend" (for whom the narrator nonetheless felt deep longing).

Martin Amis, *The Information* (1996)

A confession: I've never gotten all the way through a Martin Amis novel — including this one — but some people (my sister, for one) love this tale of two old Oxford friends-turned-writers, one of whom has "hit it big," the other of whom is madly envious and bent on revenge.

Zoë Heller, *What Was She Thinking?: Notes on a Scandal* (2003)

The creepiness factor is high in British writer Zoë Heller's pitch-perfect novel about a middle-aged high school history teacher whose "friendship" with a flighty, glamorous young art teacher — who begins an affair with one of her teenage students — quickly turns obsessive bordering on pathological.

Mike Albo and Virginia Heffernan, *The Underminer: Or, the Best Friend Who Casually Destroys Your Life* (2005)

This delicious little novel is essentially a monologue in the voice of the ultimate backstabber.

Jenny Offil and Elissa Schappell, editors, *The Friend Who Got Away: Twenty Women's True-Life Tales of Friendships That Blew Up, Burned Out, or Faded Away* (2006)

A smart if earnest collection for those who like their betrayal in essay form.

Joseph Epstein, *Friendship: An Exposé* (2006)

A meandering memoir in which the author —who claims to have seventy-five close pals—tries to figure out how we choose our friends.

Lizzie Himmel

Lucinda Rosenfeld is the author of the novels *What She Saw . . .* and *Why She Went Home*. Her fiction and essays have appeared in the *New York Times Magazine*, *The New Yorker*, *Creative Nonfiction*, Slate.com, *Glamour*, and other magazines. She lives in Brooklyn, New York, with her husband and two young daughters.